The Loss

Karlissa J.

THE LOSS
Copyright © 2020 by Karlissa J.

Print ISBN: 978-1-4866-1948-1
eBook ISBN: 978-1-4866-1949-8

Word Alive Press
119 De Baets Street, Winnipeg, MB R2J 3R9
www.wordalivepress.ca

WORD ALIVE
—P R E S S—

Cataloguing in Publication may be obtained through Library and Archives Canada

To my adventure partner, Jason, who continues to encourage me.
And to my children, as they grow and explore their world.

Decades Ago

On an island far away, a Rezumi woman stood before a Scavgan man. The woman held her massive wings at her side.

"I need to get out of here," the Rezumi insisted to the Scavgan.

The Scavgan appeared to be a thin, insignificant presence under her tall shadow, yet he held out his chest and smiled up at the mighty winged creature as though he held her future. And he did.

"A quaint village, full of friends and family," he said. "Why would you ever want to leave?"

He already knew her answer.

She growled, quaking. "I don't belong here. Your people's ships can take you far across the sea, to anywhere you desire."

"You have wings. Can't they take you anywhere?"

"I'm not one of your gladiators. Believe it or not, some of us aren't strong enough to make that journey." She bowed her head. "But your people refuse to take me aboard. You could convince them, I know you could. You arena owners seem to hold a lot of sway."

"We hold money," he said. "Money holds sway. What can I take from you? I know your reputation. You have no money. No property. If you really want my help, you need to give me something worthwhile in exchange."

She gritted her teeth. "I have one thing."

"What?"

"A child. Male. He may grow into a gladiator. His father was mighty."

"Now now, I can't go kidnapping children," the Scavgan said. "Things have to be on the up-and-up, or the Emperor may shut us down."

Though she didn't know it, the Scavgan had lied. Their Emperor appreciated the arena's entertainment too much to close it over a few illegal dealings.

"The child, I bore," she said casually. "But he's useless to me. He'll only slow me down. I want a life. I want *my* life. You can have his."

The Scavgan nodded. "Well, that's legal. If you're the parent, handing your son over to be trained as a gladiator is acceptable."

"I'll bring him to you here, tomorrow," the Rezumi mother said. "And you will get your fellow Scavgans to allow me onto their ship?"

"Fair enough," the Scavgan said. "What's the boy's name?"

"Grey Noon."

CHAPTER ONE

Katia eyed a bright yellow ripe melon, hidden away in a tangle of brush where no animals had discovered it. She held it in her paws and tugged until it snapped away from the mother plant.

This is a good size, she thought, turning to roll it back to their hideout. *The Scavgans and I can share it.*

"G... go," a high, almost shrill voice said. "No go. No go!"

Katia perked her ears, then looked down. Vortro, sitting at her feet, stared up at her through beady black eyes. This was the first time Katia had heard clear words from the worm, but not the first time she had suspected Vortro was attempting speech.

This creature, whatever it is, I don't think it's just a worm, she thought. If only the Scavgans had hearing as good as Katia's, they might stop treating Vortro like a pet. *Maybe it's my job to help them realize that Vortro is a person, though an... unusual person.*

Vortro squeaked as Katia leaned over and whispered, "It's okay, little one. I just left the shelter to find some food. We can go home now. But in the future, you shouldn't follow me out, okay? Stay home where it's safe."

"Home…" Vortro then squeaked, flipped over, and began crawling in the direction of the shelter.

Katia followed after the creature, rolling the melon.

Zan stretched out his arms, yawning.

"Where is Katia?" Zan folded his hands behind his head, resting them against the smooth cave wall. "And why does she insist on us staying behind?"

Ian's eyes held anxiety as he scanned every inch of the cave. "Where's Vortro?"

"Why do you worry about that silly worm?" Zan said. "It always comes back to us. It must think you'll be infected with parasites again, so it can crawl in and eat them. Or maybe it found a different host. Wouldn't you be happy for it if it did? When's the last time it had food?"

Ian's stomach growled. *When's the last time we had food?*

In his small fishing and farming village by the sea, Ian hadn't grown up in the lap of luxury, but neither had he ever gone hungry. Even if it required catching the food himself—which he often had, since his father and older brother had been fishermen—there'd always been something to eat.

Zan, on the contrary, *had* grown up in the lap of luxury, as the son of an important dignitary living in the capital city of the Questavan Empire. When he'd gotten hungry, the most work he'd ever had to put into getting food was asking a servant to prepare him something, and waiting until the servant returned with a plate of delectable treats.

Now they were in the jungles of Aziasha, a place that only the furry little Darian Katia found familiar. And she seemed to think she should be the only one out collecting food. For the Scavgans, Ian and Zan, this was the fifth day of letting Katia tend to their needs, and in exchange obeying her order never to leave the tiny cave where she'd housed them.

Ian's stomach again rumbled. "Maybe I should go out. The jungle can't be that difficult. I could find a body of water, make a fishing pole—"

"Ian, I wasn't complaining because I expected something done about it," Zan cut in. "I've heard enough stories of poisonous plants, poisonous animals, poisonous everything in Aziasha… I don't like staying here in the cave—it's wet and dirty and cramped—but I'm not going to risk my life out in the jungle. I'm sure Katia has us in here because she's smart enough to know the trouble we'd get into out there. Besides, if you think about how dangerous the jungle is, she's risking her life to take care of us. Let her make her sacrifice."

"That's even more reason to help her!" Ian stood and walked towards the cave entrance. "She's small and delicate, and we should be out there with her, protecting her."

"Ian, look at me." When his friend obeyed, Zan pointed to his right eye. His eyelid, a deep, unhealthy grey, was swollen shut and puss oozed from around it. "The Athai have survived the Marsh Isles for generations, where the forests are dangerous enough to host venomous bugs that almost killed us both, and blinded this eye."

Ian's heart sank. "Don't say that, Zan, You'll get your vision back. I'm sure of it."

Zan shook his head. "I won't. Katia told me."

"You may have misunderstood her. She doesn't speak our language. How did she even tell you?"

Zan sighed. "Ian, I've gotten used to this cross-language communication we've had to deal with, being stranded out here with her. Hand signals, acting things out. I've even taught her a little of our language and learned a little of hers. I'm sure of what she was communicating, Ian: I won't see through this eye again."

"When did you have this conversation?"

"While you were sleeping. You've slept a lot the last few days. Are you sure all the venom is out of your system? You seem a little… delusional."

"The venom has worn off," Ian insisted, stepping past the cave's entrance. "And I'm ready to be useful."

"Ian!" Zan snapped. "Get back in here. Even if you don't believe my eye is blinded, she told us to stay here. She freaks out every time we so much as stand at the entrance. If she were here right now—"

"She isn't! What if she's hurt? We can't just stay here!"

For a moment, the two remained silent, allowing the unfamiliar cries of unknown creatures to fill their ears.

"She's only been gone a short time," Zan said softly. He patted the spot next to him. "Come on, sit and wait a little longer. And try to speak more quietly. We don't know what may be out there listening."

Ian frowned as he took another step away from the cave.

"Ian… do you hear that?"

Ian allowed another moment of silence. "Hear what?"

"Let's start with that low gurgling sound. You hear it?"

Closing his eyes, Ian focused. "Yeah." He opened his eyes. "We've been hearing that since we got here. I thought you heard something new."

"It *is* something new, Ian," Zan said. "Do you know what makes that sound?"

"Some kind of animal."

"What kind?"

"Probably a bug of some sort."

"But do you know that?" Zan patted the spot next to him again. "Come, sit." His friend didn't respond. "Ian, you don't know this jungle like Katia does. You don't know what you're hearing, what you're seeing, what to eat, what not to touch. I'm ready to let her be the expert. Please, come back. I don't want to stay here alone."

"I'm hungry, Zan. And I'm worried about Katia. I feel completely healthy, so I won't sit around and be useless."

As Ian continued to walk away from the cave, he heard Zan again.

"Blackbloods," his friend warned.

Ian froze.

"You remember the story, right?" Zan continued. "That horror tale a Darian told us? You know what it implies: there are Blackbloods here in Aziasha, the result of creatures drinking water infected with blackwaters. Are you really up for facing a zombified monster that could infect you?"

At first Ian was ready to turn back. But he tightened his fist and gritted his teeth. "That's low, Zan. You know I'm afraid of Blackbloods."

"I'm being realistic, Ian. Come back."

Zan listened as Ian's footsteps faded from hearing. Closing his good eye, he curled up into a ball.

"I tried," he whispered to himself. "Ian, please, don't get yourself killed."

Mere minutes later, Zan sensed Katia approaching. He opened his good eye and saw her hold a yellow fruit in front of her, Vortro by her side. She rotated her ears back and forth, as though searching.

"Ian left," Zan said, moving to a sitting position.

Katia blinked, cocking one ear.

"He left." Zan pointed in the direction Ian had gone. "Out there."

Katia's eyes filled with fear. She dashed out of the cave.

Ian's stomach continued to vocalize its discontent as he wandered past emerald trees and tangled bushes. To anyone watching, his meanderings would have appeared aimless, as he never stayed on a straight course—though to his mind, his direction was intentional. Perhaps hunger, thirst, the chak venom, or his displeasure with Katia—and now Zan—accounted for the difference between what truly was and what he felt.

There has to be a pond, he thought. *Or a lake, or a river. . . and it has to be close by. A forest is never this green without water.*

So he paced, tuning his ears to the familiar sounds of water and his nose to the scent of pondweed. Instead the often raucous calls of unknown animals and the copious, dichotomous smells of multiple plants overwhelmed his senses.

I miss home. I miss the village, and I miss the sea. The sea!

If he'd been paying more attention, he'd have searched for the coastline where Katia had rescued them. He was sure their shelter wasn't too far from the ocean. But now he'd wandered far from the shelter, possibly lessening his chances of finding the ocean.

He shrugged.

I've come this far. I won't go back yet. I'm going to stumble across water any moment now. He touched his throat, suddenly recalling how sore it felt. *Maybe it'll even be drinkable water.*

Katia felt both relief and concern at how easily she managed to track Ian down. His trail, both in terms of physical tracks and broken foliage, stood out clearly against the otherwise untouched jungle.

When she caught sight of him, she took in a quick scan for danger. It appeared she alone had followed him.

"Ian?" Katia called.

Ian turned to her, not smiling. Though it comforted him to see her safe, his focus had been on finding food.

"Katia," he said, approaching her. "I need water."

She shook her head, not understanding.

"Where fish are." He made a swimming motion with his hands, putting them together and moving them left and right rhythmically. "Fish."

The Darian stared blankly.

"Fish," Ian said, louder. "I'm finding water to fish in." Kneeling, he grabbed a short stick and carved a simple picture in the dirt. "See? A fish."

Katia eyed it. "Alasay," she said in her language.

"Fish," Ian said again, nodding. "Alasay."

She gave him a quizzical look, trying to understand. *What is he saying? Did he see a fish? Did he visit the ocean? Or has he found a puddle big enough for fish to live in?*

"And water," Ian tried again.

He drew little wavy lines and Katia tried to decipher them.

That looks like our symbol for the monster goddess Yupetas, she thought. *Did he find a temple? Yupetas looks sort of like a fish, I guess. She has scales, at least, and a long body.*

Ian pointed at his squiggles. "See?"

When Katia only stared back blankly, Ian got another idea. He cupped his hands, as though holding liquid, then tipped his head back and brought them to his mouth, making a slurping noise. He ended his demonstration.

"Water." He acted it out again. "Water?"

"Water!" Katia's ears drooped, eyes filling with tears.

Oh no, she realized. *They're thirsty. But I've been feeding them lots of fruit... I thought that would stave off thirst. It does for my people...*

She remembered something her mate Anveil had told her. When Katia had asked him why some critters were only ever seen at watering holes, Anveil had told her that some creatures are so dependent on drinking water that they spend their entire life at one of the few freshwater pools.

Fish needed water, and Ian was saying that Scavgans needed water, too.

She began walking back toward the cave, turning to Ian with an encouraging smile and coaxing him to follow. He did, though his head hung low and he crossed his arms the whole way.

While they walked, Katia contemplated their dilemma. How urgently did they need water? She had been hoping to wait until the monster in these woods had left the area, but what if they didn't have that much time before the foreigners got sick?

We've waited for days for the monster to move. What if it's not going to move for a long time?

Finding the melon seemed less of an accomplishment now.

CHAPTER TWO

*T*yzak tried not to feel gloomy. He hated being sad.

As he stepped down the stairs into the *Radiant Dawn*'s galley—the kitchen and dining area—he attempted to cheer himself by listening in on the friendly conversations being carried on by those sitting at the tables with bowls full of fresh fruit and veggies. Walking farther, he focused on the bustling kitchen staff, darting around energetically as they prepared food.

Enjoying the wonderful food should cheer you up, he told himself. *After all, these veggies and fruits will go bad before too long. Enjoy these few days with fresh produce, instead of the normal stale biscuits.*

Tyzak absently went to the kitchen to receive his ration, his mind wandering to Ian and Zan. Even as he took his bowl and looked about for a table to sit, he realized that, for once in his life, he just wanted to be alone with his thoughts.

He picked an empty table and took a seat.

The captain seems to think those two are okay, he thought. *Though how could he possibly be so sure of that? Poor Ian, he's so young. And Zan, he's so... Zan.*

Honestly, Ian was the easier one to get along with. However, Tyzak surprised himself by how close he felt towards Zan.

A sad smile seeped onto his face. *Ah, to think I grew up laughing at mean jokes about Questavans, and here I am, worried sick about a Questavan friend of mine. It must be Ctzo's influence.*

Yes, Captain Ctzo was another Questavan he respected more than the average Mediocan respected anyone from that desert city. It may have been generations since the Questavans had conquered the proud Mediocans and forced them into the Questavan Empire, but for many the wounds were still fresh.

I wonder why Zan's so shy about his background. Tyzak twirled his spoon through his food. *It's plain as day he's from some wealthy, important family. But he only told Ian, not me. What would have been wrong with telling me?*

Tyzak had thought the three of them were good friends. Did Zan think he'd judge him for it?

Zan, get back here this instant so I can have a conversation with you about keeping secrets from friends.

He paused, half-hoping that his wish would come true, that Ian and Zan would appear at the galley's doorway. Instead a tall, dark, brutish figure pushed through the door: Black Night.

Tyzak never tired of gawking at the young Rezumi. If he was just a teenager, Tyzak couldn't help by wonder how big the adults of his race got. Black Night was the very first Rezumi he'd ever met.

Black Night caught Tyzak's eye and smiled. After ambling over to the kitchen to receive his own bowl of food, he came over to Tyzak's table and wedged himself into the seat across from the Scavgan.

Tyzak noted the Rezumi's meal consisted entirely of fruit: violet berries, creamy slices of who-knew-what, and something dark and oblong; all unfamiliar Aziashan fare.

"Looks delicious." Tyzak forced a cheery tone into his voice. "And how has your morning been?"

Black Night stretched out his left wing until it touched the far wall. "I always feel a little stiff before my morning workout. How about you, *pana*? How are you holding up?"

Tyzak intentionally changed the subject. "*Pana*... remind me, is that to be taken as a compliment?"

"It means 'friend.'"

"Ah." Tyzak bowed his head. "Compliment it is, then."

"Stop stalling," Black Night said. "You're going crazy without Ian and Zan, aren't you?"

Before he could reply, Chiha sauntered into the galley. The Athai woman didn't appear to have come to eat, as she never once glanced at the kitchen staff. Instead she just looked past those seated at tables.

Please don't see me, Tyzak thought, shielding his face and hoping Black Night's bulk would hide him from view. He needed space from her.

Chiha's green, feathery tail flicked back and forth as she brushed past table after table. Finally, she drew close enough to catch sight of Tyzak seated across from Black Night.

The Athai sidled right up to Tyzak.

Black Night cleared his throat. "Excuse me, ma'am, but we were in the middle of a conversation." His tone held a great deal of politeness.

"And now I join you," Chiha said, her tone holding no politeness whatsoever.

"It was a private conversation," Black Night said, his voice now carrying a hint of frustration. "Do you mind?"

"You can have your conversation after I have mine. I want to talk with Tyzak."

Tyzak gulped. "Um... Chiha..."

Black Night chose that moment to begin eating. He opened his mouth wide and his long jaws engulfed a melon. In one bite, he crushed it down to mashed fruit and sweet juice, the latter dribbling down his face.

Chiha watched with apparent fascination. When he swallowed, she commented with joy, "You are a monster!"

"A nice monster?" he asked.

"I mean a monster as in a beast. A mighty creature, fierce in battle, ground quaking beneath their steps."

Black Night chuckled. "Yeah, I guess that's me. And just so you know, I admire how well you speak Questavan." With that compliment out of the way, he added, "Now, Tyzak and I would like to speak alone for a few minutes. Is that all right?"

Chiha flicked her feathery hair. "In my tribe, warriors win respect by going after and killing monsters."

Black Night sighed. "Good for you."

"I will duel you," Chiha said.

"Pardon?"

She stood. "When I beat you, I will win great respect."

"When?" Black Night rumbled, his tone revealing just how much she'd gotten under his skin. "When you beat me? You make it sound like I *can't* beat you. And isn't it polite to ask whether your desired opponent wants to fight you?"

"Why do you care about being polite? I've heard you speak rudely to the captain."

"When am I rude to the captain?"

"Do not lie. I have overheard your arguments when he takes you away to reprimand you."

Tyzak attempted a smile. "Aha. Well, maybe I should let you two... uh... you know, I think there's something I need to do..."

Black Night paled. "My conversations with the captain are supposed to be private," he told Chiha. "Do you know what *private* means?"

"Well, you are very rude to him," Chiha said. "You must learn respect for your leaders."

Black Night raised his wings, shoulders hunching and neck shaking—a threatening posture that caused his mane to stand out. It made him appear larger than he already was.

Immersed under his hulking shadow, Tyzak instinctively shrunk back. But Chiha didn't even flinch.

Black Night growled. "My relationship with the captain is my business and his, not yours."

"You should show some respect for me," she said. "I am a princess."

"Not aboard this ship, you're not. You're nobody."

Rather than take offence, she laughed. She leaned closer to the Rezumi, curling her tail. "Come fight me, and we'll see who is nobody."

"All right," one of the other Scavgans said, rising from his table. "Take this outside, you two."

"Gladly," Black Night said through gritted teeth. "You, me, on the deck. Now."

Chiha flicked her tail. "I'll get my spear."

Nope, today would not be a boring day.

Tyzak strode over to a barrel and rested his elbows against it, staring happily out at the big, brutish Black Night and the nimble, lizard-like Chiha.

The captain was currently aboard his favoured vessel, the *Diversity*, although he'd sent a few of his crew to man the *Radiant Dawn*. But if Ctzo had known a fight like this one was about to take place, he'd likely have broken it up before it started.

I have to admit, I'm glad he doesn't know what's going on, Tyzak thought. *And I hope he doesn't catch on before it gets really good.*

Not that Tyzak liked seeing people angry and beat-up. But he was a sucker for entertainment, and this looked promising. Besides, it was all in good sport. Surely they wouldn't actually hurt each other?

He eyed Black Night's face. The giant's teeth were gritted and his brows furled, his ears pointed back in rage. Then Tyzak gazed at Chiha, chin held arrogantly high, long spear at the ready. He knew from experience how well she could use that weapon; when he'd first met her on the Marsh Isles, she threatened him with that same spear.

A hint of doubt crept in. *I certainly hope it's in good sport. If they do hurt each other, I'll seriously regret not trying to get the captain's attention.*

However, it seemed as though the other crewmembers aboard weren't about to alert Ctzo. They either went on their way, ignoring the two, or stood watching on the sidelines. A ring of spectators had gathered.

Black Night and Chiha took a moment to size each other up. Then Black Night barrelled forward, charging her. Chiha sidestepped him, flipping her spear in hand and jabbing the blunt end into his side.

Tyzak let out a relieved breath.

Yeah, this isn't serious, he thought, noting that she wasn't using the sharp end of the spear. *This isn't a matter of life or death. Just pride.*

Unfortunately, or perhaps fortunately, both contestants had a lot of pride to lose.

Black Night grunted at the jab and spun to face Chiha, only to see her slip out of view. Every time he turned, she hopped behind him.

The next jab smacked into his rear. Predictably, this enraged the Rezumi and he stormed around, pounding his hefty wings into the ship's planks, always missing the agile Athai.

Chiha landed a hit behind his ear, a rather sensitive spot. Black Night roared and swung his wings violently.

In desperation, he finally concocted a new strategy. He fell backwards, allowing his back to slam against the ground and hoping to crush her in the process.

The next thing he knew, the sharp end of Chiha's spear tickled his nose.

"Surrender?" she asked.

"No."

"Stab, you're dead." With that, Chiha turned to the crowd, waving her spear victoriously.

Black Night reached around with his wing to slap her. She caught the movement in time, however, halting his wing with the blunt end of her spear.

"Child," she said with scorn.

He muttered a dark word under his breath.

Chiha then leapt from his chest and joined the crowd. While some slinked away, disappointed with the result, others couldn't help but admire her. They became her temporary posse, following along with her as she returned downstairs to the galley.

Tyzak approached Black Night, clapping. "Bravo!"

Black Night frowned up at him. "Is that a joke?"

"Not at all. You've accomplished a tremendous feat—a feat very few have managed." Tyzak flashed a brilliant smile. "You've gotten Chiha to forget about and ignore me."

Black Night shook himself as if to set aside the sense of failure he felt, returning to his full height. "You say that like she's a puppy who follows you around everywhere."

"She *is* a puppy who follows me around. It seemed cute at first, even flattering, but I've honestly grown tired of it." Tyzak's smile faded. "Especially since I have Ian and Zan on my mind. Missing them just... well, it gives me far more incentive to spend time alone than I ever had before. I've never lost someone that close to me."

Black Night wrapped a comforting wing around his shoulder. "Hey, they're not lost, *pana*. The captain thinks they're okay. We should have more confidence in their ability to survive."

Tyzak sighed. "That's not what I meant by *lost*. I meant that they aren't here, with me, and I can't simply go visit them whenever I want, because I have no clue how to get to them or how long it'll be before I see them again."

"If it's any consolation," Black Night said, "I feel that we *will* see them again."

CHAPTER THREE

Sébérus ducked behind a large rock as a bullet ricocheted off Grey Noon's skull-like helmet. Watching the massive Rezumi beside him, Sébérus smiled.

We get ambushed, and he looks more disappointed with our attackers than angry or afraid, Sébérus mused.

Peering around the rock, he studied their opponents: Scavgans, clothed in fleece garments. Every inch of their uncovered skin sparkled with silver and gold paint. He recognized their appearance from his favourite history book. This was what remained of the once great Augai Nation.

"These have-been warriors need to lie low," Grey Noon growled. "Are they trying to get themselves killed?"

For once, the pirate-priest hadn't been the one to start this fight. The crew of *Ko'Ekua* had landed on a seemingly deserted island to rest, stretch, and investigate the worn but still standing lighthouse and small stone buildings, in case they could be used by the Ti'te'Vikans.

Apparently, the Augai had already laid claim to the island. As the crew landed and exited the vessel, the Augai poured out of the doorways and bushes to confront the invaders. Grey Noon had called out, attempting to speak with them, but the Augai clearly had no intentions of talking. They pulled out pistols, swords, and scythes and began their attack.

How pathetic.

Even as the Augai fired shots his way, Sébérus regarded them with scorn.

They outnumber us, but not by much, he thought. *There aren't enough of them to keep them alive. And what are they doing, all coming out at once in a chaotic mass? This isn't how the Augai almost won the War of Nine Leagues. I suppose they've lost their leaders since then.*

The Augai had nearly taken the Questavan Empire, leaving its people hopeless, particularly when the Empire's General Unio had fallen ill just before an important battle. But General Ctzo had stepped in to save the day, conquering and scattering the Augai.

Sébérus knew that from Grey Noon's perspective, Ctzo hadn't been the only victor. After Ctzo had won the war, the weakened and much-hated Augai had been easy pickings for every priesthood, smuggling ring, and pirate fleet with a score to settle. Rumours had claimed that the Augai had been pushed to extinction.

Apparently, a few still remained.

Sébérus heard another bullet hit the rock shielding him. "Any orders, Captain Grey Noon?"

"Just stay here and watch how it's done, Sébérus," the pirate replied.

Sébérus couldn't resist a grin. "I like that plan."

But Sébérus didn't just grin at the thought of finally seeing Grey Noon in action.

Isn't it nice that he calls me by my name? Sébérus asked himself. *The other pirates just act like I'm inferior and refuse to call me by any name except Blackblood.* He fantasized about biting one of those other pirates in the ankle. *Let's see how* they *like being a Blackblood.*

Bullets thudded into Grey Noon's armour as he charged towards the nearest line of Augai. While still a ways off, the pirate captain scooped up the beach's coarse sand with his wings and flung it into their faces. The blinded enemies stopped firing, then felt their ribcages shatter as the Rezumi clotheslined them with his massive wingspan.

Only one shooter continued to fire, and Grey Noon shielded his face with his right wing. In a fluid motion, he spun one hundred eighty degrees, his left wing landing a crushing blow on his opponent's skull. A new attacker then charged from the other side, collided with Grey Noon's wing, and fell dead.

Sébérus watched with awe as the well-oiled team of pirates fell on their adversaries with the skill of trained soldiers. The fight could only be described as a skirmish, since the ragtag Augai succumbed within moments.

Sébérus stepped out of his hiding place, bowing at the captain's feet.

"Beautiful," the Blackblood said. "A masterpiece in the art of warfare."

Grey Noon's tone in no way indicated whether he appreciated the compliment. "And next time you'll fight too."

"Well, after the appropriate training—"

"No training. You know how to follow orders. Follow mine, or die trying. That's the role of new sailors on my crew."

Sébérus managed to hide his tremor of fear. "What type of fighting will I be doing? Background, foreground, support…"

"You'll do what your priest asks, when he asks it," Grey Noon said. "But before you join in the war, you must spend some time with the gods, purifying yourself."

Sébérus sighed. *Purifying. Right.*

"There is no war without a cause," Grey Noon continued. "Your purpose for fighting must be at the front of your mind in every battle. Someday you will need to choose which gods will be your personal gods. This decision is vital and must be made with wisdom."

Sébérus bowed again. "I approach that responsibility with great solemnity, my priest."

Since you'll probably kill me if I don't.

"Meet me in the shrine in an hour," Grey Noon said, looking back towards the *Ko'Ekua.* "I need some time to meditate before you join me."

"Of course." Sébérus nodded, recalling the small room aboard the ship that housed the shrine. "When you're ready, my priest and captain, you can teach me the ways of the gods."

Grey Noon growled between clenched teeth. "What is taking him so long?"

Amidst a semicircle of sacred crystals, a faded book marked in colourful ink lay open before him. He'd removed his usual skeletal armour, laid it aside, and replaced it with the brilliant crimson and teal cowl of a Ti'te'Vikan priest. A necklace of deep green gemstones hung around his neck. Each held a symbol serving to remind him of a particular mantra. While meditating on these mantras, Grey Noon felt peace and meaning. Each prayer became his life's mission.

"For the sake of glorious Erra," he whispered, fingering a gem with his wing-claw, "may the land be enriched and cleansed, farmed by those who will offer her the sacrifices she deserves for the day she caused fruit trees to sprout and grow." He paused and then continued nonchalantly. "And for Tarair's sake, may fire destroy that Blackblood's bones if he's not here within—"

"My priest." Sébérus entered, demonstrating the proper reverence, crawling forward on his knees and intermittently pressing his forehead to the ground in a humble bow. A simple red shawl covered his shoulders.

"You are late. I expect commitment. And if I don't see it, you will die."

"Forgive me, my priest. My… pains…" Sébérus rubbed his arm. "The pains I get from… well, being a Blackblood. They're acting up."

"You would not have pain if you'd focus on the mantras." As Grey Noon closed his eyes, he pictured his mother, giving him over to the arena. "All my pains are gone now. With time, prayer, and study, yours will disappear as well."

"Er, right." Sébérus hesitated. "Ready when you are, my priest."

"I *am* ready. Are you?" Grey Noon removed himself from his current position and motioned for the Blackblood to take his place amidst the ring of crystals.

Sébérus knelt before the open book, his eyes wandering between it and the crystals.

"Now close your eyes," Grey Noon ordered. "I will recite to you the story of how our world's islands came to be."

Sébérus's mind wandered between taking note of whatever seemed most significant in the story and wishing he could massage his limbs. As soon as Grey Noon wasn't watching, he decided, he would sneak a dose of those drugs he had hidden in the storage room. Then he'd feel right again.

Yes, bringing drugs aboard the ship could yet turn out to be a fatal decision. But only if he got caught. And no one could convince him he didn't need those chemicals to ease his pain. Not even an infamous pirate-priest.

Play along for now, Sébérus reminded himself. *When the opportunity comes, you can slip away from these pirates and start a new life for yourself. In Aziasha. In Questava. Wherever you can come up with a survival plan.*

Survival. The word seemed… hollow. He didn't just want to survive. He wanted to live, to thrive. But what would thriving look like? How could a Blackblood find peace in a world where everyone saw him as either a mindless slave or a soulless mutant?

Maybe I should stay here, he thought. *At least Grey Noon respects me.*

He tuned his mind back to the priest's words.

"When Tarair finally escaped the demon Hash-jak, he came to land on the earth," Grey Noon said, finishing up his prelude to the god's arrival in their world. "But all that existed in our world was a sea of black."

A sea of black. Was that a reference to blackwaters? The nonchalant way in which Grey Noon spoke suggested this isn't what the Rezumi meant. But that was the image to flood Sébérus's mind—a world of blackwaters.

"This is why Tarair stole the demon's dark blade." As Grey Noon flipped a page in the book, the image of an inky sword came into view. "Even blacker than the blackness of the waves, the waters trembled and parted before it."

Something blacker than blackwaters? Now that was hard for Sébérus to imagine.

"Wherever the ocean parted, Tarair would grab the mountains in his bare fist and drag them upwards, so they came to float on the surface."

Sébérus chuckled to himself as he tried to imagine floating islands.

Grey Noon took no time moving on from this story to recount the other impressive deeds of Tarair. With each tale, he glowed with pride in the god's victory.

It doesn't take a genius to notice that Tarair is his primary god, Sébérus thought. *But I get to pick my own, dear priest, don't I? So tell me about someone else. Muscle-laden warriors are not my thing...*

His mind wandered back to the blackest of swords, so dark that even the raging sea of blackwaters greyed in comparison. A sword that could command the blackwaters. Did such a sword exist? What magic might such a relic be able to perform? Could it turn blackwaters to regular water, drain the blackwaters from blood and return Blackbloods to their prior form?

Suddenly, he heard a sharp growl from Grey Noon. "Sébérus!"

Clearly I missed an important question. Sébérus cleared his throat. *Well, I should convince him I've listened at least a little.*

"The sword of Hash-jak," Sébérus said. "Does it have a name?"

He turned to read Grey Noon's reaction. The Rezumi's countenance softened as he absorbed the question.

"Moakoko," Grey Noon said.

Sébérus nodded. "My priest, how do I know when I've become aware of who my primary god should be?"

"It takes most people years to discover." Grey Noon paused. "Though from the day a monk taught me the stories of the Ti'te'Vika, I knew Tarair and Erra were the two I admired most. And when I took to the seas, I memorized the list of gods who protect and bless sailors, and I offer them sacrifices monthly."

A monthly list to sacrifice to, huh? Well, no one said religion isn't work.

"So when you realized it was Tarair you would worship, did he just… connect with you?"

"Who did you connect with in these stories?" Grey Noon asked.

"May I answer your question with a question?" At his captain's nod, Sébérus continued, "Are we allowed to worship demons?"

"Absolutely not."

"May I ask the reason? Is it because they're evil?"

"Some of the gods can be less than honourable when the situation demands," Grey Noon said. "But no. You can't worship the demons because when the demons and gods went to war to decide whom the mortals should worship, the gods won. The demons are weak, unworthy of praise. The gods deserve worship. Understood?"

Sébérus bowed. "Of course. Does another god claim Hash-jak's sword?"

"Why the interest in the sword?" Grey Noon frowned. "Wait. When I said 'sea of blackness,' did you think I meant blackwaters? You like the sword because you think it defeats the blackwaters?"

Sébérus held back his ears from drooping. "You're saying the sea of black in your story doesn't have anything to do with blackwaters?"

Grey Noon let out a slow, quiet sigh. "I don't believe so, but if you ask the priest who ordained me... well, no one really knows."

Sébérus smiled. He still wanted that sword.

"You should spend the next hour in private meditation," Grey Noon said. "Don't leave until another worshiper comes to take your place."

"Of course. I thank you for your instruction, my priest. May Erra bless you." He held himself back from adding a blessing in the name of Tarair, since he'd yet to hear of Tarair bestowing anything but curses.

"Study the first twelve sacred ordinances, then read more stories of the gods."

With that, Grey Noon departed without another word.

Sébérus stared at the open page in the book, admiring the murky blade Moakoko.

CHAPTER FOUR

*I*t was a good Vasitan maintained so many connections, otherwise he'd have no idea where to begin looking for an informant to lead him to illegal blackwaters shipments. Even though he didn't know where to look, he knew who to ask.

Vasitan looked around at the mud huts, his nostrils burning with the smoke wafting up from various garbage heaps. Nearly all the souls who lived in this poor village were half-clothed and half-starved, and children with blank gazes sent languid stares his way.

Despicable, he thought. He'd forgotten such forlorn places existed.

The Council representative wiped the dark muck off his boots and kicked them against a ragged carpet below the gate of the hut he'd come to. Thankfully, this one seemed a little less dumpy than the others.

On either side of the gate rose a tall fence topped with spikes of sharp glass to prevent thieves from attempting to climb it. To Vasitan, these measures seemed unnecessary; the rings of barbed-wire within the fence itself should have discouraged anyone from even touching it.

He felt several pairs of eyes on him and knew they belonged to penniless villagers. He worried they may be coming up with a plan to steal the expensive clothes right off his back.

Well, they can have them, Vasitan thought, attempting to smooth out a crease in his jacket. *I'll never be able to rid these of the stench.*

Lamenting that he'd never be able to wear these clothes in public again, his thoughts turned to his absent son, sailing out along the frontiers with that Captain Ctzo. Zan must have had an impossible time keeping his clothes spotless on those filthy ships…

A pang hit his heart.

Zan always did care a great deal about keeping up appearances, Vasitan thought. *What in the world possessed him to become a sailor? From what I've seen, a sailor can't manage to stay clean no matter how hard he tries.*

His thoughts were interrupted by the approach of an armed guard on the other side of the gate.

"State your name!" The lad couldn't have been more than a teenager, but he spoke like a seasoned soldier, with a gruffness that didn't suit his youth any more than the large musket in his arms.

"I am Council Representative Vasitan, and you will let me in immediately."

A flash of fear filled the lad's eyes. His hand went behind his back, and suddenly several more guards appeared, each hurrying off in different directions. The lad must have signalled them.

Vasitan smiled in realization. *They think I'm here to perform an official inspection, so they're cleaning up evidence of illegal activities.*

An older man hurried out of the hut to stand beside the young guard.

"Terribly sorry to ask you to wait, Council Representative, but the master of the house is taking a bath," said the man.

"We both know he isn't," Vasitan said stonily. "Let me in right now. I'm not here for an inspection, and I don't care what illegal activities Hariner is up to. I'm here to discuss business."

"Our master would be insulted to hear these accusations." The older man's reply sounded rehearsed. "He runs a perfectly legal business and has supplied even the Emperor's ships with gunpowder and cannons. You are free to examine our facilities to your heart's content. But please, allow our master a moment to get dressed."

Vasitan sighed. "Fine, I'll wait as long as you need me to, but if this were an official inspection I would come with guards of my own and blast my way in. No excuses."

Suddenly, a man in a fine red suit appeared at the door and approached the gate. Vasitan smiled, recognizing Hariner immediately.

"Stop, stop," Hariner said, calling off his men. "No need to make him wait, my servants. If Mr. Vasitan is here to discuss business, allow him entry. Business is my thing!"

The young guard and older man exchanged a frightened look.

"Oh, come off it," Hariner remarked. "I've always known Vasitan was one of us—a crook through and through!"

Vasitan's face darkened. "How dare you—"

"If you want something, don't insult me." Hariner waved to his guards, and they set to pulling open the gate. "You're on my turf now."

When the gate was open, Vasitan stepped forward, a gleam in his eye.

He pointed at the young guard. "The legal age for an armed guard in the Questavan Empire is fifteen. This boy is clearly younger than that."

"He is not!"

"Ah, but I say he is, and in the eyes of the law that's all that matters."

Hariner paled. "Why… uh… ahem, yes, I get your drift. You there, servant. Kindly get a drink for our… most distinguished guest. Representative, I'll take you to my office. This way."

Vasitan looked around, admiring the clean walls and expensive décor. "Your office is quite appealing. Being a criminal must pay well."

"It has its perks." Hariner sat behind a finely polished desk of golden-yellow wood. He motioned to a silk-lined chair behind Vasitan. "Please, take a seat."

Vasitan did as instructed, and a servant soon arrived with a bottle of wine, pouring it into a crystal chalice. He handed the drink to Vasitan, then preceded to prepare a glass for his boss.

When Hariner received his chalice, he smiled glowingly at Vasitan. "I always drink before business. To whatever riches lie ahead!"

The two toasted and drank. However, Vasitan lacked patience to finish the formalities. Only a few sips in, he handed his drink back to the waiting servant.

"So, about my reason for coming."

Hariner sighed. "You politicians can't just relax for a few minutes, can you?"

"I will be missed if I don't return home. I haven't told anyone where I went or why."

"Smart move." Hariner relinquished his chalice to the servant. "Very well. Why are you here?"

"I need an informant. Someone who knows a lot about the blackwaters trade."

Hariner shivered. "Risky business. Never appealed to me."

"There's lots of money to be made. How could it not appeal to you?"

"Oh, I don't know. Maybe it has something to do with the fact you could get infected, become a monster, and lose your soul. Not an attractive thought." Hariner leaned forward. "And you know why there's so much money going around in that trade, right?"

Vasitan shrugged. He'd never much cared why. "I guess scientists pay a lot for the chance to make a name for themselves creating monsters."

"Sure. The scientists pay the blackwaters traders and slave traders, who in turn pay the blackwaters miners… but that's not where the *real* money is." Hariner leaned back again. "You know what Ti'te'Vika is, right?"

"A religion of the Gashaian Islands," Vasitan said. "They worship their own set of gods. Some of them are warring pirates, although some of them stay home and out of trouble."

"How about the Augai?"

Vasitan laughed. "An extinct nation that we actually thought would destroy us during the War of Nine Leagues. They're nobodies now."

Hariner shook his head. "The Unknowns?"

"A children's tale," Vasitan said. "Boogeymen blamed when a ship is discovered floating in the ocean, with its crew nowhere to be found."

"Well, I'm going to tell you right now that all three of these groups are very real, very alive, and very much growing. You know who gets the bulk of the money in the blackwaters trade? The scientists. Because there are many groups out there—pirates, religious extremists, rebellions—and they would sell their own eyes if it meant acquiring an enslaved, loyal, mindless army of drones that will fight to the death for their cause. A war is brewing, Representative. And where do you think that war will hit? Who's the most attractive target?"

Vasitan paused. "The city of Questava?"

"Exactly. And that, my friend, is why you should stay out of the trade. I purposely left the city and moved to the outskirts, because I'll be honest, I'm scared of what's coming."

Vasitan laughed. "You're joking! The Augai are extinct, the Unknowns are a myth, and do you really think the Ti'te'Vika would feel right about using zombie slaves in their war? I hear they have a pretty strict moral code."

"Mark my words, this is no laughing matter," Hariner said, pointing a finger at his mocker. "I've seen and heard things you wouldn't believe. There are a dozen or more groups fighting for a place at the top, collecting soldiers and hiding them so no one can guess when they'll be ready to strike. And when they are, they'll come straight for the capital."

The Council representative forced an end to his laughter, though a big grin remained on his face. "I did not come for your conspiracy theories, Hariner. I came to get advice."

"And that's my advice: stay away from the trade."

"How about this? Give me the information I want, and I promise to turn a blackwaters shipment over to the authorities at least once every three months."

Hariner narrowed his eyes. "And the other shipments you discover? What's your plan for them?"

"None of your concern."

"Force them to pay you or get handed over to the law?"

"You catch on quick."

"Don't have to be a genius to guess that one." Hariner rubbed his chin, contemplating. "There's something else I want. A while ago, I got a hold of some military plans for a new ship, the *Nomad*. Sold it to a shipbuilder who paid quite handsomely. He says he'd like more cutting-edge designs. Bring me the latest blueprints for the newest military ship, and you have a deal. And you'd better follow through on the other offer: taking blackwaters dealers off the market and putting them in jail. Then I'll ask the informant in question to contact you. Deal?"

"Fine, fine," Vasitan said. "He better be worth the trouble."

"Not he. She."

CHAPTER FIVE

Katia had made up her mind: the foreigners needed water, and Ian's sketch of the goddess Yupetas, whether or not he had intended to draw her, gave her the perfect idea of where to go. She recalled that a temple to the monster goddess had been erected a short distance from their hiding place.

For centuries unknown, the Darians had chosen to place their temples atop sinkholes. They'd treated sinkholes as sacred, because these caverns almost always contained an abundance of clean freshwater. They knew that on Aziasha, water could be found underground—and that had made the underground a haunt for spirits of all kinds.

Only two concerns nagged at her. One, the temple would lead them farther from her home, the tribe she had grown up in. And second, she'd heard horrible stories about Yupetas killing disrespectful visitors to her temple.

However, Katia could go a lot longer without water than the Scavgans. Even Vortro, she noted with despair, was showing a desperate need for water. She cupped the little worm in her hands, licking it profusely to moisten its dry skin. Vortro just lay there, listless, its beady eyes looking dull.

The creature's slime made her tongue go numb, so she could only continue licking for so long before she had to spit and recover for a few minutes.

Her fear of the goddess, and of how long it'd take them to reach her home, would have to be put aside. They needed water to survive, and they needed it before it was too late.

"Come on, Vortro," Ian said, looking over Katia's shoulder and watching his little friend. "Pull through, please."

Zan had been watching silently from farther back in the cave. Now, he sighed loudly and stood.

"All right, let's try something else." Zan lowered his fingers to the worm. "Go on, get into my skin. It's better than living out here."

Vortro's nose twitched, investigating the offered arm. But then the twitching stopped and Vortro again lay still.

Zan swallowed, causing a burning sensation to ignite in his throat. "That thing needs water. *We* need water. What are we going to do?" He looked to Katia, knowing she didn't understand his words but hoping she understood the situation.

With resolve, Katia stood on her back legs. She turned to Ian and lifted up Vortro, holding her position until Ian took the worm in his own hands. With Vortro transferred, Katia returned to a four-legged stance and marched out of the cavern. She looked back, her eyes ordering the others to follow.

Ian and Zan exchanged glances. Hesitantly, they followed, half-expecting her to reprimand them as they left the cave's safe shadows. Instead Katia turned ahead and led them deeper into the jungle.

With every step forward, Katia set her feet firmly, but inwardly she shivered with fear. She couldn't control her ears as they swivelled constantly, attuned to every snapping twig, every insect creaking, even her own rapid heartbeat.

The foreigners didn't know how to walk through the jungle silently. Nearly every move they made crushed a plant. They even chatted with each other, as though unaware of the precariousness of their situation.

How can I tell them to be silent? she wondered. *We don't need it to hear us.*

A low, pulsating growl echoed through the trees. Katia instinctively froze. The foreigners, too, stopped in their tracks, looking around with wide eyes for the source of the noise.

She chided herself for freezing up like that. They needed to run—now. That was the best chance they had. They had to stay out of the creature's way.

Katia prepared to make a headlong dash forward, but then her gaze fell on two silvery eyes staring at them through the bushes. She tensed. A mydisant! These mighty predators were kings of the jungle, and she'd heard more than one story of Darians being murdered by the animals.

She'd been so busy thinking about the *other* creature that she'd stopped listening for natural predators sneaking through the thickets. Now they faced a more immediate threat.

"Foreigners, get back!" Katia screamed.

She continued to yell at the top of her lungs, pretending to be unafraid and knowing that reacting in fear would get her and the foreigners killed.

Unfortunately, the strategy didn't appear to be working.

"What was that?" Zan eyed Katia, noting her frozen stance.

"It sounded... big." Ian straightened, then spoke more calmly. "But even the small insects here can make very loud noises. It might be nothing."

"Are you watching our guide?" Zan hissed. "Whatever it is, she's scared."

Suddenly, Katia let out a high-pitched yip, startling Ian and Zan. The Darian was facing the bushes, hissing violently and clawing the air. She stood on her hindlegs and pointed into the thicket, yelling furiously.

"Do you see anyone?" Ian asked. "It sounds like she's really mad at something."

Zan shook his head. "Ian, you have both eyes, and your vision was better to begin with. If you can't see it, how could I?"

The Scavgans took hurried steps backwards as a large, lithe shape with rippling muscles and silver eyes exited the thicket and walked into plain view. Its canine teeth were far too large to fit in its mouth and so they protruded on either side of the creature's upper jaw, its lower jaw fitted between them.

Neither Ian nor Zan had ever seen a creature with such large claws. Its hooked nails appeared too big even for the wide paws they jutted from.

Katia stopped yelling and backed up into Ian. Her head bobbed frantically.

The monster paced in front of the trio as though assessing how it wanted to kill them. It moved nimbly on all fours, and though terrified, Zan could only wonder why it hadn't attacked them yet. It seemed ready to spring at their throats.

But then, with incredible speed, the monster darted away, disappearing into the distant jungle in a heartbeat.

Zan couldn't believe it. Had Katia somehow scared it away?

Another growl suddenly rumbled through the forest, only this time the sound boomed from right behind them. Startled, Katia rushed off, only stopping to look back at the Scavgans and motion with her hand for them to follow.

Without thinking, they did as she ordered—just as a huge forelimb thudded down into the ground behind them, smashing the bushes beneath it.

Ian and Zan collapsed beside Katia, then turned back to see what had scared the silver-eyed predator away.

Zan's jaw dropped. "That's…"

"…a dragon," Ian finished, breathing out in awe.

Though the artistic representations Zan had seen of Aziasha's most impressive monsters had certainly left something to be desired in terms of accuracy, Zan had no doubt as to what stood before him now. This was the creature that the Questavan explorers had written about, that the general public had either doubted or feared the existence of, and that the potters and painters had felt an almost magnetic appeal towards.

The dragon exhaled through large nostrils, its calm eyes searching the ground as it lowered its stately head, crowned with a tall, back-curving crest of bone. Its heavy forefoot thudded into the ground, heedless of the foliage it crushed.

As it passed by the three tiny onlookers, Zan noticed its thick muscles and tough, scaly hide. He watched open-mouthed, both hoping and fearing that the beast would unleash a plume of fire from its mouth. He also noticed, with some disappointment, that the creature didn't have any wings.

Maybe that's good, he thought. *It's scary enough without them.*

Zan had long believed that the scariest part about meeting a dragon would be the beast's size, strength, or flames. But in this moment, what cowed him most was how ghost-like it seemed. Though huge, its patterned skin of spots, stripes, and whorls made it nearly invisible in the shadows of the jungle. The dragon occasionally stomped or bellowed, a sound that overwhelmed his ears and shook the earth, yet when it wished it could step noiselessly, moving through the forest with unnatural skill.

He breathed a sigh of relief as the dragon continued on, apparently uninterested in them. Soon the end of its long, spiked tail vanished from sight.

Katia pulled herself out of the bushes and yipped at the Scavgans. Understanding what she wanted, Zan and Ian followed her, resuming their trek through the trees.

Zan eyed Ian curiously. "You look like you have something on your mind."

"Just thinking," Ian said.

"Yeah. I'll admit, I never expected to see a dragon either."

"I'm thinking about something scarier, though."

Zan raised an eyebrow. "What?"

"Well, the Kamai have said they take down full-grown dragons in hunts. For fun." Ian watched for his friend's reaction.

Zan shook his head. "Guess I need to give Réto and Kyra more credit as fighters. If they can take down one of those things, there must be very little a Kamai can't do."

How great it is not to have a Kamai's weakness, Sébérus thought as he watched Nva's elegant black form. She was so pretty and petite, a killer in a small reptilian package. Sébérus wondered, having both Darian and Kamai blood in him, which of the two races he should feel physically attracted towards.

He quickly decided. *I'd rather marry a Darian.*

Nva lay at Grey Noon's feet, her longing eyes focused on her master. Every time he motioned for something—beckoning a sailor, requesting a small snack—she raced to carry out the command before anyone else could even process it. When she'd finished, she'd return to her former position, awaiting her captain's next move.

Does she realize how silly she looks? Sébérus wondered. *Master, master, look at me, care about me! Master, master, I'm intelligent enough to use utensils and make my own meals, but I'd rather eat scraps from your hands. Master, master, I'm*

*powerful enough to rip you to pieces, but I'd rather be your slave and do absolutely
anything you ask.*

He knew from his readings that this so-called condition was
known as a servant complex. It boggled the minds of brilliant scientists and casual observers alike: the Kamai were such intelligent, in-
ventive, capable creatures, yet they instinctively enslaved themselves
to other races. The servant complex held so great a power over their
psyche that those Kamai still living free went out of their way to
ensure they never came into contact with outsiders, for fear that the
mere encounter would lead them into self-induced slavery.

As Grey Noon walked off, his mind on a new task, Nva sent a
stabbing glare at Sébérus.

"Am I that interesting, Blackblood?" she hissed.

Sébérus smiled sweetly. "Oh, just admiring the relationship
between a Kamai and her master."

Nva puffed out her chest proudly. "Grey Noon is an incredible
master."

Unbelievable, Sébérus thought. *She's actually going to brag about it!*

"You should be grateful to be aboard his ship," Nva continued.
"The *Ko'Ekua* is this world's nearest place to the heavenly courts.
Here, justice is carried out."

Sébérus frowned at her. She had allowed Grey Noon to control her moral compass. He was her master; how could he be wrong?

"Am I funny to you?" Nva asked, her eyes narrowing. "You
smile as though... amused."

At least she had one advantage. No one else on the ship would
have read the miniscule upturn of his lips as a sign of amusement.
She could pick up on his emotions far too well for his liking.

He spread his hands. "What do you want me to say, Nva? You are an elegant creature!"

"Don't mock me." Nva admired her own talons. "Or you'll find my claws aren't just for show. I don't fear you, Blackblood. I pity you."

Sébérus barely held back a coughing laugh. "Um... *you* pity *me*? How so?"

"I know you don't belong here, and you're just using us to escape. You want us to sail you around until you can sneak off and start a new life for yourself."

He frowned. It irritated him how thoroughly she understood his intentions. But admitting it would only bring more trouble.

"Look, Nva, this may surprise you, but all I want is a chance to study under the great Grey Noon," he said.

"That is why I pity you." She smiled, a chilling sight. "You lie, and your lies will be discovered. My master is smarter than you give him credit for."

Sébérus nodded nonchalantly. "I'm guessing you've told him you're suspicious of me. What does he think of your paranoia?"

Nva dodged the question. "When Grey Noon catches you in your deception... well, you will have good reason to feel sorry for yourself, and good reason to fear your inevitable fate."

Captain Ctzo held a stoic stance and stern expression. Before him, aboard the *Radiant Dawn*, the entire crew stood, many of them blushing or staring at their feet.

"Does anyone have anything to say about the brawl that took place yesterday?" he asked commandingly.

Tyzak felt he should say something. His throat went dry with fear.

The captain continued. "You all know the rules. The only appropriate occasions for fighting are sanctioned practice duels and serious battles against pirates. Brawling is not allowed, and will be punished. Did that escape your minds when you decided to watch the fight instead of reporting it to me?"

"Sir, who told you?" a Scavgan spoke up timidly.

"That's my concern, not yours." Ctzo eyed Tyzak in a sideways glance. "Well?"

Tyzak coughed, a failed attempt to clear his throat. "Black Night and Chiha got into an argument in the galley. Someone told them to take it outside, and... well, they decided to settle their differences in... an unsanctioned duel."

"Were you there?"

Tyzak hung his head, twirling his foot against the ground in a nervous circle. "Yes."

"Were you planning on reporting to me?"

"It seemed harmless enough, sir," he said before adding, "With Chiha's attitude, and how little everyone likes her, I wouldn't be surprised if it becomes a regular event."

Ctzo responded with a silent stare. Then he turned away, allowing Tyzak to release the breath he'd been unconsciously holding.

"Next time," the captain said, "I expect such a brawl to be stopped before it gets started. You all claim you can be soldiers. You should be tough enough to handle the task of breaking apart a fight between fellow crewmembers. Dismissed."

The line divided in a hurry, each sailor rushing off to look busy in one place or another. Only Tyzak stayed behind, looking up at his captain.

"I… I really am sorry." Tyzak hung his head again.

"So, Chiha has been a problem?" the captain said in a quiet voice.

Tyzak paused to think up a polite way to handle the topic. "Well, she's arrogant, and that can lead to her being rude. And she's very… um, assertive."

"Bossy?"

"Yeah, that might be one way to put it."

Ctzo sighed. "Thank you for bringing that up."

"You hadn't noticed?"

"On the contrary. She's an angel around me."

Tyzak's jaw dropped. "An angel?"

"Yes. She's very respectful, polite, and obedient. I guess she knows who has the authority to push her around, and who doesn't. But the other members of her tribe warned me about how she'll behave when I'm not watching."

"Her tribe, meaning the other Athai?"

"And the Reea. They were the first to report the brawl."

Tyzak looked around. He very rarely saw the Reea, but the serpentine swamp creatures could turn invisible at will, so for all he knew all five aboard ship could be watching him even now. He shivered at the thought.

"Captain, may I request a new rule be made?"

"Name the rule," Ctzo said.

"A non-invisibility rule, insisting that those who can make themselves invisible shouldn't do so on a regular basis, for the peace of mind of their fellow crewmates."

Ctzo chuckled. "The Reea are shy. When they warm up to us, the Athai assured me they will make themselves visible again."

"Oh, good." Tyzak smiled with relief. "Because it really is creepy."

Kind of like our invisible first mate, Jani, he almost said.

Ctzo nodded in farewell. "I'm heading back to *Diversity* now. I'll send Kyra aboard to keep an eye on things."

"Very well, Captain."

Tyzak watched Ctzo leave. It was a little odd not having him aboard all the time. The captain was gone, Ian and Zan were gone... who would he be friends with now?

"I'm sorry," spoke a female voice, throwing Tyzak off.

He turned to face the speaker. "Pardon? Oh, it's you, dear Yakara."

The Reea's snake-like head bobbed, her long neck curving so her whole serpentine body made the shape of an S. She spoke so softly he could barely hear her.

"I'm sorry being creepy," Yakara said. "No more invisible if you want."

This is where it'd be polite to argue that she can do whatever makes her feel comfortable, Tyzak thought. He eyed her small, sharp fangs, her clawed hands, and the pincer-like appendages framing her dagger of a tail. *But if something as scary as this is slithering around, I'd really rather see it.*

He gave her a wide, bright-toothed grin. "Ah, how thoughtful of you! I appreciate the gesture. And what have you been up to today?"

She shied away, pressing the side of her face into her scales. "Nothing fun."

"Something unfun?"

"Y... yeah." She said. "Hiding from Chiha."

"Why would you do that?" Tyzak asked. "I thought you two were good friends? She said she rescued you or something like that. Never would tell me the story. And I hate untold stories. Well, unless the story isn't worth telling—"

"She knows I told."

"Wait," Tyzak said, processing her words. "You were the one who reported her to Captain Ctzo?"

"Chief Orthel would have wanted me to tell. She's mad."

"Poor darling." Tyzak patted her head. "Yeah, I don't think Chiha's too impressed with how I've been avoiding her either. Perhaps we could avoid her together. I'd appreciate the company."

Yakara slithered closer, wrapping a coil around Tyzak's legs. He gulped at the disconcerting sensation of her scaly skin.

"You know, it may be a long while before you lay eyes on the Marsh Isles again."

Yakara tightened her coil, prompting Tyzak to gasp.

"Ahem... say, Yakara, would you... um..."

His gaze locked with hers. Her unusual eyes, a glowing white backdrop with a vertical and horizontal line of red dissecting it, dimmed. She seemed to be on the verge of tears.

"Oh, darling." He petted her coil. "You miss him a lot."

"He... my master."

"That's right. The captain mentioned that you Reea have the servant complex, like the Kamai." Yakara gave him a blank look.

"You know, the servant complex. You find a master, you serve them for life…"

"Don't everyone do that?"

"No."

"Not you and captain?" Yakara asked.

"That's a temporary arrangement. He's my boss, not my master."

"But you like him?"

"He's a very good captain." Tyzak reached out to pet Yakara's head. "I think you and I will be good friends."

"Friends? True?"

"Yes. I may not be Orthel, but I can keep you from feeling lonely while Chiha is mad at you."

Yakara pressed her head against his shoulder. "Thank."

"You're greatly welcome." Tyzak grinned widely. "Now… ahem… do you mind loosening your grip just a tad?"

CHAPTER SIX

$\mathcal{V}$asitan nodded as he listened to a judge explain his woes. Here, a crowded get-together of well-to-dos didn't seem so cramped. This was Parliament's first corridor, an impressive work of architecture with a vaulted ceiling and gemstone-inlaid floor. Though technically a hallway, its grandeur and size left it feeling more like an enormous room.

Several times a year, whenever he felt like it, the Emperor threw a party here. Only his closest family, the Council, the Council representatives, the general, and the highest-regarded war heroes, captains, and judges were invited—and of course a few of their unmarried sons and daughters, looking to flirt and perhaps score a marriage arrangement to leave them in a suitable position of power.

Some days, Vasitan enjoyed these parties. On others, like today, they felt like a formality. Especially since the judges and captains used the opportunity to bring to Vasitan's attention matters that bothered them. Perhaps they were too afraid to go to a Council member directly until they'd gotten a representative on their side, and they were certainly respectful enough not to complain to the Emperor until the matter had crossed the Council's desk.

It never failed that the captains would grumble about the harbour's gruelling stairway and suggest alternative ways to transport goods to and from the harbour. The judges, at least, varied their complaints.

Even so, Vasitan's mind wandered as he listened to this judge's pleas. He pictured Zan at the party with his friends, as he'd been many times before, joking and teasing, every now and then bringing up a question or even accusation about how the working class was treated. Zan may not have been flawless, but he had always been admired, and the young women in particular had noticed his charm and sense of fashion.

"Don't you find it so?" the judge asked when he had finished his speech.

It took a moment for Vasitan to absorb the question. He cleared his throat, trying to remember the topic they'd been discussing.

"Right… I suppose I never gave it enough thought before."

"Precisely my point. The Blackblood problem isn't something people see as affecting their day-to-day lives, so it can be easy to overlook."

Ah, that's right, Vasitan recalled. *We were talking about blackwaters pirates.*

"I happen to have a peer who did thorough research on the subject of blackwaters and the increasing rate of infection," the judge continued. "He was a fellow by the name of Jakodi Jair. Now, mind you, some of his theories are questionable, but I assure you, he wasn't wrong about the most important matter: blackwaters cannot be fully destroyed, and as mining for blackwaters increases, Blackblood infections are sure to become an epidemic. But no one seems prepared—"

"Forgive me, I hate to interrupt," Vasitan said politely as his gaze roamed to Parliament's exit, a grand doorway lined with guards. "I do believe my Overseer is leaving, and I have an important matter to discuss with him."

Without waiting for a reply, Vasitan hurriedly left the judge's side and rushed to the doors.

"Mayal, Your Excellence," Vasitan called.

An old Scavgan in an off-white robe stopped and turned, revealing the pale scar marring the length of his face. "Vasitan?"

Vasitan bowed at the waist. Though as a Council representative he technically worked for the Council as a whole, Mayal was his Overseer, the person most responsible for keeping Vasitan on task, and the only one who could fire him without calling the Council to vote on the matter.

"If it pleases you, I would like to request a week off from my duties." Noting Mayal's frown, Vasitan continued. "It's my son, sir…" He looked around, making sure no one else stood within hearing range. "May I speak to you privately?"

"You may." Mayal lifted his hand, a sign that Vasitan could rise, and the two walked over to an empty corner of the spacious room.

"You see, it's my son, Zan…" Vasitan stopped, trying to summon the right words.

"I don't have all day." Mayal sounded kind, but he clearly didn't want to wait long for an explanation.

"Zan ran off," Vasitan whispered. "He got himself hired by Captain Ctzo and is now on a ship who knows where."

"Ctzo?" Mayal's eyes widened. "Why would he allow your son to do such a thing?"

Vasitan knew it wasn't entirely Ctzo's fault, but he felt the need to blame someone. "I don't know why he would be so, pardon my phrasing, so daft. But the captain took off with Zan, and I've been worried sick about his well-being ever since."

"I see." Mayal's countenance saddened. "I always thought Ctzo to be a respectable gentleman. And to think I and the rest of the Council trusted him with the flag of an elite pirate hunter."

Vasitan could have pointed out that the Council's choice to make Ctzo pay for his own crew and ship, instead of providing him with either funds or a fleet, sent mixed messages about their level of trust in him. But Vasitan wasn't about to point this out. After all, he knew that the "pirate hunter" title wasn't handed out lightly, and it came with a lot more authority than the name suggested. In reality, anyone could hunt pirates with a decent chance of not landing in jail. The pirate hunters held other rights as well. Rights of conquest. Political power. And in wartime, they held high positions in the military.

"When Ctzo returns, I'll speak with him about his poor decision regarding your son," Mayal continued. "For now, take some time off and try not to worry about Zan too terribly."

Vasitan bowed at the waist. "Thank you for your concern and your kind words."

With a final nod, Mayal continued toward the doors, exiting the hall.

"Do you have time for one more visit, Representative?" a female voice asked.

Vasitan turned to lock gazes with a young woman about Zan's age. He eyed her, noting her long-sleeved but nevertheless flattering bejewelled dress.

"And you are?" Vasitan asked politely.

The young lady grinned with confidence. "My father is the judge you were speaking with earlier. But I doubt you care about that."

"Pardon?"

"My name is Brimsta. But I doubt you care about that either. The fact that I'm the informant Hariner recommended is all you need to know."

Vasitan's eyes widened and he shot a quick gaze around the crowd. His shoulders tensed, but he made them relax. All the partiers were out of hearing range.

"You?" He looked her over again. "Not only are you a woman, you're a *young* woman. Is Hariner playing me?"

"Ouch." Brimsta's smile faded. "Thanks for the vote of confidence. But believe me when I say, I know more about the black-waters market than... well, just about anyone." At Vasitan's raised eyebrow, her grin returned. "Call it a hobby."

"Pretty sad hobby." Vasitan frowned at her. "You should be more concerned about finding a suitor."

"Well, I'm sorry that I can't wait on your handsome son to entertain me. And I do have prospects, not that it concerns you." She took a step closer to him. "I'm already bored with this conversation. Don't you want to talk business?"

Vasitan looked over the guests, searching for her father.

"No, I haven't told him about my hobby," Brimsta said. "He's a judge. You think he wouldn't lock me up in a cold, forgotten dungeon somewhere?"

"I'm sure he has more love for you than that."

"You don't know him. Now, ask me a question."

She stared up at him, waiting.

He sighed. "Fine. When and where is the next blackwaters shipment coming in?"

Brimsta folded her hands behind her back. "It's a little more complicated than that. Have you ever heard of Atzinus? Yituri? Requra?"

Vasitan shook his head.

She rolled her eyes. "If you want to know about the shipments, know the buyers. I keep my ears open for who's in the market to buy, how much, and when. Now Atzinus is the biggest buyer of blackwaters, but he's way down in Aziasha, so that means most of the market never passes through Questava."

"A lot of good that does me," Vasitan muttered. "Why do I care?"

"Focus. Word is, Atzinus has been killed by his underlings and his operation deserted. It's hard to tell with reports from Aziasha, though. They may or may not be that accurate. Another big buyer is Jakodi Jair, but he's missing and hasn't ordered a shipment recently. If he had, that would pass through Questava. So you're looking at smaller-time operations, like Yituri and Requra. They're bigger than many but without the reputations of either Atzinus or Jair."

Vasitan glared at her through narrow eyes. "Are you intentionally wasting my time?"

"Fine." Brimsta's hands moved to her hips. "I'm only trying to help. You see, some of the blackwaters scientists have given their smugglers a particular signal to use—something that confirms that they are indeed his dealers and not law enforcers posing as dealers.

Yituri and Requra both use this system, as did Atzinus. Jair had his smugglers fly a specific flag. The others kept things more subtle."

A grin slipped onto Vasitan's face. "Ah. Now you have my attention."

"I can give you an estimate on when shipments might arrive, but your best bet is to go aboard every incoming ship within this timeframe—"

Vasitan coughed. "Dear woman, do you know how many ships come into port every day?"

"I'll try to narrow it down to a two-hour period. You go aboard, see if you can locate the signal, and if you find it you've got your smugglers to blackmail. And I get ten percent of what you force out of the smugglers."

Vasitan frowned. "Pardon?"

"Please," Brimsta chuckled. "Hariner didn't say I'd be free, did he?"

CHAPTER SEVEN

Zan gasped for breath, ignoring the tangles of foliage in his path. "Is traveling in Aziasha always an uphill climb?"

He knew his guide Katia couldn't understand him, and therefore wouldn't answer, but he still felt it worth saying out loud.

Ian seemed worn out, too, slouching as he walked, though Zan guessed his friend's exhaustion was more mental than physical. His downcast eyes appeared to be full of despair.

"Ian?" Zan said. "Quit worrying. Katia knows where we're going." Ian didn't reply. "What's the matter? I thought you liked exploration and adventure."

"This doesn't feel like an adventure anymore."

"How so?"

Ian paused. "Have you noticed there's no water anywhere?"

Zan had noticed. "Maybe there's water nearby, but she's leading us away from it."

"Doesn't she ever get thirsty?"

"Look, Ian, I don't know. Katia knows this jungle. Let's just trust her."

"I feel useless." Ian pushed aside a branch. "She won't let us do anything but follow. She won't let us veer aside, or carry her, or—"

"You hate it when you don't get your way, don't you?"

Ian turned back to give Zan an insulted look. "What do you mean?"

Zan smiled. "Face it, Ian. You were the captain's favourite. You wanted to fire the cannon, you got to fire the cannon. You wanted to borrow the Kamai, you got to borrow the Kamai. If you had wanted to be the first mate, I'm sure Captain Ctzo would have replaced Mr. Invisible with you."

"His name is Jani."

"Have you ever so much as seen him?"

"No, but the captain insists he's there. And you're changing the subject. I didn't get everything I wanted on the ship."

"Well, it felt like it." Zan grabbed a branch and pulled himself over a slippery patch of mud. "But Katia isn't the captain, and more importantly, Aziasha isn't the *Diversity*. You know your way around a boat, and around a rifle, there's no denying that. But the jungle? That's Katia's department."

Ian frowned in aggravation. The two fell silent.

"On another subject," Zan said at last, "I never did learn how you got to be so good with a gun."

Ian swallowed. "It's... not the best of stories."

"I'm not Tyzak. A story doesn't need to impress me for me to listen."

"That's not what I meant." Ian shook his head. "I mean, it's kind of painful."

Zan allowed his friend to remain silent for a few moments. At last, though, Ian began to speak.

"My village is by the sea, but it doesn't have the manpower or resources to be as well-defended as the city of Questava. So we get attacked by pirates every now and then. Usually the older men in the village are able to fight them. My dad tried training me to use a gun, because he knew I may need to fight the pirates someday. But I didn't take it seriously. I was just a kid. I thought someone else would always be there to protect us."

"And something changed?"

"Yes." Ian took a deep breath. "One day I was out playing with some kids. We were in a warehouse, goofing around. Then a group of pirates burst in, planning to steal supplies. One of them saw a young kid, took out a pistol, and shot him in the leg. And while my friend was down, the pirate grabbed a broom pole and started beating on him." He clenched his jaw. "I don't know why the pirate did it. It makes no sense to me. The kid was screaming, bleeding... I didn't think. I just rushed at the pirate. I caught him off-guard and managed to take the pistol from him. I fired again and again, standing right there on top of him. But I was so shaky, my judgment so clouded, my skills lacking... I fired off every last bullet in that gun and I still hadn't killed the pirate. He just lay there, dying, his eyes full of fear..."

Zan laid a hand on Ian's shoulder. Ian pushed it away.

"It took a few minutes for him to die. My dad told me afterwards that I did well, that my friend would probably be dead if I hadn't stepped in. But I decided for myself two things that day. One, I wanted to fight pirates. And two, it doesn't matter how awful a person is: no one deserves to die the way that pirate did. So I improved my skill with a gun and joined the *Diversity*. If I need to kill pirates to keep others safe, they should at least be given a quick death."

"I... I'm sorry," Zan said. "I didn't know you'd been through something so rough."

"I don't like to talk about it. And I don't think about it a lot. I just focus on my goals: become a better fighter, and help Ctzo. Maybe I'm not as mature as you are, but I know what I'm doing and why I do it."

"Did I call you immature?"

"You called me a spoiled brat."

"No." Zan laughed. "*I'm* a spoiled brat. You're just irresistible. Why do you think I like teasing you?"

"You also said I can't handle not getting my way..."

"Well, you're not handling it well right now. You're pouting about it."

Tears ran down Ian's cheeks. "I just don't like feeling helpless, okay?"

"No one does," Zan said, softening his voice. "Well, maybe Tyzak. But I guess I've gotten used to feeling helpless since joining Ctzo's crew."

Ian frowned. "What do you mean?"

"I didn't realize how much I could do in Questava until I stepped away from Questava. Now? I don't know. Part of me wonders if I should have stayed there."

For the first time in hours, Katia spoke up. "Kuya ve ca."

Zan and Ian attempted to discern the meaning from her tone, failing utterly.

"I got nothing," Zan said.

"Me neither. But she's smiling."

"Oh. So it's good news."

"I guess."

As the silvery sun began to slip beneath the horizon, Katia came to a halt before the Temple of Yupetas.

"We're here," she told Ian and Zan, hoping that somehow her smile would translate the message.

She turned her gaze back to the temple. Its entrance appeared as merely a dirty tunnel leading down into the earth, and a single unobtrusive stone to the right contained Yupetas' squiggly symbol marked into it for any passing Darian to recognize. Unlike the Scavgans, the Darians felt no need to make grand displays of their temples.

Katia stepped into the shadow of the tunnel. A shiver ran down her spine, but she shrugged it off. The foreigners needed water. This was no time to be nervous, and besides, perhaps the temple goddess wouldn't be home. Perhaps she had died.

Or perhaps she was alive and present and deadly. If so, they would be saved only by confidence and respect.

Her mind ran through the various ways of telling the foreigners to keep quiet. Suddenly remembering something, she turned to them and held an upward-pointed finger over her lips.

Zan and Ian got the message and nodded.

The tunnel was narrow enough that the two Scavgans had to crouch to pass through, and dark enough that it could only be navigated by touch. Fortunately it wasn't a long journey, however, and when the tunnel ended Katia sniffed out the pile of sticks she knew to be waiting for them. She then patted the dirty floor with her hands until she found an oval stone and struck it against the sticks repeatedly.

The Scavgans gasped when the sticks ignited, sending a whoosh of flame up into the cavern. Around them, orange light brought to life a host of symbols carved into the wall, some of them simplified drawings of animals, plants, and landmarks. Others would look to the foreigners as nothing more than meaningless squiggles.

And through the middle of the cavern, a wide, shallow river passed by them.

Finally, they had reached water.

"Water!" Ian rushed to the river with reckless abandon, kneeling beside it so he could press his mouth to the clear liquid.

Meanwhile, Zan looked to Katia, awaiting her direction. When she didn't tell them to stop, he too went to the river, scooping up water with his hands and slurping it gratefully.

Aside from the sounds of gulping, the crackling fire, and the murmur of the river, the cavern was silent. Heaviness hung in the air, making even these sounds seem muted.

A high-pitched squeak from Vortro made everyone jump, and for Zan and Ian this was the first time they'd ever heard the worm make a noise.

"What was that?" Zan whispered.

Ian reached into his pocket and pulled out his hand. The worm stared back at him through beady black eyes. "Vortro? Was that you?"

Vortro squeaked again. The sound shattered the quiet and echoed off the walls.

"Ian," Zan hissed between clenched teeth. "Keep your worm under control!"

Ian shushed his friend, gently petting Vortro with one hand while holding it with the other. As it squeaked, Ian lowered the worm into the water. The worm floated on the surface, unmoving. Then, wiggling rapidly, it darted across the river and back again.

Ian smiled. "Zan, look at how happy he is."

"Can you blame her?" Zan said. "The poor thing was drying up."

"Her?" Ian asked, shaking his head. "Vortro is a he."

Zan splashed a bit of water over his face. "Says you."

Ian shrugged and turned to Katia. "Aren't you going to drink something?"

Her eyes locked on his, but she didn't say or do anything.

"Zan, does she seem scared to you?" Ian whispered.

His friend nodded. "I think we should leave."

"Katia, drink. Then we can go." He pointed to the water, then back to the tunnel they'd just come through.

Nodding, Katia slinked to the water and lapped it up, eyes darting around and ears swerving this way and that.

"She does seem scared," Zan said, then glanced back at the river. "It's too bad we don't have a way to bring any water with us."

Ian sighed as he lowered his head to drink some more. As he did so, however, the sound of splashing downriver made him freeze. Ian looked up. Had that been Vortro? No. The worm floated nearby, eyeing him in silence.

Katia whimpered, prompting the Scavgans to back away from the water. Even Vortro crawled out of the pool and slid over to Ian's foot, up his leg, and into the safety of his pocket.

Ears swerving, eyes darting, Katia edged away from the water.

We shouldn't have come here. Katia could no longer hold back her panic. *What have I done? These foreigners, I promised myself I'd take care of them, bring them safely back to their ship. But now...*

A slithering form broke the water's surface. Whether serpent or fish, Katia didn't care to analyze which it resembled more. She knew it was Yupetas.

In that moment, an idea came to her.

With faked defiance, she growled to the beast, "Yupetas, you worthless little worm! Get lost or I'll bite off your head!"

She turned quickly to the Scavgans, who stared with wide and confused eyes. Katia ran at them, teeth bared, aiming to back them into the tunnel. If she stayed behind to be killed, she reasoned, the others could escape.

Had the Scavgans understood her goal, perhaps they'd have been awed by her sense of self-sacrifice. However, to her, it merely stemmed from what she'd been taught as a child: the survival of the tribe is more important than the survival of the individual. And these foreigners were now her tribe.

But the success of her strategy depended on the Scavgans, and Ian and Zan merely raised their eyebrows, frowning down at the sweet little creature as she bluff-charged them, clearly wondering what in the world had gone wrong with her.

We're dead. Her ears drooped. She didn't find the situation humorous for one second. *I can't save them.*

Suddenly, the jaws of the Scavgans fell open, their eyes rising to the cavern's ceiling. Katia followed their gaze, then jumped backed. Without the slightest noise, Yupetas had slipped out of the water and crawled along the limestone ceiling to hang just above the Scavgans, her tongue flicking rhythmically. Massive and muscular, with dozens of clawed legs and a head wide enough to swallow both Scavgans whole, Yupetas examined the trio through glowing, cross-shaped pupils.

It was a Reea.

Katia narrowed her eyes, her fear dissipating briefly as she studied the being. Yupetas had more legs, and she was so much larger, but she was undoubtedly a Reea.

"Ma'am, are you from the Marsh Isles?" Katia spoke in a gentle, friendly voice.

Yupetas hissed, the sound echoing off the walls of the chamber. "I am born of darkness, and to darkness I will go. And into darkness, you will be swallowed." Her mouth opened, revealing daggerlike teeth.

She's no goddess, she mused. *She's just an insane Reea!*

Insane or not, though, this creature would kill them all. Unless there was a way to reason with her.

Her thoughts were interrupted by a series of loud squeaks from Vortro.

Yupetas closed her mouth. Flicking her tongue out, the Reea looked around for the source of the squeaks. "What sort of being is this?"

Katia didn't stick around to answer. Seeing an opportunity, she darted through the tunnel, back to the surface, all the while mentally begging the Scavgans to follow.

As she exited the tunnel and tumbled out into the jungle, a body crashed into her from behind.

"Ouch," Zan muttered as he lifted himself back into his feet. "Sorry."

Katia relaxed a little. He must have tripped. When she looked around, her heart filled with relief at the sight of Ian. Even the little worm Vortro was sticking its head out of Ian's pocket.

She waited for a moment, watching the tunnel, but instinct told her that Yupetas wouldn't be giving them any more trouble.

We're alive! Katia sighed deeply, then gazed into the jungle around them. *Back to figuring out a safe path home.*

CHAPTER EIGHT

*T*hough it had been only a month ago, it seemed like eons since Ctzo had experienced his strange supernatural vision of Mocjoa. Having been infected with Jair's venom, he had been lifted by Jani and transported to the islands of the Mocjoa, where his wound had been healed. Then he'd woken up back amongst the Athai tribe.

After the experience, he'd had the Kamai bring him his scrolls so he could chart the islands he'd seen. He now examined one of those scrolls. The image on the parchment was an approximation, but it contained every detail Ctzo had been able to remember. There was a cluster of four islands, the largest being a nearly perfect circle, and the smaller three forming a triangle just to the north.

Though his eyes remained on the scroll, in his mind he pictured the woman who'd tended to his wounds. He hadn't caught her name, but she had been bug-like, with spidery fangs and elbowed antennae. He'd only attempted to sketch her form a few days ago, and he was less than satisfied with the results.

A knock on the door awakened Ctzo to the world around him. He knew from the familiar knock that Réto awaited at the other side of the door.

"Come in," Ctzo called absently, his eyes still on the map.

The latch lifted and revealed Réto perched along the frame of the door, ensuring he had some distance between himself and the floor. Kamai couldn't take off from the ground, so they generally attempted to remain on platforms or other high points, allowing them to take flight at a moment's notice.

"Another ship is approaching," Réto said. "The crew awaits your orders."

Ctzo nodded. "Perhaps the pirates are finally returning."

"Perhaps. I haven't seen any regalts for a week."

Upon arriving to the oceans surrounding Aziasha, Ctzo had warned his crew that the area lay deep within pirate territory. Many factions and troublemakers roamed these waters, hoping to collect on resources gleaned from Aziasha's rich jungles—particularly hoping to gather, steal, or sell blackwaters.

However, the ocean had been oddly empty of ships. Ctzo had learned from firsthand experience why the local pirates docked at this time of year. It was regalt mating season. The massive sea monsters, as big as ships, occasionally came to the surface to perform their courtship ritual, the males battling each other in writhing masses. The curious fish found ships fascinating, too, and it had been an unnerving experience when one had toyed with the *Diversity*.

Perhaps the mating season had come to a close, and the pirates were returning to their former activities.

Standing, Ctzo followed Réto onto the main deck. As the captain came to a stop by the ship's railing, the Kamai landed on his shoulder.

Sure enough, across the water a ship was quickly coming into focus. Ctzo took out his spyglass and peered through to the distant ship. Waving atop the masts were flags of red and black, an unfamiliar design. As he watched, however, the mysterious vessel lowered its flags. When the flags were out of sight, new ones arose in their place, with a checkered red-and-yellow design.

"What's that?" Chiha stepped up beside Ctzo, watching him keenly.

"I don't know whose flags they were flying, but they've clearly seen us," Ctzo said. "Now they're flying communication flags."

"What are those?"

"There's a sort of language of flags, developed by sailors so we can communicate at a distance. They're using the Questavan style, signalling that they wish to talk." Ctzo turned to find the rest of the crew watching him. "Load the cannons and prepare to fire. Aziasha may belong under the governance of the Questavan Empire, but pirates still rule it. This may be a friendly ship, or it may be a pirate attempting to trick us." He caught the eye of a specific crewmember. "Signal to *Radiant Dawn* and *Night Light* that they are to take up positions to the port of and behind the vessel, respectively. We'll pull up to its starboard."

Without a word, the fellow headed to the crow's nest. Chiha followed, scurrying up before her crewmate could even get halfway.

I should train the Athai to handle some of these tasks, Ctzo realized. *Things would go much faster that way.*

He continued to watch the vessel through his telescope, spotting the crewmembers of the mystery vessel running about and tying up the sails. He frowned, curious.

They don't wish to flee. That could be a good sign.

But then his gaze found the ship's captain and he smiled in familiarity.

"Réto, tell the crew not to load the cannons," Ctzo commander. "This one is an ally."

A short time later, Ctzo, Réto, Kyra, and a pair of Athai boarded the recently arrived vessel.

"Captain Ctzo!" greeted its Scavgan captain, a tall man wearing a red and violent overcoat bedecked with jewels and medals. "What a pleasant surprise!"

Ctzo nodded politely. "Captain Ryan, it's been a while. I thought you'd retired."

"I did." The older Scavgan approached and gave Ctzo a warm smile and firm handshake. "Alas, the Empire wants fine woods and other imports from Aziasha, and less experienced captains tend to either avoid the trip at all costs or never return from it. I thought you might be a pirate, but then I caught sight of those colourful sails and one of my crew informed me they'd heard that Captain Ctzo had gone into pirate-hunting… aboard a very unique vessel." Ryan eyed the *Diversity*, a grin playing over his lips. "Unique indeed!"

"Well, it's good to see a familiar face," Ctzo said with a nod.

"Since you're here," Ryan said, "may I ask for your help?"

"What's the problem?"

Ryan pulled a small scroll from his pocket. "I was hired by merchants who sailed to Aziasha almost a year ago. They managed to befriend a tribe of Darians and make a business deal: very rare Darian-made fabrics in exchange for Questavan tools. The merchants promised to return the next year, but unfortunately their captain fell ill and they weren't been able to find a replacement. They finally convinced me to take the helm and fulfill the deal." Ryan unrolled the scroll. "This includes the terms of the deal, the name of the Darian tribe, and their chief's signature. I also have a map directing us to the tribe's location."

Ctzo nodded. "Are you having trouble finding them?"

"Oh, we found them. Unfortunately, a band of pirates found them first."

Seated upon Ctzo's shoulder, Réto tensed, sensing a fight could be at hand.

Ctzo's gaze hardened. "What happened?"

"The pirates kept us from landing," Ryan said. "There are too many of them. They had four brigs to our one. Some of my crew even saw a few of the Darians caged up. We don't know if the others have already been shipped off to a Blackwaters scientist."

"And your mission?"

"If we can't free the Darians and fulfill our trade agreement with them, the crew says they at least wish to avenge the tribe. We've been deliberating a plan of attack." Ryan placed a hand on Ctzo's shoulder. "But with you and your three ships—"

"Four," Ctzo corrected. "You may not have seen our small cutter."

"Four then. That will greatly increase our odds."

Ctzo nodded. "Take me to your quarters. We can discuss strategies there." The captain turned back to Réto. "You can let the crew in on what's happening. I'll keep Kyra with me to discuss battle plans."

"Will do." Réto nodded a farewell to his mate, then took off and flew back toward the *Diversity*.

They walked down to the captain's quarters and settled down behind a large wooden desk.

Before continuing, Captain Ryan took a few minute to size up the crewmembers who had come aboard with Ctzo. His gaze settled on the green-scaled Kyra.

"Which one of these officers is your first mate?" Ryan asked.

"None of them."

"Well, shouldn't he be discussing plans with us?"

Ctzo gave a nearly indiscernible shrug. "I suppose he's tending to other matters."

Frowning, Ryan studied Ctzo through narrowed eyes. "Oh?"

Ctzo's gaze fell on a map spread across Ryan's desk. He then leaned forward and ran his finger over the words *Darian Tribe*.

"This is where the prior captain met the tribe?" Ctzo asked.

"Yes."

Ctzo eyed the terrain surrounding the shoreline site. It seemed typical for Aziasha: a long beach area separating jungle from ocean.

"It's too easy for the pirates to hide themselves in the jungle," Ctzo said. "We'll need to draw them out to sea, where the battle can be waged on our terms. And we can send scouts into the forest to determine how many of them there are, and the current condition of the Darians."

Ryan nodded. "As usual, your plan sounds wise. My only concern is, how will we draw them out to sea? And once we do, can we handle all their ships?" He brought out a set of little yellow-painted wooden boats and placed them around the tribe's location. "This is their fleet: four brigs. We now have my ship, *Treasure Quest*; your sloop, the *Diversity*; your two larger ships, *Radiant Dawn* and *Night Light*; and the little one, *Cherish*."

As he listed each ship of the fleet, he placed little red models on the map.

After examining the map further, Ctzo felt more confident. "As long as we get them into open water, I believe we can handle them. However, to minimize risk, it may be worth picking them off one by one. But before we plan further, I think we should send out a scouting team."

"I agree. Would you like me to pick some of my men for the team?"

"That won't be necessary," Ctzo said gently. "No offence to your men, but I think a Scavgan scout is more likely to be spotted." He motioned to Kyra, who was perched on his shoulder. "I usually send my Kamai to do the scouting. They can change colour to camouflage themselves, and they're small and quick."

"If you think it wise, I could take one of the Reea with me," Kyra suggested. "Their ability to turn invisible makes them great scouts, and we'll be able to cover more area more quickly."

"Good idea," Ctzo agreed.

"Right." Ryan eyed Kyra. "When she's done, we'll meet back on my ship to discuss our next move."

"If it's no trouble, I think I'll stay aboard until she returns," Ctzo said.

Kyra indicated the closed door to the captain's quarters, and one of Ryan's men got the message and opened it for her. With that, Kyra glided out.

"Now, if you'll forgive me," Ryan said, "I have something to discuss with my men."

Captain Ctzo raised an eyebrow but didn't object. "Of course."

Once Ryan had left, Ctzo nodded to his own men. "Head back to our ships and let the crew know what's going on. Make sure everyone is informed, including the Reea. They'll need to be ready in case they have a role to play."

His men each gave low bows and departed the room.

Ctzo nearly jumped when he turned and suddenly caught sight Jani standing beside him. The sturdy angel's blue hair tumbled over one of his eyes.

"I'm here," Jani remarked.

"Yes, you are." Ctzo awaited further information, then asked, "Why are you here?"

"A change needs to be made. Captain Ryan needs to have full confidence in your abilities, and he won't if he doesn't meet your first mate."

Ctzo sighed. "Well, there's nothing to be done about that, is there?"

Just then, Ryan returned with a few more of his men. He locked eyes with Jani immediately.

"Oh," said Ryan. "You must be the first mate."

Ctzo's jaw dropped. He could see Jani? "Ah, yes. This is Jani."

"A pleasure." Ryan reached out a hand, and Jani took it firmly in his own.

"The pleasure is mine," Jani replied courteously.

Watching Ryan closely, Ctzo picked up no signs that Ryan found Jani's unusual appearance startling. "I... I suppose you're wondering what race he's from."

Ryan gave Jani a look-over. "Yes, your skin is a very pale blue. Are you from one of the remote desert tribes? Perhaps from the western shores of Scavgan's Island? You look as though you've spent some time at sea, young though you are."

"I am a foreigner to your people," Jani answered cryptically. "But I do have some experience sailing, yes."

"Well," Ryan replied, "I'm sure Ctzo is glad to have your help."

Tyzak thrust the tip of his rapier into the air before him, his face holding a broad smile. He parried an imaginary foe, refamiliarizing himself with the feel of his sword.

Sighing happily, he brought the rapier up to his face. "I missed you, old friend."

Yakara stood nearby, her crest alternately lowering and rising as she watched the Scavgan through cross-shaped pupils. "Why this?"

"Why this, my dear Yakara?" Tyzak thrust the blade through the air again. "There's soon to be a battle. And if I can help it"—he lowered the blade and stood straight, smiling brilliantly—"I will be at the front lines."

"You will be behind me," Chiha interjected. She stood atop the ship's railing, clearly unafraid of slipping into the sea.

Tyzak rolled his eyes, not even turning to face her. "I thought you had gone to the *Diversity* with Captain Ctzo."

Chiha let out a sharp puff of air. She turned away, staring ahead to the bowsprit. "Moving from ship to ship is easy. It's only a jump or a swim away."

I have to admit, her athleticism is impressive, Tyzak thought, at last letting his eyes rove across Chiha's figure. *Who else would say it's "easy" to leap between ships or swim through the ocean from one to another?*

Kyra arrived, gliding through the air and landing smoothly upon the railing next to Chiha. Her serpentine eyes met Chiha's black gaze.

"Your captain has special orders for you and the other Athai," Kyra announced.

Captain Ctzo stood before a collection of Athai, Scavgans, and Darians in Captain Ryan's quarters aboard the *Treasure Quest*. Ryan and a handful of his men stood with them.

"Here's the plan," Ctzo began. "Upon each ship there will be a captain, messengers, commanders, and soldiers, in addition to the regular crew and cannon crew." He pointed to two Darians and a Scavgan in turn. "You will captain *Radiant Dawn*, you will captain *Night Light*, and you will captain *Cherish*. I will be aboard the *Diversity* as usual. Now, communication in battle will be vital: we don't want to crash into each other or accidentally fire upon each other, and the more organized our attack, the better our chance of success."

Ctzo waved at the Athai.

"I've chosen you as messengers, alongside the Kamai, because you can quickly travel around and between ships, and you have a better grasp on our language than the rest of your fellow Athai."

The Athai nodded, and Ctzo divided the group so that each ship would have a few messengers.

"As for the commanders and soldiers, you will be ready in case we board enemy vessels," Ctzo continued. "You've all had plenty of opportunity to hone your fighting skills and seamanship. I expect to see you perform admirably. I'll be selecting a commander for each contingent of soldiers. Finally, some crew will be loading and firing cannons, and others will stand by in case we need to adjust the sails. I'll personally direct each crewmember to their role."

Ctzo nodded towards Ryan, who took over the briefing. "Ctzo's scouts found that most of the pirates have returned to their ships, and that they plan to soon abandon their base, leaving the Darian tribe encaged. I suppose we can be grateful that these pirates have just enough of a conscience that the idea of slaughtering or selling their captives doesn't appeal to them." Ryan pointed to the large map covering his desk. "The pirates abandon their base in two days, then take off together as a fleet. Captain Ctzo and I agree that we'd like to keep this battle out to sea, so we'll wait for their departure until we attack."

"Of course," Ctzo broke in, "we're not going to assume they won't change their minds about killing or selling the tribe, so we'll have scouts continue to monitor the pirates until they take to sea."

Ryan traced an imaginary path along the map with his finger. "While our scouts free the tribe, others will return to our fleet with details on the pirates' heading. Now, *Diversity* and *Cherish* are the fastest of the fleet, but *Cherish* has little firepower and can't handle many hits. So the *Diversity* will approach the enemy first. She'll be in and out, damaging as much of the pirates' sails as she can before slipping away from the action. With the enemy sails damaged, our stronger ships—*Treasure Quest, Radiant Dawn,* and *Night Light*—will arrive as a line. We'll come up along the port side of the enemy ships and fire upon them. Should they retreat, we'll follow. But if we're close enough to fire on them, they're close enough to fire on us—so most likely they will return fire. We must be prepared for the onslaught."

Tyzak's mind ran through all the instructions and battle plans Captain Ctzo had reviewed with his crew only hours before.

My, our captain runs his fleet like a well-oiled machine, he thought, staring out from the starboard side of *Radiant Dawn.* He squinted at the seas, shadowed by overcast sky, and sighed. He could only occasionally locate the rest of the fleet in the high, rolling waves. *The problem with a machine of this size, of course, is that one can't enjoy the whole picture at once. But who am I to complain? I've received the best role!*

He reached for and tightened his rapier's handle, the blade still tucked within its scabbard. Then he pulled his fingers away from the sword so he could grasp his musket with both hands.

Sure, firing the cannons would have been fun, but it's the ground work, the dirty work that I'm here for.

He had a rough idea of where each of the other ships should be, including, if all went as planned, where each pirate ship stood. However, all he could see off the side of *Radiant Dawn* at the moment were roiling waves.

He wasn't aware exactly what orders passed from Ctzo to the rest of the fleet, and he only got his first inkling of the battle when the sound of cannon fire began to ring out, and return fire followed. He could only make a guess as to who had shot first, his enemies or his allies.

But that hardly matters, he thought as he braced himself below the ship's rails. *They haven't even gotten within musket range yet.*

Suddenly, a ship pulled into view, an unfamiliar brig populated by men who looked as rough as the waves they sailed upon. Tensely, Tyzak gripped his firearm. It was heavy and threatened to slip from his sweaty grip.

Then came the command to fire, and he and other members of the crew popped their heads and muskets over the railing and quickly fired. They ducked as a hail of musket balls spattered the railing, decks, rigging, and sails.

Just as they got ready to fire off another salvo, Tyzak heard the captain give the command to board the enemy ship. Discarding his firearm, he was one of the first to leap onto the other vessel. Rapier drawn, he made for the first pirate he saw, trusting his shipmates to cover his back and flanks.

With an upswing, he knocked away his opponent's blade then dropped and swept the man's legs out from under him. As the pirate fell, Tyzak thrust upward and the pirate fell on his rapier blade. He shoved the dead pirate to the side and withdrew his sword, seeking a new opponent.

Suddenly, hot pain seared through his leg and he dropped to the deck. He looked at his left leg and saw blood oozing from a hole that went right through his flesh. His shipmates appeared to have the pirates on deck busy. Frowning, he tried to discern where the shot had come from.

Then he spotted it. Upon the crow's nest, he saw the glint off a musket barrel.

A sniper. Clever.

He got up, ignoring his wounded leg, and made his way toward the crow's nest, intent on returning the favour. Before he got there, however, a huge shadow flew overhead and he heard the sniper cry out as he fell into the ocean's depths. Tyzak looked up and saluted Black Night for the assist.

Before he could get back into the battle, he heard the captain issue an order for the soldiers to hold up their blades. The pirates had noticed they were grossly outnumbered and outgunned and had wisely decided to surrender.

After their victory, Ctzo and Ryan sat together inside Ryan's quarters aboard the *Treasure Quest*.

"I'm glad we were able to aid you in your mission," Ctzo said, enjoying a long sip of tea. "This tea is wonderful. Where'd you get it?"

"Medioca, of course." Ryan sighed. "Ah, it's been too long since I was stationed there. Incredible food, beautiful views. You and I met in Medioca, didn't we?"

"We did." Ctzo nodded, thinking back to those days. "It feels like eons ago."

"Does it really?" Ryan chuckled. "You're too young to be saying that!"

Ctzo smiled. "What do you have on me, twenty years?"

"Enough years. But I suppose we met before you'd become *General* Ctzo." Ryan eyed a scar on his own arm. "We probably have enough memories from the War of Nine Leagues between us to fill a book or two."

"It's more than that." Ctzo hesitated, staring into his cup. "When you met me... I was a different person."

Ryan raised an eyebrow. "Oh?"

"You wouldn't have seen it. We barely spent time together until I moved up in the ranks. But when I was first stationed in Medioca, I was a... less than willing recruit."

"Oh, right. I'd forgotten you were one of those soldiers drafted from prison."

Ctzo stared silently at a small box upon one of Ryan's shelves. "That little chest appears Miedocan."

"Isn't it a beauty? A man in Medioca gave it to me. I think he hoped I'd marry one of his daughters. I did love his eldest." Ryan took a sip of tea, then sighed. "Ah, but there's no place for wives or children in the life of a traveller, is there?"

"I... don't know." Ctzo tensed, then stood. "I suppose we both have work to do."

Ryan frowned at his abrupt change of mood. "Did I say something?"

"I was just thinking. Forgive me. A few of my crew have gotten separated and are likely wandering the island of Aziasha. I'm hopeful that I'll encounter them again sooner rather than later."

"Is that so?" Ryan also stood. "Then I don't blame you for being eager to get back to your search, but at least allow me to take one more wander about the *Diversity*. She seems a curious marvel, and a fine ship."

"She is." A smile creased Ctzo's lips. "She certainly is."

As their time together came to a close, the crew of the *Diversity* gathered around Captain Ryan and his first mate, shaking hands and wishing farewells.

At Tyzak's turn, the Mediocan grinned brightly at Ryan. "Thank you for requesting we aid you in this affair. Ah, if only we happened across others in need of our assistance. Captain Ctzo may be content with exploration, but I do enjoy a good fight!"

"Don't be so eager to rush into battle," Ryan warned Tyzak. "You'll have plenty of pirates to fight soon enough, I guarantee it." Turning to Ctzo, he shook the fellow captain's hand. "If I return to Questava before you, I'll be sure to tell them of all the good work you've been doing here."

"It's been a pleasure seeing you again," Ctzo said. "Are you sure you don't want my fleet to escort you at least a little further from Aziasha?"

"You've done more than enough, thank you." Ryan nodded at Jani, who stood at Ctzo's side. "You keep doing good work for your captain."

Jani returned the nod, but said nothing.

With that, Ryan was lowered onto a longboat and sent back across the waters to his own ship.

"He's right, Tyzak," Jani said.

Tyzak, unfamiliar with the Scavgan beside him, eyed the formally dressed fellow. "Pardon, sir, but aren't you missing your ride?" He pointed towards the departing longboat.

Jani shook his head, then clarified, "I'm Jani, the first mate."

"Oh!" Tyzak reflexively offered his hand, then pulled it back. "Er, uh, of course. That's right. I've seen you around," he lied, chuckling.

Jani stared him down squarely. "You may not be so eager to rush into battle when a serious one comes." He looked down at Tyzak's leg. "Visit the doctor."

"Oh, it's fine," Tyzak said, chuckling. "Curiously, I barely even felt it."

"To Doctor Savato. Now."

Tyzak sighed. "Very well. If you insist."

CHAPTER NINE

Sébérus watched as yet another grey island passed into view. That was the one hundred twentieth island. The Gashaian Islands were numerous indeed! Many of them had been little more than grey or black monoliths rising above the waves. Others had been green with a carpet of grasses, or speckled with tough-looking, stumpy bushes. A select few held eye-catching forests of orange, yellow, red, or even pink.

Turning from the ocean, Sébérus caught the eye of a fellow crewmember. "Masipitus, are there any maps of Gashaia aboard?"

The indigo-skinned Scavgan raised an eyebrow. "You know my name?"

"Indeed. Any chance you could return the favour?"

"Most find my name difficult." Masipitus smiled. "But if you remember it, I suppose it's only fair I memorize yours."

"Sébérus," the Blackblood said. "Now, do you know the answer to my question?"

"Sébérus. Right. No maps. A physical map could fall into the wrong hands. No one in Gashaia wants to become a part of the Questavan Empire. Well, none of the Gashaians who live this far from Scavgan's Island, anyways. The captain has our pathway to the High Temple memorized."

"And how well do you know our path?" Sébérus pressed.

The Scavgan shrugged. "I've been aboard the *Ko'Ekua* for years. What would you like to know? How long until we arrive at our destination?"

Sébérus waved his hand dismissively. "I've already overheard the rest of the crew talking. With this weather, we'll likely arrive in four days. No, I want to know how far we are from the Kamai Kingdoms."

Masipitus smirked. "Far."

Disappointing, Sébérus thought. *I'd hoped to sneak off in a longboat and try entering Kamai territory. Of course, there were flaws with that plan. What would I do if they didn't accept me?*

"So, the Kamai live very far from Aziasha and Scavgan's Island," Sébérus said. "Yet some have journeyed that distance?"

"Kamai love to explore," Masipitus said. "They wouldn't dream of staying in one place, unless the master they'd bonded to insisted on it. But if you want to know more about the Kamai, you could always ask Nva."

Sébérus harrumphed. "Frankly, I doubt she knows her own self that well."

"Careful. She has a bit of a temper. And she is a Kamai. You wouldn't want to get on her bad side."

Spreading his wings and whipping forward his tail, Sébérus showed off his massive fangs. "What do I look like?"

Masipitus regarded him. "You look like a Blackblood. Guess one wouldn't want to get on your bad side, either."

With that, Masipitus departed.

Sébérus turned his gaze back to sea, disregarding his previous plan to settle amongst the Kamai. *I suppose my current course is acceptable. When we arrive at the High Temple, there should be more ships, a chance to strengthen my wings... and opportunities to escape and search out someplace where I can be accepted.*

Yes. That plan would be good enough.

What a brilliant strategist I am. Vasitan's face held the widest of grins as he walked aboard a small and worn vessel. By the look of it, he guessed the captain likely couldn't afford to pay him much. *Then again, he won't be able to afford not to pay me.*

The captain met Vasitan on deck, faking a warm smile. "Good evening, Council Representative. Have you seen the two full moons in the sky? Beautiful, are they not?"

"Indeed." Without stopping, Vasitan continued towards the stairs belowdecks.

"A drink?" The captain rushed to his side. "Surely you've had a long day, inspecting ship after ship. Why not spend a moment with me in my quarters? It'll give you a chance to sit back and enjoy yourself."

Vasitan didn't slow as he stepped down the stairs. "I'm here to check your cargo. And check it I will."

The Council representative stopped when he reached the storage room, pausing to admire a bit of green paint stroked in a half-hazard splotch along a barrel. The barrel stood alone...

Brimsta had said that meant the needles of blackwater were stored in the galley, hidden within bags of flour.

He quickly departed the storage area, forcing the captain to turn sharply to follow him.

"Are you done your inspection?" the captain asked hopefully.

"Hardly. I need to check your food stores."

"Suit yourself." The captain didn't sound worried as they entered the galley, but he raised an eyebrow. "Ahem... so, after you finish your inspection, perhaps you'd still like that drink?" He gaped as Vasitan headed straight for the stored flour and opened bag after bag. "What are you doing? You'll spill it!"

"Here!" Vasitan held up a capped needle, wiggling it in his hand so he could hear the liquid swishing inside. "Ah, the sound of money! Wouldn't you agree, sir?"

The captain paled.

Vasitan carefully put the needle back in place. "So you're carrying an illegal blackwaters shipment, are you?"

Gulping, the captain said nothing.

"Perhaps we should go up to your quarters and share a drink. You look like you need one. Then we can discuss the future."

Katia closed her eyes and soaked in a deep whiff of the unique flower with black-rimmed petals. Though tiny, the flowers held great significance. They grew only within a small region, and their presence told Katia she remained on the right path.

Thank you, Anveil, for pointing out these little flowers to me.

She pulled back a little from the blooms, admiring their lovely forms scattered inconspicuously along the edge of a thick bush.

"We're getting closer!" she called to the Scavgans.

Katia surged ahead, then slowed and frowned. Looking back at the Scavgans, she saw beads of sweat dripping from their foreheads, heard them gasping, and noted how they slouched as they walked.

I guess they can't keep up my pace. She shrugged. *I suppose I'm tougher than I thought. Oh well, I can rest for their sakes. It may take longer to reach my tribe, but we'll reach the village eventually.*

Captain's Journal, the second day of Thyen.

It's been exactly a month since we last saw Zan, Ian, and Katia. How much longer must I wait to see them again, Kyaté? Jani said it would be months. That could mean anywhere from another month to several or... I don't want to consider the possibility of anything longer than that.

At least our fleet has made good progress. The winds have been in our favour, although I can't credit the winds alone for our smooth sailing. The *Diversity* has proven herself a quality vessel, easy to steer and fast with the wind. I've been amazed at how well she's held up in open water. She feels as sturdy as any frigate. I don't know whether to thank the shipbuilder who crafted her or my carpenters who spruced her up, but either way, I've been very satisfied with this vessel.

The rest of my fleet, too, has been of great aid. *Cherish* can forge ahead, scouting for pirates without being spotted, allowing us to surround enemy vessels before they even know we're there. I think if *Diversity* had sailed alone, some of the pirates we've faced would have put up a stronger fight, believing victory easy against such a small vessel. However, the presence of *Night Light* and *Radiant Dawn* have ensured their fear and our continued victories.

Ryan's prediction about many pirate battles lying ahead has proven true. Thus far, we've defeated five ships. One schooner fled too quickly for us to catch up. Another attempted escape, but we reencountered it a day later and sank it, taking the pirate crew aboard.

This last month has taken us almost full circle around Aziasha. Every now and again we cast anchor and take some of the crew ashore to find supplies: food, water, wood. The Darians have been absolutely essential in this work, directing teams on what to collect and where.

One curious feature about Aziasha is that all its water lies underground. Supposedly, the island rests upon numerous water-filled caverns. Sometimes the ground caves in, and where it does, fresh water becomes available, and Darians often worship at these sites. Oddly, no one settles near water, though, for fear of the many beasts and aggressive tribes that also come to drink. Everyone takes their fill and moves on. Darians, though, can survive long without water—possibly longer than the rest of us.

Every time our longboat hits the shore, I look up past the tangled jungles to the knifelike mountains that pierce the sky. Aziasha is barely larger than Scavgan's Island, but I don't doubt it's harder to traverse. I wonder how the rest of our crew is faring.

Ctzo put down his quill, closing his ink jar so it wouldn't spill if the ship happened to roll. Standing, he looked around the room that'd been his home for his time at sea. Through the row of windows lining one corner of his quarters, he could see the suns filling the sky with glorious light.

The wooden floorboards creaked as he stepped along them. His room was lightly decorated: a few cabinets, a chest on the floor, his well-used desk, a single dresser for his clothes, a small stand housing an old candlestick, and his bed, tucked cozily into the corner.

He came to a stop before the dresser, admiring a small collection of keepsakes upon it. One, a zaia made of tightly woven beads, he'd seen at a market in Medioca; he hadn't been able to resist purchasing it. The second was an ornate spyglass, a thoughtful gift from a fellow captain. The third item was his favourite: a sea shell, large and trumpet-shaped, with orange and brown stripes. He'd been lucky enough to find it on an empty beach, though he couldn't recall which beach exactly.

I wonder if Qeysta would like it. The thought crossed his mind unbidden, alongside the image of a woman with sparkling blue-green eyes. He pushed the memory aside. *There's no point in wondering. She'll never see it.*

He sighed deeply. Perhaps he should rest for a while. He trusted no pirate ship could sneak up on them in such fine weather, and his crew had seemed lively and alert when he'd last visited them. They could handle a bit of time without him.

He sat upon his bed, his hands brushing the rough red fabric of his blankets. He lay his head upon the stiff pillow, closed his eyes, and took in a deep breath. He hardly noticed the room's familiar wooden scent. In their long journeys overseas, this boat had become home, as much a welcome house as any land-based construction Ctzo had dwelt within.

With his legs curled, since the bed wasn't long enough for him to stretch out, Ctzo didn't bother to cover himself with the scratchy blanket beneath him. He took another deep breath, welcoming each chance to rest, even for a moment. Being the captain—leader, strategist, planner, encourager, and mediator—took its toll. And truthfully, as much as he attempted to leave the wellbeing of his missing crew in Kyaté's hands, Ian, Zan, and Katia always remained at the back of his mind.

Sleep crept upon him and soon he could hear Jani's warning about the Mocjoa echoing through his mind.

"Don't underestimate them. You need to know what the islands look like in order to find them. But you will not be finding the Mocjoa; they will find you. And few of their race are as kind as the two who saved you."

Suddenly, a voice broke through his dream-like state.

"Captain?" asked Réto.

Ctzo startled and opened his eyes. "Hmmm?" He realized he'd fallen asleep. Rising, he noted his dim surroundings and realized it must be evening. "What is it?"

Réto's yellow, snake-like eyes stood out sharply from his black scales. His tone, though soft, carried a sense of foreboding. "Come on deck when you're ready."

"I'm ready." Ctzo slipped out of bed with ease, nodding to the Kamai. "What have you found?"

CHAPTER TEN

*R*éto sat upon Ctzo's shoulder pads as they crossed the deck, passing crewmembers who stood whispering to each other. Some turned to eye their captain, either with calm curiosity or apprehension. Standing beside the rail, the captain looked out upon the crimson waves, so coloured by the last sun that had begun to dip below the horizon.

Rocked by the sea, two frigates floated quietly. Sails open to the wind, they carried along sluggishly. Not a soul could be seen on any of the decks.

"What's their story?" Tyzak came to stand near Ctzo. "Looks like it could be a haunting one."

"Perhaps their crews were taken prisoner," Ctzo said casually, "or killed by pirates who didn't have enough crew to man them. So they left them behind."

"Without sinking them?" Tyzak asked.

Ctzo pointed to a few crewmembers. "You, come with me. Bring weapons. The vessels may have supplies, or they may have pirates hiding belowdecks. Tyzak, you too."

The Mediocan nodded, a cheery smile lighting his face. "It would be my pleasure! Are you taking Jani, too?"

"Hmm?" Ctzo asked.

"First mate Jani." Tyzak pointed to the man across the deck. "That's him standing over there in the corner, watching Black Night, isn't it?"

"Yes." Ctzo cleared his throat. "I just... wasn't sure if you could see him."

Tyzak smiled, folding his arms over his chest. "Look at him! Slips into the shadows without even trying! The fact no one seemed to catch sight of him until recently proves how good he is at hiding in plain sight. Sometimes I look for him but don't find him. Then I do another sweep, and lo and behold, there he is!" He stroked his chin. "The Darians always see him, we think. Not that they would tell the rest of us."

Ctzo doubted even the Darians could see Jani, but he wasn't about to correct his crew.

Tyzak rambled on. "We asked them if they had ever seen him before, and you know what they said? 'You Scavgans all look the same.' Really, Captain! Do you believe that? I think it was meant as a joke, but all the same—"

"Tyzak, would you please fetch Chiha for me?" Ctzo said in a tone of command.

"Oh. Of course." Tyzak only walked a few steps before he called out, "There you are, Chiha! Our captain desires your presence."

Chiha bounded over gracefully. She bowed at the waist before Ctzo. "You asked for me?"

"I'd like you to scout ahead. Grab your spear and go investigate the ship closest to us." As she departed to carry out his orders, Ctzo caught sight of Jani walking towards him. "Yes, first mate?"

"Bring Black Night." Jani nodded his head towards the Rezumi.

Ctzo raised an eyebrow but didn't argue. "If you believe he'll be of help."

"No." Jani smiled warmly. "But he's coming down with a case of cabin fever, and some new sights will do him well. Also, it'll make him less difficult for you to handle."

Following Jani's gaze, Ctzo's eyes landed on Black Night, who was pretending to wrestle the small grey Darian, Oti.

"Perhaps they should both come," Ctzo thought aloud. Raising his voice, he called to the Rezumi. "Black Night, I'm sending you aboard the vessel. Take Oti with you. But keep a close eye on him."

Black Night barely looked away from his Darian playmate as he nodded. "Sure. Oti, follow me!"

The captain's gaze fell back on Tyzak. "Once Chiha returns from her scouting, you and I will be the first ones to board the nearest ship."

Grinning happily, Tyzak bowed at the waist. "It would be my honour, sir!"

In a few minutes, Chiha bounded back aboard to report to Ctzo. "No one alive, no one dead. But I found blackwaters on the galley floor."

Tyzak shivered and Captain Ctzo nodded grimly.

"We're going to have to show caution then," Ctzo said. "Chiha, investigate the next ship." As she raced off, he continued his instructions. "Tyzak, you're with me. The rest of you, stay with Jani. Black Night, follow behind. Make sure Oti remains under your lead."

If he'd have looked over his shoulder, Ctzo would have caught Black Night's concerned expression, but the captain remained focused on the strange ship as he carefully crossed the gangplank. Tyzak followed closely behind, and Jani and the others came after.

Black Night hesitantly took up the rear, Oti perched on his broad shoulders.

The two Kamai circled the air around them. "What should we do?" Kyra asked her captain.

"For now, continue to scour the ships from the air," Ctzo said. "If serious trouble arises, I'm sure you'll hear it."

"Will do," Réto said in agreement.

As Tyzak stepped belowdecks on the heels of his captain, descending into darkness, he noted the stairs creaked eerily. At least, he considered it eerie. But Ctzo marched silently on, and Tyzak bit back any comment.

He placed his weight on his left leg and felt a sharp pain, then gently eased off it.

Heartless pirate, wounding my poor limb, he thought, smiling through the discomfort. *At least I was avenged. Victory was ours!*

Tyzak's forehead hit a hanging lamp. After a quick massage, he pulled down the lamp.

"Captain, I found a lamp. Perhaps we can get it lit?"

"Well done." Ctzo took the device and soon had it working. "No point going any further without one of these."

Continuing into the depths of the ship, they walked through the galley, tiptoeing around the mostly tidy room. A few shattered clay vessels seemed out of place, though, and Ctzo gave them a closer look.

"Blackwaters," the captain said.

A growl echoed through the room and Tyzak quickly turned to look behind him. There, he saw Jani and the few crewmembers with him.

"Black Night? Was that you?" Tyzak asked.

"No." The Rezumi's voice came from outside the room, back towards the stairs.

"Get down here," Ctzo ordered. "The rest of you, spread out and have your weapons ready. Watch your step! There could be more blackwaters on the floor."

Black Night stood at the bottom of the stairs, still wanting to keep the light of the upper world within sight. His burly figure trembled as a puff of air hit his face, and his massive wing struck out towards the source of the movement. He found only the wall.

"Trying to get me?" Chiha asked disapprovingly. "You missed."

"Why did you blow on me like that?" Black Night snapped. "I could have killed you."

"No, you are too slow. Tell the captain I found much more blackwaters on the other ship." She waited. "Well?"

"I'll tell him later. I think they found a Blackblood. Do you know what that is?"

"Like Jair?" Chiha shrugged. "We have Blackbloods on the Marsh Isles, too."

"Most aren't like Jair," Black Night said matter-of-factly. "Most are mindless monsters that don't know anything but pain and how to inflict it."

Again, Chiha let out a sharp puff of air. "You stay in the shadows hiding from your imagined demons. I will go and see."

Captain Ctzo placed the lantern in the centre of the galley floor, then drew his pistol. Tyzak caught himself backing towards the light and forced himself to stop, though his rapier remained pointed ahead.

He heard that same low, vibrating growl and, watching his captain, Tyzak couldn't believe how steady the man remained. As the growl drew out into a long moan, Ctzo guided himself toward the sound and stepped forward calmly.

Tyzak made a move to follow after his leader, realizing that someone had to have his back. Instead, though, Jani came up behind and to the left of Captain Ctzo. He, too, appeared unafraid.

First mate or not, I can't be shown up so easily, Tyzak decided as he moved in closer to Ctzo's right.

A howl rang through the air, causing many to startle.

"Why are we standing still?" Chiha demanded.

Pistols held by shaking hands swung her way, followed by annoyed reprimands as the crew realized they weren't facing a Blackblood.

"Chiha," Ctzo ordered, "up here with me."

She bounded forward almost gleefully. "Yes, master."

Master? Tyzak frowned. *She is a lot more respectful when the captain's around.*

Ctzo stood next to a darkened doorway with Jani, Tyzak, and Chiha. As the captain progressed through the door, someone further back picked up the lantern and brought it closer.

Suddenly, a glowing-eyed Scavgan fell through the doorway, and the room filled with gasps. The four in front drew back as Ctzo's pistol aimed steadily at the creature's head.

The creature was very obviously a Blackblood, oozing oily liquid from various cuts in its skin. Despite being mere inches from Ctzo, it appeared not to notice him, nor any of them. Muttering in animal-like grunts, its eyes went to and fro without locking on anyone. It whimpered, then curled into a ball.

Tyzak was prepared to strike, his rapier aimed and his arm tensed.

"Stop!" Chiha said.

He flinched as her hand touched his shoulder.

Calmly, Chiha moved closer to the Blackblood, singing softly. Tyzak couldn't understand the words, as she spoke in her own language, but the soothing rhythm brought to mind a lullaby.

"What are you doing?" Tyzak snapped.

"Can't you see?" Chiha's gaze remaining on the Blackblood. "He is in pain."

"And we will be too, the moment it bites one of us."

"Let her try to communicate," Ctzo said. "He could be like Jair, capable of speech."

Tyzak shrugged but kept his rapier poised as Chiha continued her soothing song, her voice echoing through the room. The

Blackblood's gaze remained on the ground, though his mutterings slowed and soon hushed completely.

A shiver went down Tyzak's spine as Chiha reached out and touched the Blackblood's forehead. He very nearly grabbed her hand and pulled her back.

"You could get infected," he hissed.

Chiha paused her singing. "Only the blood can poison, Scavgan. His forehead is clean."

She's either very brave or very stupid, Tyzak thought.

A growl vibrated from the Blackblood's throat, followed by a whimpering sob. Suddenly, it rose and screamed and Chiha pulled back.

Ctzo got between her and the Blackblood. His pistol raised again, but to Tyzak's amazement he held back from firing.

"If we're going to capture him, we're going to need ropes," Ctzo said. "And where is Black Night?"

The crewmembers farther back passed along the question, then passed forward an answer: "He's gone to get the Kamai."

Captain Ctzo visibly bit his tongue.

Jani passed Ctzo a stretch of rope. "We can try to bind it," the first mate said softly, "but there's no knowing how it'll respond to such an action."

"Until it attacks, we don't have a need to kill it," said the captain. "But neither can we risk everyone's health by allowing it—"

A clawed hand shot past Ctzo and towards Chiha. Tyzak didn't wait for an order. His rapier struck through the Blackblood's chest. The creature looked his way and Tyzak felt his heart stop in his chest as he stared into those amber eyes. Did he see relief in that yellow gaze?

The Blackblood fell, dead, and Chiha choked back a sob.

Tyzak looked at the crumpled body. His sword arm quivered. He felt a tinge of remorse, something he'd never felt in previous battles. "I—"

Chiha's arms engulfed him. "I know," she said between tears. "I know you had to. Thank you." She looked down at the Blackblood. "It just seems… not fair. It's… not fair, to have to live and die like that."

Tyzak gently embraced her, his eyes downcast. "No. It's not really fair, is it?"

CHAPTER ELEVEN

*A*bsently, Sébérus ran his Blackblood hand along a stone pillar, his mind turning from the pillar to his hand. He flexed his massive claws, noting their strength and cutting edge. The wing-bones stretching from his arm pulled taut until his right wing lay outstretched; then he pulled them back, folding his wing against his side.

Moments like this, when he could indulge in playful curiosity of his own body, encouraged him. So often it seemed that he was fighting the aches and pains of being a Blackblood.

Perhaps it won't always be that way, he thought. *Today I haven't given myself even one shot of the drugs I snuck aboard. And yet I feel wonderful!*

Taking his eyes off his arm, his gaze rose to the ceiling high above and its intricate carvings. Three-dimensional images flowed along the roof, drawing his focus to the centre where he saw a radiant orange sun, painted in various hues and complex designs.

Atzinus's fortress had been designed with cold practicality in mind. The many temples of the Ti'te'Vika, on the other hand, were the work of an artist.

Grey Noon had once been trained in the ways of his faith in this very temple. The Blackblood couldn't say whether this temple was one of the largest or most impressive, only that Grey Noon favoured it above all others, dubbing it the High Temple, though it's real name was Kavat'ti'ray, meaning "the transcendence of the suns."

Not long ago, Grey Noon had vanished into a separate room off this one. Sébérus had seen his captain and a small assortment of other Ti'te'Vikan priests—some Rezumi, some Scavgans—enter that room for a priestly meeting.

I'd be curious to know what they're talking about. The thought had crossed his mind several times, but so had the realization that the group likely didn't wish to be disturbed, nor would they want eavesdroppers listening in. Sébérus had thus resisted the urge to stand outside the doorway and listen in. Thus far, at least; his self-restraint was wearing thin.

He finally strolled confidently to the doorway and stood just outside. He'd only briefly encountered most of the priests in the room, but he had quickly memorized each of their voices.

The most recognizable of the voices was soft and aged, with a constant tone of calm. It was Pazu, an elderly Rezumi of near-white fur. Pazu, a high priest, had once been Grey Noon's mentor. In fact, he'd been the one to rescue him from the arena and lead him to the Ti'te'Vikan faith. Yet one would never guess that Grey Noon had learned religion from him. Pazu was as docile and friendly as Grey Noon was aggressive and domineering. Sébérus imagined the two clashing on most topics of faith, yet Grey Noon carried an obvious respect for his old mentor.

Brasher and younger was the voice of Terr, a radical who followed Grey Noon's line of thinking… though Terr seemed to have less common sense and fewer war instincts than Grey Noon.

A few other priests shared the room, adding comments here and there. But for the moment, the conversation focused around Pazu, Grey Noon, and Terr.

"It can be done," Terr said with confidence. "And I'm not the only one who thinks so. Grey Noon?"

"I agree," Grey Noon said. "But it will take strategy and planning. The timing isn't right."

"Maybe not today or tomorrow, but it's very near at hand," Terr continued. "I and a few other priests have gathered nearly enough Blackblood soldiers to make an attack on Questava. Imagine if we pooled our resources, perhaps got various rebel factions to attack at the same time as us!"

Sébérus's ears perked.

"Hmm," Pazu deliberated. "I've never been keen on the use of Blackbloods as soldiers. The poor souls have been tormented enough."

"The Blackbloods have nothing else to live for," Terr argued. "And most of them were Darians before. A backwards pagan people if I ever met one."

I wonder, Sébérus thought dryly. *Just how many Darians have you actually known?*

"We need a bit more time," Terr continued. "A bit more time, a few boatloads more of Blackbloods. Then we'll be able to start our war on Questava."

Sébérus leaned into the door. "So you really are planning on attacking Questava," he said aloud.

The room's occupants turned in his direction with startled gazes.

Grey Noon bristled, his voice dark and dangerous. "And what makes you think you're welcome to join this meeting?"

"I have questions," Sébérus said.

"You may ask them after the meeting!" Terr snapped.

Pazu raised his wing. "Calm yourselves. I believe there is no wrong time to ask for wisdom and understanding. What do you wish to know?"

"I'd heard rumours that the Ti'te'Vika planned to attack the city of Questava." Sébérus strode forward unabashedly, pretending not to notice Grey Noon's frown. "But I hadn't decided whether the rumours were true. Tell me then, why go to this kind of trouble?"

An elderly Scavgan spoke up first. "The Questavan Empire thirsts for more land. No matter how far it expands, it is never satisfied. Over the centuries it's gone from a small desert kingdom to consuming the entirety of Scavgan's Island. And now its eyes roam further, to neighbouring islands, and Aziasha, and even into Gashaia. When will its hunger end? Never. Such an empire will slowly make its way to our doors. And if it continues to gain strength, there will be no stopping it from devouring us when it arrives."

"That is one concern, yes," said Pazu, hesitating. "The other is Questava's privateers. Pirate hunters are paid handsomely for capturing Ti'te'Vikan ships, even those which never attack. We've had to become more defensive of our own people, even aggressors, as the empire persecutes us for our faith. We'd be happy to leave Questava alone, but the Emperor seems not to know who is an enemy and who merely shares the world with him. Some of our order seek vengeance for their fallen friends."

Sébérus turned his attention to Grey Noon. "Is that your interest, my captain?"

"Empires rise and fall," Grey Noon said, waving a massive wing. "What I care about are souls, and the lies Scavgan religions propagate. Kyaté's Temple is an affront, a pestilence. That's what I wish to see destroyed."

Sébérus cocked his head. "Isn't the temple in Medioca, not in Questava?"

Grey Noon nodded. "It is, but the last time I and other priests attacked it, soldiers from Questava stood in my way. In particular, a certain captain."

"Ctzo Mainaia." Sébérus nearly whispered the name.

"Yes." Grey Noon lowered his brows, growling.

Sébérus realized he must have spoken in a tone of awe and admiration. "I've… read about his military exploits. He is an impressive leader, to be sure."

"He got lucky," Grey Noon snapped. "In winning the War of Nine Leagues, and in stopping our attack on the Mediocan Temple. But he's backed by the empire itself. Medioca may be conquered territory, but it provides many resources and enriches the lives of the Questavans. They want to see its people hard at work in vineyards, fields, and markets. If that means keeping them cheery, allowing them to worship at their own temple, then Questava will spend resources keeping said temple in good repair. And in guarding it."

"Ah." Sébérus nodded, understanding. "To get through to Medioca, one must first get through Questava."

"Exactly," Grey Noon said. "It may take time to conquer Questava, but we're not the only ones itching to do so. Whether it's the Ti'te'Vikans, who see the glory of the fallen capital, or another group, the city's fall means Medioca's fall is a short time away."

Or you could convince Questava to destroy the Mediocan temple themselves, Sébérus considered. I'm sure there's a way. An amusing idea.

"Who are these others you speak of, these rebels who would like to see Questava fall?" Sébérus asked. "And what is their motivation?"

"Blackwaters pirates want to see their trade made legal," Grey Noon explained. "I doubt they care to see the empire fall. They just want to put their own leaders on the throne and on the Council. Supposedly the Augai are gearing up for revenge, but from what I've seen they're nothing but rabble dreaming of the impossible. There are various other groups gathering warriors, either for a stealthy assassination, outright war, or an extended plundering. I think people are just sick of being ruled by the empire, for one reason or another. The people tend to bore of powerful leaders."

Questions scurried through Sébérus's mind. "What's the end goal then? When Questava falls, what rises from the ashes?"

"I don't care," Grey Noon said casually. "I just like the idea of seeing their temples turned to rubble, and Kyaté's Temple unprotected. As I said, the blackwaters pirates and other rebellions will put their leaders on the throne. The Augai? It is claimed they merely want to watch Questava burn."

"Why did they attack during the War of Nine Leagues?" Sébérus's wondered. His research hadn't gleaned any answers to this question.

Pazu gave a slight shrug. "The same reasons, I gather, that many have dreamed of attacking the Questavan Empire. The empire conquered them, and they wish to conquer back."

Fair enough, Sébérus thought. Though some nations and tribes had joined the Questavan Empire willingly, most had needed to be convinced—by force.

"But the conquering of Scavgan's Island by the empire was finished generations ago," Sébérus said. "Why wait this long?"

"You wait until you're strong enough," Terr said, nodding towards Grey Noon. "Your captain spent years as a slave in the arena. He didn't bother killing his masters until they thought he was broken. Until they had their backs turned. And until he was strong enough."

"Wounds don't always heal in one generation," Grey Noon said. "Some take far longer."

A pang entered Sébérus's heart, and his face fell.

"Are you all right?" Pazu asked. "Something the matter?"

"Forgive me." Sébérus bowed low. "I should allow you to get back to your meeting."

"You should." Grey Noon managed to keep the growl in his voice soft. "But if Pazu forgives your interruption, I can as well. Now, please return to the rest of the crew in the commons room."

"As you wish." Sébérus's head remained bowed as he sidled out, not lifting it again until he had stepped through the doorway. Then he turned back toward the shining sun on the ceiling.

Grey Noon had said that wounds didn't always heal in a single generation. But what would it be like to belong to a people, a group? One he was passionate about, so much so that the scars of generations past became his scars, their pains his pains, their wars...

A sigh escaped his lips and the ache in his heart moved to his chest, which he rubbed absently. Instead of easing, the ache turned to a sharp pain.

He gritted his teeth. *Curse this weak Blackblood body!*

Perhaps instead of the commons room, a short trip down a nearby hall, he'd return to the ship and get in a short nap.

Perhaps the wounds of one generation are more than enough for me.

CHAPTER TWELVE

*K*atia eyed the jagged mountain peaks with apprehension. She had crossed them while with Anveil's tribe, and she could do it again—this time with the two Scavgans. Already she'd had to alter her path several times in order to account for the fact that the Scavgans couldn't climb trees, but there was no way around these mountains. The Scavgans would have to follow her.

She peered into the darkness far below, tensing as her claws gripped the stone pinnacle beneath her feet. Ears twitching, nose sniffing, she sensed… nothing. Hopefully no valley serpents.

Raising her head, she looked behind and below where the Scavgans were hidden amidst jungle foliage. She'd vaulted ahead of them to reach the steep stone cliff, leaving them behind as she surveyed the heights.

Her gaze journeyed up the daggerlike peaks which rose in long, snaking formations. The rock beneath her feet towered proudly above the jungle branches, yet it was but a mere child next to its formidable parent mountains.

Katia shook her head, brows lowering. How was she going to get the Scavgans through this?

Ian's eyes widened as he looked around the jungle for signs of their Darian leader.

Behind him Zan panted noisily, in and out, allowing his weight to slack against a sturdy tree. He swallowed, then squinted at the burning in his throat.

"Did you see where she went?" Ian asked. He stepped a few paces, then halted, eyes roaming the forest. Crumpling to the ground, he took a foot in his hand and rubbed the tense muscles. "Do your feet hurt as much as mine?"

"Everything hurts," Zan gasped. "And I'm so tired."

"Cheer up." Ian rose and laid a comforting hand on his friend's shoulder. "Part of surviving treks like this one is remaining positive."

"Surviving." Zan chuckled. "That's dark. I always assumed we'd survive this, with Katia's help. Now you're making me worry."

Katia emerged from the bushes and the Scavgans' eyes fell on her. She smiled, then waved for them to follow. "Getting close."

The Scavgans exchanged frowns.

"Funny." Zan lifted himself away from the tree and trotted after her. "I think I recall her saying that several days ago. Don't you?"

Ian nodded. "Katia, what does 'close' mean?"

"Close." Katia's smile broadened. "Um… close. Follow!"

She disappeared into the bushes, leaving no sign of her path.

Zan and Ian pushed through into the bushes, one foot in front of the other, keeping their arms close to their sides as they ignored the sting of scratching branches. By now, their skin had been criss-crossed with scrapes. Why fear a handful more?

Their jaws dropped when they came to the grey cliffs. Katia crawled spider-like up the rough surface, placing each foot without fear, always finding some minute crack or protuberance that could hold her weight.

Zan hesitated. "Does she… expect us to follow her?"

"I think so."

They returned their gazes to the sharp incline. Katia now sat far up, staring down on them and calling gently but loudly for them to follow.

Ian was the first to hesitantly grasp a fistful of rock in his palm. The cliff felt slick despite the many chips within the rock. He pushed a foot up, then slid back down.

Zan, meanwhile, walked along the length of the cliffside. He looked up at a cleft in the rockface. "Ian, do you think we could make it up from here?"

Ian nodded. "Good thinking, Zan. If we squeeze into this crevice, anchoring one foot on one side and the other over here…"

"We should be able to push ourselves to the top," Zan finished.

Ian went first, wedging himself within the cleft and hoisting himself up step-by-step. Sharp bits of rock scratched up his knees and hands, but he did his best to ignore the pain and blood.

Finally, he pulled himself up onto a ledge and sighed, his eyes rising to another cliff mere meters in front of him.

Perfect. More climbing.

At least he noted a narrow ledge along the cliff leading upward. It wouldn't be easy to walk along it, but it looked passable.

He heard Zan grunting behind him, working his way up the crevice. He looked over to watch his friend's progress—and realized just how high up he stood.

Ian didn't like heights, but this was no time to let fear get the best of him. He couldn't focus on it. It was either climb, or abandon hope of returning home.

He waited for Zan, then helped his friend up the final few feet before walking with him to the narrow ledge.

Katia, meanwhile, had already mounted the cliff. She was calling down at them with encouragements in her native language.

Ian and Zan climbed the ledge and soon crested the cliff face. Ian's mouth fell open. Before them lay a riddled passage of spires, valleys, and cliffs. He couldn't tell if they were climbing one shockingly uneven mountain or a chain of several mountains pushing against each other, with dark valleys in between.

Again he saw Katia in the distance, and his eyes searched out a path towards her.

"I think I see a trail we can take, Zan. Follow me."

Zan gulped behind him. "Uh… right. I'll follow you."

Ian picked his way carefully along a row of descending stones as though they were stairs. If they continued this way for a bit, they would reach a path that would take them to Katia.

He hesitated before taking his next step, however, realizing that the path he had identified, the one that had seemed the only obvious choice, was too narrow to traverse for a long stretch. They would have to find another way.

It took everything within Zan not to panic as he stepped from stone to stone. The path was precarious, the heights dizzying.

"One step at a time," he whispered over and over. "One step at a time."

But taking one step at a time became harder as the final sun dipped below the mountain and the world darkened.

Zan finally reached a point where he was no longer confident that he could see the next step before him.

"Ian, I–I can't see."

Ian reached out and touched Zan on the shoulder. "Yeah. I think we need to stop."

"Here?" Zan trembled. "On the side of a cliff?"

"We can't go forward. I don't think we have a choice."

Zan settled down on the tiny patch of ground they stood upon.

"Maybe one of us could nap at a time," Ian suggested. "The person who's awake can hold onto the sleeper so they don't slip off the cliff."

Zan wanted to argue that the sleeping person might just pull them both down. Still, what other choice did they have?

Something furry brushed again his arm, and Zan realized Katia had returned to them, tucking herself between him and Ian. It felt good having her nearby. Maybe she would have a better way to protect them on these heights.

"So, who sleeps first?" Zan asked.

The Scavgans attempted to sleep, but it was useless; they were too afraid, and there was no way Katia could close her eyes when she had the foreigners to look after.

As soon as the morning light became bright enough to see by, the three travellers arose and continued their trek. Katia vaulted ahead, scouting for any signs of impassable terrain so she could direct the Scavgans onto a more advisable path.

Her heart raced as she watched the Scavgans slowly pick their way around the mountain pass. She hadn't given thought to how dangerous the journey would be for these two-legged creatures. The threat of valley serpents seemed irrelevant at this point; the foreigners were struggling against the very mountains.

Looking down into the darkness between the many spires, she realized how much the valleys themselves appeared like snakes, slithering between the heights. Falling into those depths would be death for Scavgan and Darian alike.

I've never seen a real valley serpent, Katia thought. *I don't believe Anveil ever did, either. I wonder if the stories about them gobbling up travellers were actually warnings about those who fell from the cliffs.*

In her mind's eye, the valleys became hungry, toothy snakes with skins as black as shadow. Their gazes focused on Ian and Zan, their gaping maws awaited the travellers. One little slip was all it would take.

She shivered. *Keep focused, you two...*

Despite the fear of falling, Ian couldn't help but take his eyes off his feet for a moment to stare out at the world around him. The cliffs seemed almost magical, and no mountain he'd seen could compare to the narrow winding valleys and complex heights he now stood upon.

If I could fly, he thought, *I'd dip up and down these valleys and rise to the highest spiracles. It'd be like riding the massive waves of a stormy sea.*

"What's the holdup?" Zan asked, his words snapping Ian back to reality.

"Sorry." Ian looked back to his feet. "Just enjoying the view."

"Yeah, I know what you mean. It's… beautiful."

Here we are, Ian thought, placing his foot another few inches ahead. *One misstep away from death. And we still want to take a moment to enjoy the very mountains that might kill us.*

Thinking of the mountain this way—as something beautiful and exotic instead of menacing and terrifying—made the rest of the journey that much easier. Up ahead, Katia patiently beckoned them forward. Her presence gave him confidence.

He nearly startled when a patch of grass appeared between the rocks. At last, after a long downward trek, they had arrived at the jungle floor. Ian sighed with relief when his feet hit the soft grass. He took a few more steps, then looked back to see Zan jump the meter that remained.

"That was… something," Ian said.

Swallowing, Zan panted. "I—"

Ian's eyes widened as he noticed Zan's dizzy expression. He grabbed his friend's arm. "Zan? Maybe you should sit for a moment."

Not arguing, Zan allowed Ian to lead him under the shadows of the jungle canopy. Katia sat nearby, smiling assuredly.

"We can rest?" Zan asked her wearily. She nodded, seeming to understand. He leaned back against a tree, closing his eye. "Good."

"I wonder how much farther we have to go," Ian remarked as he took a seat beside Zan, curling his legs against his chest. "But I don't know how to ask. I don't even know where she's taking us."

Zan allowed a half-smile. "I'm not sure I've ever been fond of surprises, but I guess I'll have to get used to them." He sighed deeply, closing his eye. "One step at a time, I suppose."

"Yeah," Ian said. "One step at a time."

Zan's hand brushed his own right arm. Feeling something, he reopened his eye and peered down at the spot he'd just touched. After a moment of examination, Zan plucked something tiny and black from his arm and held it in his palm.

"What do you suppose this is?" Zan asked.

Ian leaned in. "You mean you've never seen a leech before?"

"A what?!" Zan tossed the offending bloodsucker to the ground. "No, I've never seen one. Don't they like really wet habitats? Remember, I've spent my whole life in the desert."

Ian shuffled his feet. "I just mean... well... I've been finding leeches on me ever since we arrived in Aziasha."

Zan sighed. "I don't know whether I've just been too tired to notice, or if losing an eye affected my vision more than I thought!"

That ended their conversation, and Zan didn't bother to search for more leeches. His eye closed again and he quickly dozed off. Ian wasn't far behind.

CHAPTER THIRTEEN

"*I* trust you had a pleasant journey?" Council Member Mayal asked as he sat in a grand chair with colourful cushions.

Vasitan nodded. "Yes, sir."

Truthfully, Vasitan's carriage driver had been rushed and caused some near-accidents on the way. But he wasn't about to waste a Council member's time with such insignificant complaints. His eyes did a quick sweep of Mayal's private office—the lovely paints and exotic décor—before he continued, "How may I serve our Emperor?"

"It's come to my attention," Mayal said, sitting straight and dignified, "that shipments of blackwaters have been slipping through our harbours unnoticed."

Vasitan's heart skipped a beat. "I can assure you, I've been faithfully completing my rounds."

Does he know I'm involved? Is he suspicious? I know I've milked money from several ships as of late... Have I been working too fast?

"I know you've done your job," Mayal continued, allowing Vasitan the slightest sigh of relief. "But the pirates are clever. Blackwaters are a menace to our world, and I've told the Emperor that I will personally ensure their trade and sale is slowed, if not outright halted."

Nodding rapidly, Vasitan realized how serious this was.

"I've heard rumours of a few blackwaters scientists at work on nearby islands," Mayal said. "I'm collecting more information and recruiting pirate hunters to see that their operations are ended. Burned to the ground."

"That's brilliant, sir!" Vasitan said quickly. "I mean, that you've been able to find such information when sources are usually so tight-lipped."

"Well, you can thank Captain Ctzo and his crew of pirate hunters for giving me the clues I needed to get started. He sent me a witness who'd once been in the blackwaters trade, selling to a scientist named Jakodi Jair. That scientist, it seems, is now deceased. We've taken over his fortress. But the witness had a few other bits of information that made all the difference."

Behind his back, Vasitan clenched his fist. It seemed he could blame Captain Ctzo for two things now—for taking his son, and for alerting the empire to certain pirates and scientists.

Is he on a personal mission to ruin my life? Vasitan wondered, even though he knew that wasn't the case. *But what an unlucky coincidence.*

He had to make sure he didn't panic. The heat would wear off. He just had to back away from the trade for now, and in a year business could continue as before.

"I will aid the Emperor in whichever way you see fit, my master."

CHAPTER FOURTEEN

*K*atia released a long, haunting cry. It carried through the jungle, through the bushes and shadows. Ian and Zan both held their breath, waiting.

A series of raucous hoots answered back. Katia leapt up, calling louder, and then several voices answered in unison.

Out of the jungle bounded Darian after Darian of greater fur colour variety than either Ian or Zan had thought possible: blue-greys, orange-reds, muted yellows, rich maroon, and a host of greys and browns, not to mention patterns including stripes, spots, and splotches.

They circled around Katia excitedly and crowded the Scavgans, reaching up to grab the foreigners' hands. Ian and Zan found the crowd pulling them into a nearby thicket. Noting Katia's massive smile, neither fought back, though they wondered who these people were and where they were being led.

At length, the thicket gave way to a clearing where the ground underfoot was no longer a tangle of jungle growth, but well-trodden red soil. Trees and larger bushes remained, complemented by simple huts of crisscrossing wooden poles.

Ian and Zan at last exchanged understanding glances.

"It's her tribe," Ian whispered.

Zan nodded. "I guess this is where she's been leading us—to her home."

Seated on the red dirt in a haphazard circle, Ian and Zan were served platters of fruit in nearly every colour and shape imaginable. The two hesitated only slightly at the unfamiliar sights and smells. Their growling stomachs encouraged them to abandon their fear and start chowing down. Dripping, gooey messes soon tumbled down their chins, but they ignored the urge to hunt for napkins. Katia's tribe didn't seem worried about tidy eating, only occasionally licking pulp from their own hands.

When the meal finished, the Scavgans were half-dragged to a large stone basin partially filled with water. Bugs and dead leaves floated on the surface. The Darians handed them gourds before pouring the water over their hands and into their mouths.

Ian and Zan were too thirsty to care about the quality of the water. When they realized they were being encouraged to drink, they chugged it down. Ian paused only to pull Vortro from his pocket and pour water over the worm, which had once again began to dry out. Vortro immediately perked up from the attention.

As soon as their drinking slowed, Ian and Zan again found themselves being led, this time into a hut. Two woven mats lay upon the dirt floor and the guests were laid down on the mats and tucked under blankets.

"Sleep." Katia stood amongst the crowd of Darians, smiling at the Scavgans. "Time to sleep."

"Your journey has been a long one," the white-furred Darian named Sina said to Katia in a tone of awe. The dishes had long been cleaned, the visiting Scavgans sent to bed, when Sina looked at her friend with bright pink eyes.

"Yes," Katia said, sighing. "Recounting it all makes me realize just how long a journey it's been." Her hand played through the dirt in front of her. "I... I miss Anveil."

Sina placed a hand on her friend's shoulder. "I sensed that. I'm sorry you lost him."

Katia felt no shame at the tears trailing down her cheeks. "Yet I've been braver and stronger than I ever felt possible." She took a moment to admire the stars above. They sparkled in the sky, a dim quarter-moon adding its glow. "I suppose life moves on."

"Have you enjoyed being with the foreigners?"

"You wouldn't believe the stuff they expect me to eat!" Katia smiled and rubbed her belly. "Some things, I've missed very much. Like good fruit."

The two shared a short laugh.

"Sleeping on the ship, too, was difficult," Katia went on. "That is, their giant canoe. It rocks and creaks. It's so much harder to fall asleep there than in a nice, warm hut."

Sina giggled. "Sometimes the huts are too warm. But isn't your husband's tribe nomadic?"

"True. But Anveil was always good at finding a comfortable cave or log or other shelter to sleep in." She considered what had happened to that tribe. "Perhaps they'd allow me to rejoin them. Though it wouldn't be the same without Anveil, and I honestly don't know if I'd trust them to welcome me without him."

There was a moment of silence.

"So you really aren't staying," Sina said at last.

"What?" Katia realized she hadn't seriously thought about it. "I mean, I haven't… um…"

Sina's pink eyes glistened as she stared at her friend. Then, hardly loud enough to be a whisper, she said, "It's okay."

"Hmm?"

"You need to leave. I can tell. Katia—"

"No!" Katia stomped her foot. "This is my home. This is where I want to be. This is where I'm happy. This is where I'm safe."

Sina shook her head. "Deep inside, you know this isn't where you belong."

Now Katia's eyes glistened, and a tear rolled down her cheek. "But life is so much simpler here. I can be carefree and unafraid. I can be… happy."

"And yet you'll always know that you abandoned the life you were meant to live. It isn't about being unafraid and comfortable. We're meant to grow and become stronger. Katia, I think you're meant to be a hero. But you can't become that here."

Katia's tears flowed freely. "I know what I'm supposed to do, Sina. I know I'm supposed to go with the foreigners, to return to their ship. But I'm scared." She looked up at the simple huts and emerald foliage. "I feel at home here."

Sina put a comforting paw over Katia's. "You will feel at home with them. Someday. I know you will."

"How will I tell the others in the tribe that I'm leaving?"

"They already know. We always sensed it. And we all want the best for you." A bittersweet smile lit Sina's face, and she embraced her friend. "You're going to become something amazing, Katia."

Closing her eyes, Katia absorbed the feeling of her best friend's hug, knowing full well how unlikely it was that they'd meet again in this life. "I will miss you all."

"You will not be forgotten," Sina promised. "You weren't forgotten when you married Anveil, and you won't be forgotten as you travel to the farthest forests and waters. It is your fate. It saddens us now, but it will bring you joy in the long run."

The next morning, Ian awoke to voices chattering outside the hut in a foreign language. He moaned and rolled over. The bed was a bit bristly and the blankets made him itch, but this was still the best night's sleep he'd had in a long time, and he wasn't ready to wake up.

"Ian?" Zan called from his sleeping mat.

"Mmmh," Ian muttered back.

"Ian, we can't stay here forever."

Ian's eyes remained closed as he heard Zan get up. "What do you mean?"

"The sooner we find the ship, the sooner we can get home. We'll have a good breakfast and pack up something to eat on our journey. I saw some Darians with drawstring bags we could buy from them, assuming we have anything of value. Why didn't I buy jewellery from the Marsh Isles like Tyzak? For being weird and a bit crazy, he had a smart idea there. Do you have anything we could give them?"

"Sleep," Ian replied groggily.

"We'll need water too," Zan continued. "Maybe they'd let us have a few filled gourds. Katia can hopefully help us get packed."

Ian felt a pang hit his heart. Katia. Based on how they'd welcomed her, she evidently knew the tribe well... which meant that if he and Zan wanted to move on and find the fleet, they'd have to say goodbye to Katia.

He really wasn't ready to get up and face the day.

It didn't take Zan long to accomplish his goals. Katia helped him pack gourds full of water and bags of fruit. Ian followed along behind, feeling like he had to force himself to lend aid.

When everything was finally ready, the Darians lined themselves up and each gave Zan and Ian a firm hug.

With the goodbyes complete, Ian turned away from the tribe. He couldn't bear to look at them, to let them see the tears streaming down his face. And he hadn't seen Katia in the line-up.

Smiling, Zan nudged his shoulder. "What are you crying about?"

"Won't you miss Katia?" Ian asked.

"Nope." Zan laughed at the glare he got from his friend. "Katia's coming with us!"

Ian's expression turned into a blank stare. "Uh... what?"

"Why do you think she's been hugging all her friends goodbye?"

"She's..." Ian's eyes searched the tribe until he spotted Katia and locked eyes with her. He opened his mouth, then closed it. The look in her eyes said everything.

As Katia's tribe gave the trio a final set of hugs, they clung onto the Scavgans' legs and shouted farewell blessings.

"May your new life be a rich one," Sina said as she gave Katia one last embrace. "You will be missed."

A sob escaped Katia. "And may you be ever safe and prosperous."

"Do you remember the way to the shore?"

Katia nodded. "Yes. We'll follow along the coastline until we meet more Scavgans. We'll find another ship... that is, their canoe... and return to the sea."

Pulling away, Sina smiled at her friend. "That is a wise idea. You are smarter than you ever believed, dear Katia. And these foreigners have you to thank for their survival."

Katia's heart raced. "Once we leave the safety of the village, we'll be back into dangerous jungle."

"Only for a brief time. And this patch of jungle is one of the safer places. You've made it this far. You can make it through there."

At last, Katia backed away from Sina, tears falling unhindered from her eyes. "I think the foreigners are anxious to continue our journey." She sniffed. "Goodbye, my best of friends."

"Goodbye, Katia. And best of travels."

Katia's mind remained on her people even as she trekked through the jungle, towards where she knew she'd find shoreline. She played back old memories as she walked, wondering about her friends and family. Her thoughts were so distracted that when she finally returned her mind to her current situation, she realized with surprise that they'd travelled for hours and the suns had nearly set.

Finding an old, hollowed-out log, she settled into it and motioned for the Scavgans to rest just outside.

They'd made good headway, and as Sina predicted there was no trouble in sight. At this rate, they'd be on the beach by the next night.

The next evening, before the suns had set, Ian felt sand squishing under his feet. Looking out through the foliage, he glimpsed the ocean's glimmering blue waters. He knelt, taking in the sight as he enjoyed deep, relaxed breaths.

"We're here," Ian said.

Walking past him, Zan stopped just beyond the reach of the sloshing waves. "The way you said that, you'd think we were home. We still have to find the fleet."

Ian noticed the dryness in his throat and was grateful when he recalled the guards filled with water at their disposal. The thought that his thirst could be so easily cured made him able to ignore it.

"Yes, I guess we do still have a long way to go," Ian said. "But can't we celebrate little victories?"

"You're right." Zan placed a hand on his friend's shoulder. "We're getting closer. Katia, where next?"

Ian caught her yawning as she settled into the warm sand. It made sense that she'd be so exhausted after leading them such a long way, across so much of Aziasha. She deserved some time off.

"Let's relax for a bit," Zan said, sitting next to Ian. "It's been a while since we really rested."

Zan startled awake to find himself stretched out in the sand, the cool darkness of late evening surrounding him. Ian lay nearby and Katia stood watch, gazing out to sea. He shook his head as he sat, having forgotten where they'd fallen asleep. The three had been so worn from their journeys through the jungle that sleep had come easily.

His gaze landed on Vortro. The little worm had crawled out of Ian's pocket and now slithered along its master's back, nosing around with its triangular face.

Is it just me or has it gotten bigger? Zan wondered.

He marvelled that the creature hadn't starved. Were there more parasites to feed on, or had it been eating something else?

He soon got his answer. When a small bug landed on Ian, Vortro lunged at it.

For a moment, his ears tuned to the sloshing of the waves and gentle songs of jungle wildlife. This spot felt quiet. Perhaps most of Aziasha's animals remained inland, away from shore.

A small critter scuttled across the sands and Zan watched it absently, noting how different the world looked with only one eye to see it through.

Ian yawned and rolled over, and Zan thought for a moment that his friend must be awake. But when he called, Ian didn't respond. Katia, too, had fallen back asleep, her head rested against her arms.

Hearing voices from the nearby jungle, Zan tensed. Even Katia startled awake, her ears held high in rapt attention. As Zan listened more closely, he recognized the language of the newcomers: Questavan.

Zan shook Ian's shoulder. "Ian, get up. We have company."

The voices seemed to be getting closer. Ian's eyes blinked open, and Zan pulled his still-groggy companion to his feet. Katia snuck towards some bushes, motioning for the Scavgans to follow. With Vortro slithering on his skin and Ian in his arms, Zan stepped into the bushes and crouched low, turning to watch for signs of the strangers.

Within minutes, four Scavgans walked out of the jungle, shouting animatedly at one another. Though Zan couldn't catch their words at first, he guessed by their tones that the conversation wasn't a pleasant one.

"Do you know nothing?" one of them yelled at another.

A third pointed toward the sea. "Look! The boat's not here. Guess we'll just have to walk back."

"High tide," the first said irritably. "Do they not have high tide where you come from?"

The second Scavgan put up his hands defensively. "I thought we pulled the boat far enough onto the beach that the tide couldn't reach it. Sorry. And what's this 'where you come from' business? We're both from Questava!"

The fourth at last spoke, his voice soft enough that Zan had to focus hard to discern his words. "You've only been here for a short time. Get used to the way things work. No one here cares where you're from…"

Zan shook his head, unable to make out the rest as the group re-entered the jungle and walked away.

His stomach growled but he ignored it, his gaze following the shoreline. He could see for some distance, but there was no sign of a ship or any other habitation.

"Maybe they have a base inland," Ian said, as if reading his friend's mind.

"Should we follow them?"

For the first time ever, Zan saw Katia shrug. Perhaps leading them to the beach had been the completion of her plan and she didn't know where else to go.

Zan stood. "All right, let's follow them. Maybe they're not pirates and they'll be kind enough to offer us a place to rest, and a bit more food and water."

His stomach growled again. He reached into their pack, pulled out a fist-sized fruit, and quickly munched it down.

"And if not?" Ian asked.

Zan smiled. "I'm sure we can find a way to steal something. Come on, before we lose them."

Katia didn't argue with Zan and Ian as they snuck through the jungle after the strange Scavgans, though her senses remained on high alert. There was something about these people that bothered her. It was their scent, she decided, though she couldn't place the odour.

Understanding the way of Scavgans was Zan and Ian's area of expertise. They'd trusted her to lead them through the wilderness, and now she had to return that trust.

Nevertheless, her uneasiness grew. She *knew* that smell. It was recognizable yet unfamiliar, haunting.

Maybe I'm just imagining things, she thought.

A dark puddle appeared in front of her and she jumped aside, imagining it to be a pool of blackwaters. But no; she relaxed as she realized it was some drink, something that had spilled from a bottle a Scavgan had left lying on the ground.

But that scent! She realized it had been blackwaters, and she'd smelled it all over those Scavgans. She felt sure of it. She'd only encountered blackwaters in small puddles on a few occasions, and the odour had never really stood out to her. It had been so faint.

So why did it seem so strong now?

The trio reached a clearing and Zan and Ian carefully peered through the bushes. Both gasped in surprise.

Curious, Katia pushed forward until she could see. Already the sounds of Scavgan voices had reached her ears—and suddenly she could see why the smell of blackwaters was so strong.

Several dirtied Scavgans stood around the entrance to a cave, each of them covered from hatted head to booted foot in leather gear. Trailing from the mouth of the cave were railways lined with carts. Scavgans pushed empty carts back into the cave, and carts filled with tiny clay vases came out of the caves.

A few carts lay abandoned on the ground. One, filled with shattered vases, revealed what was being carted out of the cavern.

"Blackwaters." Ian murmured, his eyes narrowing as he took in the scene. "It's a blackwaters mine."

Zan grabbed his friend's shoulder and pointed. Ian's jaw fell open when he saw what Zan wanted him to see: walking towards the mine was Jakodi Jair, the blackwaters scientist himself. He had glowing amber eyes, rough and dark Blackblood skin, clawed hands, and that unusual tail which ended in a spear-like stinger framed by narrow pincers.

Jair acknowledged one miner with a smile, than continued into the mouth of the cave. His dark form quickly vanished into the shadows.

Zan slipped the pack of supplies off of his shoulder. "I'm going to take a closer look."

"What?!" Ian said. "I don't think that's a good idea. There's—"

"—not too many of them." Zan was already starting to slip out from the bushes.

Ian and Katia exchanged looks. He couldn't tell from her expression what she was thinking.

"Zan, you can't just," Ian whispered. But Zan was gone, ducking behind an overturned cart.

He can't go in there alone, Ian realized. He gave Katia a nod as he handed their supplies to her. Then he followed after Zan.

Expecting to be caught at any moment, Ian's heart pounded violently in his chest. Yet he trailed Zan from one minecart to another. The workers were too absorbed in their activities to notice. Or perhaps Zan and Ian had just gotten lucky. Either way, the duo successfully inched their way into the mine.

Once inside, Zan whispered, "No sign of Jair."

Ian surveyed the dim setting lit by hanging wall torches. "How about I do a quick check further in? It's better that one of us gets caught than both of us."

"Go ahead," Zan relented. "Try to be fast, though. I'm going to follow if you take too long."

CHAPTER FIFTEEN

Sébérus massaged his arm, trying to distract himself from the pain by gluing his eyes to the pages of the Ti'te'Vikan religious texts. He sat on the deck of the *Ko'Ekua*, where he'd hoped to get a private moment to study while the other crewmembers remained at the temple.

The sharp aches coursing through him at the moment were far from unfamiliar. They were just part of being a Blackblood, a creature mutated from its original self, with a body trying to adjust to every change on a physiological level.

He gritted his teeth at his once-minor headache, which had gradually increased and now throbbed unignorably. He closed his eyes, sighing as he set aside the book. He needed rest.

Sébérus turned his head, though his eyes remained closed, letting instinct guide him belowdecks and in the direction of a hammock. He dragged himself into it, groaning all the while. After plopping down on the hammock and twisting and turning for several minutes, he came to a firm conclusion: *This is pointless.*

Though his senses told him he was alone, he still felt the need to open his eyes and perk his ears, scanning the room for any signs of life. When he'd satisfied himself, he reached into a stack of old clothes. As he'd hoped, no one had touched the rags. Dealing with someone else's dirty laundry wasn't high on his crewmates' list of desires. No one suspected their real purpose: to hide the strong painkillers he'd snuck aboard.

Sébérus kept his motions quick as he prepared and then injected the liquid. He'd used the same needle over and over, reasoning to himself that his blood was already so poisoned that it didn't matter whether he used a clean needle. Maybe he was wrong, maybe he was right, but he only had one syringe. It would have to do.

Allowing a sigh of relief as the drugs began to take effect, Sébérus quickly hid his stash.

He jumped at the sound of tapping behind him and swirled to face the noise.

There stood Nva, her serpentine eyes glinting. Her head shook slightly and her clawed foot tapped the floor. "Do you want to explain to me, or shall I get the captain?"

High Priest Pazu sighed heavily as he wondered how to deal wisely with the current situation. Sébérus's crime could not be overlooked. Sneaking drugs aboard the *Ko'Ekua* was a desecration. The ship had been dedicated by the Ti'te'Vikan priests, set apart for the propagation of their faith. And the crew aboard it had thus far maintained full respect for the vessel.

Grey Noon, in his zealous way, would no doubt call for blood.

However, Pazu had always felt pity for Blackbloods, especially those who had the illness forced upon them by profit-seeking scientists.

I have no doubt the creature's suffering is great, Pazu thought. *What else would drive him to take such risks?*

In the little time he'd spent with Sébérus, he hadn't gotten to know much of the Blackblood's personality. Still, he couldn't help but pick up on a sense of the creature's arrogant craftiness. Maybe that came from his Kamai aspects. Nva certainly had come across as arrogant and conniving from time to time.

Pazu heard a large figure walk up to the door. *Ah, my old apprentice has returned. No doubt in a foul mood.*

As Grey Noon entered, growls vibrated dangerously through him. "How could I have been blind to this? Nva never liked that Blackblood. I should have trusted her instincts. To think he'd be daft enough to bring drugs onto my ship!"

The older Rezumi sighed sadly. "It is a terrible tragedy."

"Tragedy?" Grey Noon snapped. "The only thing that could possibly be considered tragic is the gruesome manner in which that abomination is about to die!"

"Calm yourself." Pazu stretched out his wing. "Perhaps death isn't the way to solve this."

Grey Noon's eyes widened, then narrowed. "Oh?"

"You told me he's a very clever fellow. Strategic, shockingly intelligent."

"Yes." Grey Noon sighed. "It would be a shame to lose an asset like that. But is he really an asset when he can betray us so fearlessly?"

"He'll learn to fear you. Everyone does, my child." Pazu looked out the nearest window. "Sometimes it worries me. But in this instance, it's probably for the best. The Blackblood has used us for his own ends."

Again, Grey Noon growled. "He can't have expected to get away with his drug habit forever. He likely planned to leave when he got the chance."

"Arrogance can blind anyone." Pazu watched the orange leaves on a tree shift in the breeze. "As can pain. If he'd been thinking more clearly, I'm sure he'd have realized how likely it was he'd get caught."

"And such arrogance should cost him his life. Do you disagree?"

"Lately you don't seem to care too much whether or not I disagree with your ways. Why does it matter now?"

Grey Noon's voice softened. "I care about and respect your opinions. In many ways, High Priest, you saved my life."

Pazu closed his eyes. *Yes. And you've used that freedom to take the lives of many others.*

Was Grey Noon right in assuming piracy and war were the answer to the empire's reign? Perhaps in Pazu's old age, he had grown too accustomed to how the world worked, rather than being willing to take the risks necessary to change it for the better. And yet he couldn't bring himself to feel at peace about the matter.

He allowed it to slip from his mind, and refocused on the task at hand.

"Yes, this Sébérus has committed a terrible crime," Pazu acknowledged. "And you are free to make an example of him by ending his life. But—"

"You think I could do better? Find another way to punish him that would benefit me more?" Grey Noon cocked his head, contemplating. "Interesting idea. I'll give it some thought."

Grey Noon walked over to Sébérus's jail cell and stared down at the smaller creature, his massive shadow darkening all but the Blackblood's glowing yellow eyes. Those eyes stared back at him, but the Rezumi couldn't read the expression.

After a moment, Grey Noon growled. "The punishment we've settled on is far gentler than you deserve." He thought he detected curiosity in Sébérus's gaze. "You have two choices. You may be executed here and now. As I said, it's the least of what you deserve. Or you can help us plan our war against Questava."

Silence hung in the air.

"Quite frankly, people rarely surprise me," Sébérus said. "Yet you just did. I was convinced it hadn't even crossed your mind to let me live. You are ever a source of awe for me."

"Am I supposed to be flattered?"

Sébérus closed his eyes. "What makes you think I could come up with strategies better than your own?"

"You're a genius. And you have motivation: the threat of my wrath. Those two factors should be enough. Besides, the current Questavan government has outlawed the very existence of your kind. According to them, you should be killed on sight. If you help us, I can ensure those laws are changed. You can live in freedom."

"Who says I don't want to die?" Sébérus snapped hastily. He turned to face the back wall of his cell.

"If you did, you would have ended your life already. Instead your ambition drives you on. And I have no doubt it will continue to do so." The massive pirate captain then turned, leaving his prisoner with a few final words. "I'll give you a bit of time. But I'll be back here in several hours. By then, I'm sure you'll have enough ideas to impress me."

Sure enough, mere hours later Sébérus stood before the assembly of priests. A chain linked him to a heavy ball which he could barely drag around.

"You've been given a choice." Pazu looked Sébérus over solemnly. "Have you devoted your mind to helping your master, or have you chosen death?"

Sébérus eyed each of the priests in turn. He sighed. "I've got a few ideas… but to carry them out, we'll have to return to Aziasha, and to Atzinus's fortress."

CHAPTER SIXTEEN

*C*tzo's mind wandered as he stared out at the rippling seas, the wind sending the smell of saltwater up his nostrils. He pictured a map of Aziasha's coasts and mentally marked where he knew their fleet to be.

Perhaps this is unwise, he considered, his gaze following the calm soaring of a seabird. *We're on the northern side of Aziasha now, but we lost Ian, Zan, and Katia on the Marsh Isles, far south of here. What are the chances they've travelled so far from where we last saw them?*

He stepped back from the ocean, deciding that they should turn around, return to the Marsh Isles and the Athai tribe. Perhaps the lost crewmembers were safe with the tribe, enjoying their hospitality.

Kyra flew over and landed on Ctzo's shoulder. "A crewmember spotted a few ships flying Questavan merchant flags. Should we investigate?"

Ctzo considered her question. "If we can see them, they should be able to see us. If they don't approach us, there's probably no reason for us to approach them. Let Réto know that we're changing course—we'll head back around the coast to the Marsh Isles. I'll get the crew to rig the sails appropriately."

"What did you find?" Zan whispered as Ian slipped back behind the old minecart.

"More miners." Ian curled up beside his friend. "Six, I think. I expected more."

"I guess blackwaters mining is dangerous work. Not a whole lot of volunteers."

"And if you listen to what the miners are saying, they don't think they get paid enough for it."

"I don't think you could pay me enough to work with blackwaters." Zan stared at his feet, thinking. "Any brilliant plans?"

"Getting out of here sounds great."

"Not until we find Jair!" Zan snapped. "We can't just abandon this opportunity to get him back."

Ian shook his head. "How are the two of us going to keep him prisoner?"

"I didn't say he had to be a conscious prisoner." Zan peered around the corner of the old cart. "I'm guessing you didn't find him?"

"I'm guessing he's left the mine. Or maybe he went farther back. I don't know. I really think we should get out of here, Zan."

"Wait! There!" Zan whispered excitedly. "He's walking up to that guy in the purple jacket. Do you think that's the mine supervisor?"

Ian sighed. "Zan, please…"

"We can't leave now. Too many miners. We'll be seen. We'll have to wait them out."

Jair approached the mine supervisor calmly, his tail flicking back and forth. He didn't even look at the man as he walked towards him, his gaze instead journeying around the dirt walls and wooden carts.

Jair briefly closed his eyes, fixating on his superior senses. As a Blackblood, he'd learned to enhance his senses: he could detect the slightest breeze, vibration, shadow, and ray of light—and he could feel the invisible energy currents that pulsated through every living creature.

He sensed two figures cowering behind an abandoned mine-cart nearby.

Must be miners attempting to squeeze in some extra respite from work, he mused. He didn't blame them. Visiting the mines had never appealed to his more cultured attitudes. *What a grimy, slave-driven mess of a workplace. Oh, why must progress be forged in such dismal lairs?*

Jair refocused his attention on the mine supervisor, who stood before him.

What a grimy, slave-driving mess of a man. Why must progress be forged in the lairs of such dismal individuals?

The Scavgan before him, a man of dark blue skin and cold white pupils, nearly growled at Jair. "Are you even listening, creature?"

"No," Jair replied. "No, I was not listening. Did you have anything important to say? If so, please speak more concisely, and place your pungent breath elsewhere."

The mine supervisor clenched his fist. "I'm used to being respected."

"As am I, dear sir." Jair didn't even flinch.

At last, the other man unclenched his fist. He glanced away. "My… apologies, sir."

Jair inwardly savoured the victory. *Oh, what a joy to be a Blackblood! No one wishes to get on your bad side.*

"So, I'm sure neither of us has the time to dilly-dally," Jair pressed. "Why don't we keep this conversation brief and pointed, to the benefit of us both?" He flicked his snake-like tongue as he surveyed the mines. "I would like a ship full of blackwaters for my own personal use, thank you."

Frowning, the mine supervisor looked hard at Jair. Then a smile slipped over his lips, and a deep chuckle rumbled through him. "That's crazy!"

"Excuse me?" Before he knew what he was doing, Jair grabbed the man's throat in his claws, imagining what it would be like to poison this pompous fellow—

What am I doing? Jair quickly withdrew his hand. If he'd been capable of blushing, his face would have been flush with embarrassment.

"Ahem… my apologies," Jair said. "Temper got away from me."

It seems to do that a lot these days. He pushed the discouraging thought from his mind. *I'm just stressed, that's all.*

"Look, dear fellow, I've been stranded on Aziasha, wandering these woods week after week. I'm about ready to find a more comfortable living situation. A ship will do me well in reaching said situation. My ride to Aziasha has long since departed without me. So, will you provide me with a ship?"

The Scavgan grumbled. "We have a smaller vessel you can take, but how much blackwaters will you need? The ship can only carry so much. And whether or not you care, sir, I have a business to run. I can't go around handing out my product for free."

"Of course," Jair said. "And I will send you payment for services when I am able."

"Right." The mine supervisor sounded doubtful. "Go meet my man Gry outside. I'll be with you in a moment."

"Thank you." With a swish of his tail, Jair turned to the mine's entrance.

Once outside, Ian and Zan didn't breathe easy until they'd escaped into the shadows of the jungle foliage where Katia awaited them.

Ian gave her a warm smile. "We're back, safe and sound."

Nodding, Katia then slipped further into the jungle, motioning for the others to follow.

Zan sighed irritably. "I still can't believe we missed Jair. Again."

"Zan, the last time we went after him, you lost an eye."

"If we could capture him—"

"There were too many miners. Maybe we'll get another chance some other day."

The trio exited the jungle as Katia led them towards the beach, but Zan continued to gripe under his breath. "We're supposed to be pirate hunters, and we can't even catch one lousy blackwaters scientist."

Ian shivered, wrapping his arms around him. As the suns dipped lower, with the lowest nearly touching the horizon, the air became cooler. He hadn't noticed it last night. Perhaps he'd been too worn down to care. Or perhaps the chill breeze sweeping over the sands hadn't been present last night.

He glanced out to sea, eyes playing over the rippling waters. Then he focused on a dark shape hovering over distant waters. A ship!

His pulse quickened. Was it bringing in more blackwaters miners? Or perhaps supplies? He opened his mouth to alert Zan and Katia, but something held him back. The ship seemed somehow familiar... yet there was no logical way to tell from this distance...

Ian's jaw dropped. "Zan! The ship!" As the boat came closer, his face broke into a smile and he jumped up and down excitedly. "It's the *Diversity*! They've found us!"

"But why would they come here? I mean, we were on the other side of Aziasha when they lost us."

"Who cares? They're here!" Ian waved his arms, then stopped when he realized they were unlikely to be seen. "Should we light a signal fire?"

Zan shrugged. "Ask Katia. I'd risk it, but maybe she has a better plan."

When Katia finally understood what was going on, she dashed towards the sea. Stopping where the waves washed over her feet, she yipped loudly and excitedly. When that didn't seem loud enough, she hollered. Ian and Zan joined her, waving and shouting, and Vortro chimed in with rapid chirps.

The moments seemed to pass as slowly as hours—until finally the *Diversity* made a sharp turn, the wind catching her sails and carrying her straight towards the waiting sailors.

Ian didn't bother containing his excitement.

As Captain Ctzo walked down the gangplank to meet them, his stride as stately as ever, Ian ran over and threw his arms around his captain.

To the teenager's surprise, Czto laughed.

Ctzo put a hand on the lad's shoulder. "Welcome back! When Kyra said she'd caught sight of you three on the beach, I found it hard to believe. It is good to see you again!"

As *Radiant Dawn* came to rest ashore, Tyzak ran down her gangplank, slipping and falling the final few feet. He then rushed headlong towards Ian and Zan. Just as they stepped back from Ctzo, Tyzak was there to engulf them in a tight hug.

"Never," Tyzak said as he squeezed Ian and Zan in his arms. "Never, ever, ever disappear like that again."

Katia yipped happily as she landed on the deck of the *Diversity*. At first, she wasn't sure whom she wished to greet, but she gasped as Oti pounced on her, hugging her tightly.

"You're back!" Oti shouted.

She patted his shoulder. "You... um... thank you."

You're not embarrassed to show your happiness? she wondered.

She was even more startled at the feeling of wetness as tears dripped down onto her from Oti's eyes.

"Oh, Oti." She hugged him close. "There, there, I'm back. You're all right."

As a shadow fell over them, Katia looked up and smiled at Black Night's cheery face. He gently stroked her with his wing.

Home. She was far from her tribe, and forever separated from Anveil. And yet warm feelings of comfort and joy ignited within her. *This is home. . . these people, these ships. Thank you, Sina, for encouraging me.*

CHAPTER SEVENTEEN

"*A* blackwaters mine?" Ctzo asked Ian and Zan as they stood in the captain's quarters.

"The mine isn't far from here," Zan said. He fiddled with the simple patch covering his right eye. Doctor Savato had put it together rather hastily, and it often slipped from its place. "The mine supervisor mentioned having ships. Have you seen them? They would likely be docked nearby."

"We passed some ships flying Questavan merchant flags," Ctzo confirmed. "I was suspicious, but they never approached us and we decided to leave them be."

"You know who else is here?" Zan asked. "Jair! Ian and I were chasing him when we got separated from the rest of you. I guess he wandered across the island to here. A stroke of luck… for us."

Ctzo raised an eyebrow, frowning. "Quite the surprise. Are you sure he didn't follow you?"

"I don't think so," Ian said. "I think Katia would have noticed. It was a long and at times arduous trip, especially when we had to navigate around the mountains. Right, Zan?"

Zan nodded. "I'm with Ian. Katia would have noticed. *We* would have noticed."

"In that case," Ctzo said, "it is indeed surprising you've encountered Jair so far from where we left him."

Zan leaned forward eagerly. "Perhaps this means your God Kyaté is giving us another chance to capture him?"

"Perhaps." Ctzo nodded. "To be honest, I'm less concerned about recapturing Jair and more concerned about shutting down that mine. If we take out the source of the blackwaters trade, we'll save many lives. I'm not as worried about the damage Jair could do."

"Right," Zan said, hesitating. "I guess I'm just annoyed that he's evaded us so far. You're right, the mine should be our priority."

"What can you tell me about the mine?" the captain asked. "How big is it? How many workers?"

Ian considered. "It's not huge. I mean, in physical size it's decent, but there are very few workers, and a lot of damaged carts have just been abandoned. Handy for us, since that meant we were able to sneak around."

"Maybe it used to be bigger," Zan suggested. "The number of carts was disproportionate to the number of workers. Perhaps someone got infected at one point, causing workers to quit?"

"The mine is inside a cavern," Ian said, "and the cavern is lit by torches. The miners wear lots of protective gear. The supervisor had a purple jacket."

"We never heard how many ships they have," Zan added. "But Jair was wanting to take one ship, loaded with blackwaters, and the mine supervisor told him there was a smaller ship he could take instead."

Ctzo straightened up. "Then the first thing to do is to scout out the area. I'll send Yakara to take a look around."

Zan frowned, not remembering who Yakara was. "Oh, right. She's one of the Reea, isn't she? One of Chiha's friends?"

"Yes." Ctzo nodded. "Though lately she seems to spend more time around Tyzak. She's not usually visible, but she follows him around and attempts to speak to him whenever he'll initiate the conversation."

Ian looked around the room. "How do we know when a Reea is following us?"

Ctzo shook his head. "I'm mostly aware of their activities because First Mate Jani, the Kamai, and the Athai have a sixth sense for them. If you want to find her, check with Chiha or Tyzak. And you'll need Chiha here to translate."

Hours later, Yakara's radiant red pupils watched the bustling miners from her hiding spot in the jungle. She flicked out her serpentine tongue.

Kyra, perched upside-down against the trunk of a tree, eyed her curiously. She hadn't lost her fascination with the Reea. Eight short limbs with clawed hands carried Yakara's snake-like body. A crest of spines ran from her head down her back, and her long tail ended in a spear-like stinger framed by two narrow pincers. Kyra had learned from Chiha that the Reea's venom—released at will from its claws, spines, fangs, and stinger—was actually the creature's own blood. Hence, a Reea was hesitant to use it. In fact, for all their frightful appearance, most Reea had shy or even nervous personalities, leaving them to rely on camouflage as their main defence, disappearing into the scenery around them.

That ability made Yakara perfect for this mission.

Kyra, too, could camouflage at will, but the Kamai couldn't do it as well. Kyra would have to rely on her stealth, agility, and keen instincts to accomplish the task ahead: spying on the blackwaters miners and finding their points of weakness.

She turned her attention to the miners as they busily went to and from the cavern. They were few in number; that was an obvious weakness. Each had a sword strapped to his side. Their protective gear, designed to lessen the risk of Blackblood infection, likely offered little defence against traditional weapons.

Another obvious weakness was their focus. Each time a pair of miners brought out a cart filled with clay vases of blackwaters, they did so slowly, their eyes never leaving the wagon except to gauge the immediate path ahead for any patches of uneven terrain.

I suppose that's how Ian and Zan were able to sneak into the mine unnoticed, Kyra thought, surveying the scene once more. *Still, Kyaté must have been giving them His favour.*

"Yakara, I'll search for Jair by the beach," Kyra whispered softly in the language of the Marsh Isles. "You search in the caverns and then meet back here when you're done. Understand?"

Yakara nodded.

"Am I speaking clearly?"

"Yes, you speak my language very well," Yakara replied. "I wish I could learn yours as quickly."

Kyra spread her wings and dropped from the tree trunk. Her wings caught the air and she glided off in the direction of the sea.

Yakara wasted no time completing her objective. Without a sound, and invisible to the eye, she slipped past the miners and crawled into the depths of the cavern. At the mine's back, she discovered a line of machinery, all of it rusty and foul-scented. She found few Scavgans—only two, one operating a lever, and a second holding a vase as blackwaters poured into it. At this second fellow's yell, the first one pushed the lever upwards. The flow of blackwaters stopped.

Interesting, Yakara thought as she eyed the machinery, wishing she understood the complex network of metal.

No sign of Jair, though.

She slithered back out of the cavern to report to Kyra.

"The miners are few in number," Kyra recounted to Ctzo, Jani, and Réto upon her return to the captain's quarters aboard the *Diversity.* "Facing them on land shouldn't be a problem. However, we'll have to surround them to ensure none flee into the mine or jungle."

"And their ships?" Ctzo asked.

"Three cutters—presumably, one is being given to Jair—and a small frigate."

Ctzo nodded. "Then this isn't a large operation."

"They all have weapons, just as Ian and Zan reported," Kyra continued. "They may not have much training in using them, however. They likely just carry them in case of a fellow miner being infected by blackwaters."

"Sounds simple enough," Réto said. "Any ideas, Captain?"

"Surround them, as Kyra suggested." Ctzo considered. "The Athai and Reea should be perfect for that task. We'll divide into groups, each coming from a different direction..."

Half an hour later, Ian crouched in the jungle, a pistol in hand. He carefully picked his way forward, attempting to remain as quiet as possible as he snuck towards the mine. When he paused to listen, he could hear the miners chatting casually. He tuned his ears for the sounds of his shipmates moving through the jungle but couldn't be sure he detected them.

Good. If I can't hear them, the miners shouldn't—

The sound of loud footsteps headed his way sent his heart racing. He looked around for a place to hide.

Too late.

A miner stopped just short of him, his mouth falling open the instant he sighted Ian. Ian raised his pistol, pointing it at the miner.

"Don't move," Ian said.

The miner trembled. "Look, our boss is a reasonable fellow. Just talk to him. I'm sure he can get you whatever it is you're after."

Does he think I'm a pirate?

"If you don't give me trouble," Ian whispered, "I won't give you any. My boss is reasonable, too."

"Then for Asha's sake, put down the gun," the miner murmured. "I'll get my boss and you can get yours and they can talk this out."

Ian glanced over at Zan, who crouched behind a bush a few meters away. Zan shrugged.

"There's two of you?!" the miner exclaimed in realization. "How many others?"

"Get on your knees," Ian ordered, keeping the pistol pointed his way.

After he'd fallen to his knees, Ian rummaged through the miner's outfit and removed the weapons he found. He piled them next to a tree. "Zan, I'm going to stay here with him until the signal."

The miner looked around apprehensively. "There are more of you, aren't there? Look, we really don't want trouble—"

"Keep quiet." Ian turned from his prisoner to face Zan as his friend moved ahead through the foliage. Zan soon vanished from sight.

Ian could hear his heart beating as he waited. The miner swallowed audibly. Then a loud whistle sounded from the direction of the mine.

"That's our cue." Ian got behind his prisoner and motioned him towards the noise. "Stand up."

The two shuffled through the bushes before emerging into a clearing. As planned, Ctzo and his crew stood in a circle around the stunned miners, the mine supervisor among them. Reea blocked off the entrance to the mine and Athai and Scavgans stood between the miners and the jungle. The crew held weapons—pistols, swords, and spears—and aimed them at the miners.

The mine supervisor shook his head. "You know, you didn't need to go to the trouble of surrounding us. And you certainly don't need to be pointing guns at us! We surrender, for goodness sakes. Put away your weapons!"

The captain made no signal to his crew. Ian and the others kept their weapons poised.

"We didn't know how much trouble you'd give," Ctzo replied calmly. "Better to be safe."

"My thoughts exactly." The mine supervisor pointed to a cart full of blackwaters vases. "Do you know how dangerous this stuff is?"

"Yes. Why are you mining for it?"

"It's risky work, but it pays."

"Your work endangers others," Ctzo said. "Including the natives of Aziasha. They often get turned into slaves using your product."

The supervisor shrugged. "Not my problem. I don't tell people how to use this stuff. If you want to punish a buyer, there's one creepy guy who was here not long ago asking after my wares. He keeps coming back."

"Jakodi Jair." Ctzo nodded once. "I would very much like to see him. Any chance you know where he is now?"

Cursing under his breath, the mine supervisor took one last look around. "He was just here a moment ago, I swear."

Kyra's serpentine eyes swept the area. "He may have sensed us coming and turned invisible."

Ctzo motioned to specific members of his crew. "Go search for him in the jungle."

Ian saw Zan get up and turn to head deeper into the trees. He also noticed Chiha and Yakara bounding off in different directions.

"As for the mine itself," Ctzo continued, "those of you with explosives, get to work."

A few more crewmembers emerged from the foliage, bundles of explosives in hand.

The mine supervisor's face paled. "No! Do you know how much that machinery cost? How long it took to set up? How many lives were lost in the process?"

Ian shivered. People had died setting up this mine? Perhaps, more accurately, the blackwaters had infected them.

"I'm more concerned about the lives that can still be saved," Ctzo replied grimly. "Now, as for you and your workers, there are few enough of you that I may be able to comfortably imprison you within the brig of my ship, should you refuse to become obedient crewmembers."

"I'll become part of your crew!" one of the miners spoke up. "I'm sick of this job anyways."

Others voiced their agreement. The mine supervisor just shook his head and bit his lip.

"If you show yourselves cooperative," Ctzo assured them, "you will gradually be freed from your confines."

The captain's gaze lifted to the mine, and the crewmembers who'd set the explosives deep within the mine now emerged, smiling and nodding.

Chiha streaked through the jungle canopy, only pausing every now and then to consider the path ahead. These trees weren't like the ones on the Marsh Isles. They were smaller and less firm. She had to take more care where she placed her feet, and she nearly lost her footing several times. There, at least, she found one blessing: these trees were shorter than the ones at home. If she did make a mistake, at least she didn't have as far to fall.

In one hand, she held her spear. Her ears were attuned to the sounds of the forest, her eyes searching for any signs of her quarry.

Sure, Jakodi Jair could turn invisible—just like the Reea he'd given himself the blood of. But that didn't mean she couldn't find him. The Athai and Reea had practiced mock battles for years, in celebration of the historic battle that had ended not in bloodshed but in unity between the two peoples. She knew how to find the invisible.

A twig snapped out of place and Chiha's spear darted towards her unseen target, thudding into the trunk of a tree.

Jair fell backwards and landed awkwardly on the ground, changing the colour of his skin back to black. He quickly recovered, smiling as he caught sight of Chiha.

"Ah. Now you are without a weapon." He held up a clawed hand. "While I am not!"

Effortlessly, Chiha vaulted over Jair's head and into the tree behind him. She recovered her spear and turned back to face him in one fluid motion.

Jair narrowed his eyes. "One weapon does not a formidable opponent make. For as you can see, I have many ways of damaging you."

Even as he spoke, Jair inched backwards.

"You are afraid," Chiha said. "Why should I fear a frightened enemy?"

"Obviously I fear for my life." Jair continued to move away from her. "If I am captured, the end is nigh. For what Scavgan would allow a Blackblood to go on living? So you see, I must escape. I have no other option."

Chiha gritted her teeth, creating a loud grinding noise. "Speak simply! You waste your words!"

"If I get caught, and you return me to Questava, I will be killed."

"Why?"

"The law states that Blackbloods must die."

"All Blackbloods?"

Jair nodded. "All. So you see why I must run, little lizard?"

He turned and dashed off into the forest, but Chiha's spear flew into his path. Jair dodged it without slowing down.

Chiha grabbed her spear off the ground, then paused. Her mind filled with the image of the Blackblood they'd found on the ship. Alone, confused, and cursed. And she remembered the abrupt ending to its life.

She stared at her spear, then looked up into the tangled bushes. She could still hear Jair's progress through the shrubbery.

Turning away, she set herself on a path back towards the mine.

One Blackblood has died already, so one must go free. It seemed the only fair choice. She didn't dwell on how Jair could yet be a source of danger. *I will tell them that he escaped. No. . . I will not tell them a thing. Perhaps that would be best.*

CHAPTER EIGHTEEN

*G*rey Noon's fleet, led by the black ship *Ko'Ekua*, left behind the temple and journeyed through the many islands of Gashaia. At last they exited the island range and navigated toward Aziasha's northeast corner and the imposing towers where Atzinus had once earned his reputation as the top blackwaters scientist.

Sébérus had expected that seeing Atzinus's fortress again, devoid of its master and the cruel people who had served him, would bring some amount of pleasure. Instead he felt only annoyance at his predicament as the imposing towers and wall came into view.

Likely there was some way to outsmart Grey Noon and escape to freedom, but to what end? He'd be an outcast, a mutant, a monster to whomever he met. The pirate captain, for all his anger and self-righteous indignation, at least respected Sébérus's intelligence. In fact, Grey Noon was the only one besides the old priest Pazu who didn't even seem to care that Sébérus was a Blackblood.

Besides, he still had a throbbing pain and panicky sense of withdrawal filling his head. Grey Noon had unceremoniously dumped all of Sébérus's drugs overboard, which meant he had no way to treat his constant aches and pains. Sébérus now found it overwhelming to dream up more than one plan at a time.

As the fortress came closer and the ship pulled into harbour, he submitted himself to helping Grey Noon with his plan—breaking the city of Questava, weakening the empire as a whole, and if all went well avenging himself on Captain Ctzo.

And I so admired Ctzo. Sébérus sighed, dragging himself down the gangplank, with Nva following from the sky to ensure he behaved himself. *I suppose war turns potential friends into mortal enemies. Besides, there's no guarantee Ctzo himself wouldn't hate me on sight.*

He walked past the docks and into the unguarded fortress. Grey Noon followed behind with a contingent of pirates.

Once they'd all entered, Sébérus came to a halt. His amber eyes studied the towering fortresses around him.

Grey Noon turned to speak to his crew. "Gather all the Blackbloods you can find. Do not harm them. If they are aggressive, resist them, but know that their blood is not to be spilled." His wide wing encircled Sébérus. "Bring each and every Blackblood here to Sébérus."

Sébérus felt his jaw tensing. What would it take to gain his freedom? How easy would it be to simply sink his teeth into an unarmoured portion of Grey Noon's wing and spread his unfortunate sickness...?

No. Sébérus held himself back. *Rezumi have resistance to Blackblood infections.*

Besides, he'd probably break his teeth. Rezumi skin was thick and tough. Grey Noon probably didn't even need his armour to win most battles.

He searched the skies for Nva, someone else he desperately wished he could bite. She was likely faster and more agile than he was. He may have Kamai features, but being part-Darian slowed him down.

He soon gave up his search and returned his eyes to the ground. The pirate crew had scattered by now, leaving Sébérus alone with his master.

"Your plan is… interesting." Grey Noon seemed loath to say the words. "I'm actually interested in seeing if you can pull it off."

Sébérus bit back his reply.

"You have earned my respect." Again, it wasn't the type of compliment Grey Noon relinquished easily. "I hope you can learn to respect me."

"I do," Sébérus muttered. "I respect that my plan hinges on you allowing me to live long enough to carry it out."

"So I'm not wrong." Grey Noon looked down on Sébérus with a self-satisfied smirk. "This isn't just about pleasing me, or my revenge on Ctzo, or even the future of Questava. This is your chance to get back at the world for the wrongs done to you."

"Hardly," Sébérus snapped a little more forcefully than he'd intended. "This is about making the world a better place. I'll never be able to live in peace—none of my kind will—unless people learn to see Blackbloods differently."

"And will they? When all is said and done, will they actually see you any differently?"

"They'd better."

Sébérus watched as the first Blackblood was led up to him. The captive came without a fight, his eyes staring forward blankly. He was dragged via a chain, the pirates guiding him and keeping a good distance. The creature had once been a Darian, one with a light build and large ears. A second pair of ears grew behind the first.

"What is your name?" Sébérus asked.

"Kaio." The Blackblood blinked slowly and spoke in a small voice. "Where... where is master?"

"You don't have a master anymore."

Kaio seemed incapable of understanding. "Is... is he on a trip?" Though full-grown, the Blackblood seemed to have the mind of a young child.

Sébérus sighed sadly. "Do you know where any of the other Blackbloods are?"

When Grey Noon and his pirates had slaughtered Atzinus's employees, the Blackbloods on site had been ignored, left to their own devices.

"Here's another one of them," said a pirate as he approached, leading along another half-coherent ex-Darian.

"Kaio, do you know where any of the other Blackbloods are?" Sébérus asked again.

The other Blackblood didn't answer. Instead he began to quiver. "What are you doing here? Where are our masters?"

"Kaio—"

"Are they... gone? Forever?"

"Yes," Sébérus said firmly. "Gone. Forever."

"Oh." Kaio looked to the sky for a long moment. Then his muscles relaxed and he sighed. "That's... nice."

A collection of Blackbloods crowded one of the fortress's small rooms. Food had been brought out by Grey Noon's pirates and the Blackbloods now sat around eating, dazed expressions on the faces of most.

Sébérus watched them sadly. His gaze rose to the pirates, now gathered outside the door and whispering questions to each other.

And to think these Scavgans expect such broken people to become warriors.

The whispers ended and Sébérus caught sight of Grey Noon's massive shadow through the doorway. Sébérus stood and walked in that direction.

"We'll give them time to eat, drink, and rest," Grey Noon said when Sébérus approached. "As you suggested."

"Right." Sébérus nodded. "Follow me, and I'll show you Atzinus's lab. His notes should be enough to give me a starting point."

A few minutes later, they stood in Atzinus's main laboratory, freed from its previous master. As Sébérus entered the familiar grey room, his eyes roamed the desks and shelves filled with books, bottles, beakers, and an array of strange equipment. An acrid scent wafted through the air, likely from one of the many chemicals stored on the shelves.

Grey Noon growled, his gaze focused on the chemicals. "How many of these bottles contain drugs? All of them?"

"You can't destroy them!" Sébérus realized his tone probably sounded desperate. "I mean, these chemicals are vital to the creation and alteration of Blackbloods. Hence, they're vital to our plans."

"Just what are our plans, then?" Grey Noon asked. "You told me earlier that we'd be stealing Blackbloods to use as soldiers."

"But not in the way others would use them. In most cases, Blackbloods are brainwashed and prepared to serve as cannon fodder. The Blackbloods we'll be employing will fight of their own free will. They will be loyal, faithful—"

"And followers of the Ti'te'Vikan faith?"

Sébérus faltered. "Y—yes."

Ah, this stupid headache has me distracted. Any other time, I'd have seen his question coming and been prepared with an answer.

"You will be their priest, and they will be your people," Sébérus said after a moment. "But first we have to collect them. When they come to realize we've rescued them, we'll earn their trust. Then they'll be ready to fight on our side." He motioned to the shelves of chemicals. "Blackbloods created by scientists often have their bodies altered in various ways counter to their natural forms. If we can combat even a few of these mutations, it will ease their physical and emotional suffering. Physical, because the mutations fight the natural design of their bodies. And emotional, because once they're brought closer to their previous form, they will find comfort in knowing they're at least a little closer to their true selves. They will be grateful."

"Then we will give them spiritual food," Grey Noon said. "And they will find strength in knowing the gods."

"Yes."

"Your plan is wise." Grey Noon looked around the room. "And the chemicals…"

"We need them to help alter the Blackbloods."

"Do you know how to do that? You're a brilliant creature, but are you a blackwaters scientist?"

"I can learn," Sébérus replied, his tone confident. "As I said, Atzinus's notes should give me the starting point I need. And I can begin by... well, by practicing on the Blackbloods here."

Sébérus tensed at his own words. It seemed so cold to consider these people test subjects, but he had to start somewhere in learning how to improve the lives of Blackbloods. He could use animals instead, but it seemed cruel. Still, perhaps he could find some rodents around the fortress...

While his mind wandered, Grey Noon read him carefully. "Get familiar with the Blackbloods and the dead scientist's notes. I will be expecting regular updates from you."

"Of course," Sébérus replied as he headed towards the door.

"Where are you going now?" Grey Noon asked. It sounded casual but he clearly expected an answer.

Do I always need to give an account to you?

Sébérus held back the snappy remark. "I'm just going to familiarize myself with the other Blackbloods, of course."

Sébérus found the collected Blackbloods together in one room, a few Scavgan pirates standing over them.

He turned his attention to one of these pirates. "Is this all of them?"

"All we found," the pirate answered. "Thirteen total."

Not very many. Sébérus scanned the crowd. *Atzinus was busy in the months before his death. I don't know some of these faces.*

He did recognize Lym, however. Larger than a true Darian, Lym's bulging muscles were hard as rock. All male Darians had horns, but Lym's curved into multiple spirals, and he had an extra pair spiking through his forehead.

Lym looked around curiously, but never took a step as Sébérus paced around the room.

Then there was Kaio, the new and unfamiliar Blackblood with a wiry build and second pair of ears.

Sébérus came to a halt in front of the smaller Blackblood. "Kaio, what role were you designed for?"

Kaio cocked his head. "What?"

Sébérus pointed at the extra pair of ears. "Are you a tracker of some sort perhaps?"

"I'm nobody," Kaio said gently. "That's even what my name means: *nobody*."

"Not in Gashaian," a pirate murmured.

Kaio's left ears perked up. "What?"

"He's right," Sébérus affirmed. "In one of Aziasha's tongues, your name may mean *nobody*. But in Gashaian, kai means *I am*, and ko is placed before a word to emphasize its significance. Combine those, kai and ko, and you get, *I am significant.*" He placed a hand on Kaio's shoulder. "And you are significant to me, Kaio. I'd like you to be my right-hand assistant. Would you enjoy that?"

"I'm sorry," Kaio said, sounding ashamed. "I'm left-handed."

A smile slipped over Sébérus's lips. "Perfect. You can be my left-handed right-hand assistant."

"Oh, good. Yes, I would enjoy that greatly."

Sébérus pointed to the other Blackbloods. "Keep an eye on them and make sure they understand we're here to help them." He sighed, rubbing his forehead. "I... I need a moment. I'm going to be on Grey Noon's ship. He's the giant I was speaking with earlier."

Kaio nodded. "Yes, new master. I can watch everyone."

Some time later, Sébérus laid upon his back on a softly swinging hammock, staring up at the wooden planks of the ceiling. Without his drugs to fall back on, he found sleep to be the next best cure for his Blackblood aches. Not that he really slept; he just lay there, giving time to his thoughts. It seemed better than forcing himself to grind through his pains.

He was confounded by one question: what was a Rezumi's weakness? Muscles. Size. Durability. Flight. The Rezumi were an incredible race. Not only that, but Grey Noon had a decent amount of brains to match his physical prowess.

Still, every race had a weakness. Several, actually.

The Kamai were naturally brilliant, with agility, flight, and large fangs and sharp claws. But their emotional dependence on the leadership of another race held them back. And they were perhaps the smallest in size, which could be a disadvantage.

Scavgans had ingenuity and the empire to their name; they dreamed big and worked hard. Physically, though, they weren't exactly impressive. Their bipedal stance and delicate hands likely aided in their ability to construct, but it also left them defenceless when unclothed. Their agility was mediocre.

Sébérus had encountered few Darians in his Blackblood life, and the only ones he'd seen were captives in Atzinus's fortress: desperate, panicked, and helpless. What he'd seen of the Darian race told him they could climb well, run fast on all fours, and had small yet effective fangs and claws. They seemed a step up from Scavgans physically, but a step down in size and ambition.

And Rezumi. What to say of them? They were the largest race. They could fly well but required a strong wind or else they'd drop from a decent height and land in water before they could achieve lift-off. They were tough, with higher resistance to disease—including Blackblood infections—and had skin thick enough to repel bullets. No, they weren't invincible, but they certainly weren't pushovers.

They lacked the quick mind of the Kamai, but also lacked the weakness of the servant complex. They weren't fighters by nature and instinctively adopted a heavily fruit-based diet. Yet that didn't mean they couldn't be taught war: years in the arena had given Grey Noon the battle skills he needed to take out multiple enemies at once.

So what *were* the weaknesses of the Rezumi? Sébérus sighed aloud. Nothing that seemed particularly useful to him. But maybe he was asking himself the wrong question. Perhaps it'd be better to ask: what was Grey Noon's weakness?

CHAPTER NINETEEN

"There's something eerie about watching a featureless sea," Zan noted.

He and Tyzak stood upon the deck of the *Diversity*, looking out to the ocean. The fleet had veered away from land and now cruised the empty ocean to Aziasha's north, taking advantage of a good wind.

"Whatever do you mean?" Tyzak asked.

Zan's eyes soaked in the wide, blue expanse. "The captain said we're currently going about five knots. A good speed in this wind. So you'd think it would look like we're making progress." He squinted, then shook his head. "It... it looks like we're standing in place."

"It does!" Tyzak released a brief chuckle. "My, you truly haven't been at sea for a while."

"I don't think travel is for me." Zan sighed. "Nor exploration. Trekking through Aziasha was a nightmare. And it feels so frustrating being at sea, like there's no progress to be made. It doesn't seem like I can change Questava from here. Not in the way I can while I'm there."

"And that's your goal? You're thinking too small. We're out to change the world, not just Questava! And we'll do that with each new discovery we make, each enemy ship we sink…"

Zan allowed a half-smile. "So you understand how Captain Ctzo views the world. Well, I can't say I see it the same way. It took sailing across the world, and being stuck in the jungle for a while, to realize that I'm not helpless back home. I can make a difference there. And I think being there plays to my strengths better than the physical challenges of the open seas and unexplored territory. I'd rather be bringing up discussions on poverty, imperial attitudes, and our understanding of the world."

Tyzak grimaced. "I always hated debates. In Medioca, we often say that your family is your place. And your family is in Questava."

"Yes." Zan sighed heavily. "Won't my father be happy to have me back in Questava, attending parties and attracting the attentions of young, well-to-do women?"

"Attracting attentions?" Tyzak smirked. "Somehow, I doubt that. Charm is not your thing. Though it would be amusing to watch you attempt it."

"I'll have a line of women back home hinting that I should propose to them. That should prove that I can be charming."

"Oh, I see." Tyzak's expression turned into a pouting frown. "You're only charming when you care to be."

"I think only women find me charming. And there's no women to charm around here."

"There's Katia."

"Not that I'm racist, but I'm not marrying a Darian. Besides, we don't speak the same language."

Tyzak searched his mind for other female crewmembers. "Kyra?"

"She's married!"

"Chiha?"

Zan raised an eyebrow. "Since when is she a member of the crew?"

"You didn't know she'd be joining us?"

"I did." Zan smiled. "I just didn't know anyone could get her to work!"

"The captain has a way with her." Tyzak shrugged widely. "Who knew?"

"Well, I can't flirt with Chiha, because she's your girl."

Tyzak crossed his arms. "She's not my girl. She doesn't even like me anymore."

"A lot has changed since we left."

"Yep. And you know what the best part is?" Tyzak grinned, pointed to Zan's damaged eye, and with a sweep of his arms continued, "You get to wear an eyepatch!"

Zan frowned. "Really, Tyzak?"

"What? Everyone knows eyepatches are impressive!"

"Well, I'm glad at least you think so. Because my father is going to be upset."

Tyzak's two eyes and Zan's one eye returned to the tossing blue seas.

"So, tell me a story," Tyzak said. "The captain took you and Ian into his quarters for a long chat. What was discussed therein? And what adventures can we expect next?"

"Honestly, I'm not sure. The captain is set on searching out the Mocjoa. And I'm not really sure what to think about that."

"How so?"

"His... spiritual encounter with them. How many people were there to witness his supposed rapture? Are we sure he didn't just pass out and dream it up?"

"Ian was there," Tyzak said simply. "He didn't see the angel like Chief Orthel did, but he saw the captain disappear. Make of it what you will."

"What you said about your family being your place... do you believe that?"

"I do indeed."

"But you're here," Zan said. "So far from your family."

"Ah. In territory, not in spirit!" said Tyzak. "We are merchants, and merchants search for new and better markets. Think of all the trade that could happen between the Marsh Isles and Scavgan's Island! If we do discover these mysterious islands of the Mocjoa, all the better!"

"You believe you're honouring your family by being out here?" Zan sighed. "If I go back and confront the way we live in Questava, I'll be dishonouring my family."

"Quite the opposite." Tyzak locked his gaze with Zan's. "My friend, I believe you'll be doing your family a great honour. Those who come after you will be blessed by your refusal to remain silent. What could be a greater service to your family than that?"

"Perhaps."

The conversation ended at that, and Zan left Tyzak to head belowdecks. As he walked, he found himself rubbing shoulders with an unfamiliar Scavgan of sky-blue skin.

"Are you... First Mate Jani?" Zan asked.

"I am." Jani smiled warmly. "Welcome back!"

"I don't think we've officially met." Zan offered his hand, then gave Jani a moment to shake it. "You don't know how glad I am to finally see you. Between the captain's obsession with finding the islands from his dreams and the invisible first mate, I was convinced I was working for a madman. A likable, honourable madman, but a madman."

Jani nodded once. "Here I am."

"Here you are." Zan smiled. "And as I said, that's a relief."

Suddenly, Zan looked up to see Ian walking toward them. His eyes were weighted with worry, his face downcast as he approached.

"What's happened?" Zan asked.

"Something's happened to Vortro."

While the captain's eyes were fixated on the many sea charts laying across his desk, Jani's calm blue gaze remained on him.

Ctzo shook his head. "I've looked over these a million times, all the records I have of Questava's explorations, and even fictional maps of make-believe kingdoms. Nothing resembles the islands I saw in my vision."

Jani nodded, but said nothing.

"Where do I even begin?" Ctzo said the words as if to himself, but he soon turned to his first mate for an answer. "Well?"

"What do you know?"

"Not enough to work with."

"But what do you know?" Jani pressed.

Ctzo sighed. "The Mocjoa aren't on Aziasha, or the Marsh Isles. The Gashaian Islands are vast and could easily include the islands I saw. But if that were the case, wouldn't the Kamai or Rezumi be familiar with the Mocjoa? How could a race remain hidden there?" He closed his eyes, trying to picture the islands once more. "A grey sea. That's what throws me off. I've never seen a sea that grey before. The seas surrounding the Gashaian Islands are shallow, so their waters look green-blue. The closest I've seen to a sea that colour is north of Scavgan's Island. But I've been told that once you get past the dozens of small islands in that direction, there's nothing but open water. Our ancestors tried sailing that way, and most of their ships sank." After a moment longer, he muttered, "Very few have tried heading south from Aziasha. The Marsh Isles are considered to be the bottom of the world. I wonder what lies south of them?"

He looked around and found that Jani was no longer in the room. He sighed.

"Well, that's the best I have to go on." Ctzo reached over to a little model ship and placed it atop a map of Aziasha, moving it down to the far south. "We'll return to the Athai on the Marsh Isles, gather supplies, then continue into the unknown reaches of the farthest south."

Zan rested a comforting hand on Ian's shoulder as the two entered Savato's medical room.

Most ships hired a surgeon who was also a carpenter. Instead Ctzo had hired a scientist and doctor named Savato. He'd wanted someone who would take seriously the task of learning about Darian traditional medicine. And the captain had expected from the beginning that their quest would take them to little-known lands, where he felt a scientist could be of greater help than an extra carpenter.

The old doctor frowned as he caught Ian's concerned expression. "What seems to be the matter?" His gaze flowed past to Zan. "Are you here to have me check on your eye again?"

"No." Zan nodded at Ian. "This is about his pet, Vortro."

Ian cupped something gently in his hands. "I pulled him out of my pocket this morning, and I found this."

Savato leaned forward for a closer look. A nugget-shaped object lay still in Ian's outstretched palm.

Ian gulped. "Is—is he—"

Savato burst out laughing. "Marvellous!" He swiped the object from Ian's hands. "Who would have thought? The Athai didn't mention... no, come to think of it there was that story the one fellow told me. But nothing else in their legends about this little good luck charm suggested—"

"Is he dead?!" Ian yelled above Savato's exuberance.

Calming himself, the doctor examined the object carefully. "No, I believe I see a bit of movement. Here." He grabbed a lit candle and, to Ian's horror, held it close to the nugget. "Yes, I see movement inside the casing. No worries, he's developing fine."

Zan grasped Ian's shoulders. "Maybe you should explain what exactly this *thing* is."

"It's a pupa." Savato smiled at Ian. "I'm sorry if I frightened you. I just find it exciting, this new species and all the surprises it brings." He gently presented Ian with the pupa. "Vortro is doing fine.

Ensure he remains somewhere safe and dry. But not too dry. Some humidity in the air will do him well for when he's ready to emerge."

"Emerge?" Ian looked with awe at the sleeping pupa. "Vortro… isn't really a worm, is he?"

"The worm form you're accustomed to was just the larva. Many bugs have a wormlike form before they undergo drastic changes in the pupa." Savato paused. "The Athai I spoke with gave me no indication that anything like this was possible. I'm going to ask around, see if I can learn what he'll turn into."

"Great," Zan muttered, removing his hands from Ian's shoulders. "We still have a bug to carry around."

Ian looked down lovingly at the pupa. "Don't worry, Vortro, I'll take good care of you."

Savato cleared his throat. "The pupa is a delicate stage in a bug's life. Don't blame yourself if something goes wrong and Vortro doesn't pull through to adulthood."

Nodding, Ian pulled Vortro closer. "Thank you."

Savato gently brushed past the two younger Scavgans. "Now, I'm going to see what I can learn."

Savato returned to his lab a few hours later, spent and a bit confused. He settled down into his large chair, sighing heavily and closing his eyes.

I'm getting too old to be out at sea. He pushed the thought from his mind. *What am I saying? My brain is as nimble and absorbent as ever. And I'd rather spend my last days adventuring the world than lazing around at home.*

His eyes remained closed as he sorted through the various conversations he'd had recently. Most of the Athai had been as confused as Ian about Vortro's transformation. How seriously then should he take the one story?

One Athai had shrugged at Savato's questions.

"My grandfather told me that the choeina live in villages in dark places of our world after they grow limbs," he'd told the doctor matter-of-factly.

"Villages?" Savato had pressed.

"In dark places." The Athai had hesitated, as though unsure he recalled all his grandfather's words. "Like, in the nightmares of the people."

Ah, yes. Another reference to the choeina being spirits of some kind. It was funny. Most Athai associated the choeina with good luck and health. So why would one story liken them to dark spirits? Piecing together another culture's understanding of life was proving more than a little complicated.

"I suppose," Savato muttered to himself. "Yes, I suppose we can always just wait and see what our darling little Vortro reveals..."

His mind trailed off, and he fell asleep.

CHAPTER TWENTY

*W*eeks had passed since Jair's visit to the blackwaters mine. He cursed his luck as he wandered the jungle.

Ever unfortunate, running into my old general time and time again. Do the gods find it humorous, bringing us together? Brushing aside a large frond, his foot landed in a shallow puddle. The warm water consumed his senses for a moment. He swallowed, only now noticing the dryness in his throat. *Even Blackbloods thirst...*

Staring down at the puddle, he noted the brown, muddy look of the water. He then fell to his knees, stuffing his face into the murk and gulping greedily. He shortly drained the tiny body of water, feeling no less thirsty after having done so.

He growled. Realizing how animalistic he sounded, he laughed at himself.

Jair frowned as he looked out into the jungle. Up ahead, between the trees, he glimpsed what seemed to be a wall of rock.

A cliff, he realized as he came closer. His path appeared to end right at its foot.

He walked alongside the cliff face, no particular destination in mind. He was too preoccupied with his thoughts to care much about finding either a place to rest or a way off Aziasha.

Though I should eat something. Yes, a morsel or two would be good.

He frowned when he came to a section of rock that had been cleared away. Within it, a narrow tunnel led into the darkness.

Curious, Jair stepped inside. As he progressed through his unlit surroundings, a sharp, sulphur-like scent became apparent, growing stronger. He ran his hands along the earthen wall until the wall fell away and he sensed that he'd entered a larger room. Fragments of broken pottery cracked under his feet and a sticky substance oozed around them.

Pottery and blackwaters, he realized. *Blackwaters that have been burned in a strong fire.*

Fire could not destroy blackwaters completely, but it did reduce it and change the consistency.

The pottery made him think this might have once been a storage room, but clearly it was no longer in use. He sensed no one else around.

Overwhelmed by the smoky scent, he closed his eyes and navigated himself through the pitch black to a stairway on the other side of the room. He walked up it and soon found himself back in the sunlight. Around him, tall walls framed various corridors. Looking up, stone towers rose into the sky.

A fortress! He walked a ways, turning down one path after another. This place wasn't small.

Jair sensed Scavgans at the other end of the hall before he saw them. He stopped, then sensed someone coming up from behind him. He was surrounded.

Halting, he eyed the Scavgans. They were dressed like sailors and had their pistols raised.

Shaking his head, Jair muttered irritably, "Such rudeness. When did it become acceptable to greet lonely visitors with such deadly force?"

He eyed each of the strangers in turn, and his face turned to a strange half-smile.

"Curious. I am a Blackblood, and you are not. Yet you scowl at me with neither fear nor respect." He sighed, lifting a clawed hand, and pulled back his lips into a toothy smirk. "You must be volunteers! Oh, I do look forward to working my magic on you!"

"Don't bother," a voice said. "You'll have your hands busy with other work."

Jair's gaze turned towards the source of the voice. A Darian-like Blackblood stared back at him, although he was so short that he barely came up to Jair's waist. The creature spoke boldly, however, and his ears rested casually against his neck. He even had wings folded in at his side!

Jair's eyes widened. "It… can't be…" He trembled. Emotions bubbled up within him—awe, disappointment, anger—as his thoughts became frenzied. "Atzinus… a Kamai's blood… no, he couldn't have… not possible…"

He screamed.

Sébérus's ears went back as Jair released a blood-freezing screech. The pirates alongside him, hardened as they were, flinched and cowered. But Sébérus remained calm and composed.

"You... you..." Jair growled. "I both hate you and am fascinated by you. How dare Atzinus... how did he...? Never mind. To what do I owe the pleasure, sir?"

"Sébérus. I'm one of Atzinus's... projects."

"Ah, yes, I guessed as much. How is he these days?"

"Very dead. Though I'd assumed you'd heard the rumours."

"Well, one can't believe all the rumours that tickle their ears." Jair considered further what he'd just heard. "Dead, you say? How unfortunate."

"I'm not crying," Sébérus said.

"Oh, good. Neither am I. And I hate to have to fake sympathy."

"You are Jakodi Jair, the mad blackwaters scientist my master raved against."

Jair smiled. "Well, my reputation precedes me! Mad, you say? I suppose I do lose my temper every now and again, but I assure you I'm not always angry. Did Atzinus describe me as mad? I suppose he'd only have negative comments for his most serious competition."

"Competition?" Sébérus shook his head. "I hear you work on a volunteer basis. How many Blackbloods have you actually created?"

"Animals can be more readily volunteered than people," Jair said. "And I believe in giving the despairing and suicidal a second chance on life, so... I suppose I don't need to explain it to you. Suffice to say I've made enough Blackbloods in my time, most of them animals."

"If you're eager for more work," Sébérus said, "I have an offer for you."

Jair clapped eagerly. "Oh! Are you here to give me Atzinus's secret to creating a masterpiece such as you?"

"No." Sébérus massaged his forehead. "You can have that, eventually, if you can find it in his mess of notes. I'd like your help improving the conditions of the Blackbloods in my care. I'm no blackwaters scientist, and though I could become an expert with a little time… well, you already are one. And I have other matters to oversee."

"I would be honoured! But first," Jair said, beginning to walk away, "allow me to return home to my laboratory—"

The gathered pirates, who had been standing around quietly, suddenly stepped towards the scientist, reminding him of the weapons they held.

"Ah." Jair sighed. "No, you are right. Quite pointless. Captain Ctzo has likely had my home turned upside-down and—"

"Did I hear someone mention Captain Ctzo?" Grey Noon's voice boomed as he rounded a corner and joined the group.

Jair's gaze rose to meet the Rezumi's eyes. "Wow. You are magnificent."

Grey Noon leaned towards Jair. "You've met Captain Ctzo?"

"Oh, I was under his command during the war," Jair said with a wave of his hand. "But if you mean recently, since he's stood under the blue sails of the *Diversity*… too often."

"Where and when did you last see him?" Grey Noon pressed.

Jair frowned. "Weeks ago, here on the northern coast of Aziasha. Why?"

A smile overtook Grey Noon's face. He rose, looming over the scientist. "I have unfinished business with him."

CHAPTER TWENTY-ONE

Sometimes when Ctzo closed his eyes, memories snuck into his mind uninvited. This time, they were images of a baby girl, so small and light, held snugly in his arms.

Ctzo opened his eyes and found himself staring out at the rolling waves. The sky was cloudy and a mild fog hovered over the sea. He startled when he sensed Jani at his side.

"Anything to report?" Ctzo asked.

Jani was silent for a long moment and Ctzo wondered if he'd been wrong about sensing the being beside him. He turned to look and discovered his first mate, too, staring out at the sea. The man's face held an unreadable expression.

"There are changes in the air." Jani's tone was solemn, his voice barely above a whisper. "Changes that neither you nor I have the power to stop, though we may try."

"Good changes? Or bad changes?"

"Changes." After a moment, he added, "I must go belowdecks. I will return shortly, if I can."

"Very well."

When Jani had departed, Ctzo returned his gaze to the ocean. Jani was a fellow of many riddles. However, he'd grown so accustomed to Jani's oddities that the conversation soon left his mind.

Ian leaned over the railing of *Diversity*, smiling as the ship sped alongside a group of zaia. The streamlined creatures zipped through the water, barely creating any spray as their backs and dorsal fins broke the water. These zaia were smaller than any he'd seen before, about as long as Ian was tall, and the protruding canines on their lower jaws were hardly visible. Their blood-red skins seemed startling against the pale blue shallows.

"Ian!" Tyzak called excitedly.

The young Scavgan didn't pull his eyes from the zaia. "Yeah?"

"You're going to want to come quick," came Zan's voice next. "It's about Vortro."

His heart skipping a beat, Ian jerked upright and faced his friends. "What's happened?"

"Vortro's fine." Zan began heading for the lower decks while Tyzak pushed Ian along. "Savato has him in his lab. The weird critter is starting to emerge. I'm guessing you're going to want to see that."

When they had gathered in the lab, Ian leaned in close. Savato pulled up a chair so he could be seated for the event.

The pupa quivered. A split appeared in its shell, and then a segmented, night-black hand reached out.

"The worm has hands?" Zan shook his head. "Gross. I don't think I want to watch this."

Ian's wide eyes remained fixated on the pupa as a second hand broke free, flailing as though searching for a handhold. The pupa wiggled as its captive pushed and pulled in an attempt to break free.

"Should we help?" Ian asked with concern.

"No, no," Savato insisted. "It's only been a few minutes, boy. Let the process continue."

At last, the clawed hand pried along the edges, scraping and pulling, creating a long rip through the casing. A round head with wide silver eyes then wiggled out. Spidery fangs had formed around Vortro's new mouth, and antennae stood erect from its head, probing around in a manic motion.

The eyes locked onto Ian and he felt a wave of shock roll over him. More than just intelligence sparkled in those eyes: recognition and awareness filled them.

"I—Ian!" the creature spoke. The word was a little garbled as it echoed from the creature's spider-like mouth. An unintelligible squeal followed, then tears filled its silvery eyes and dribbled down its fangs. "I—Ian..."

The creature struggled against the pupa until its body and legs were also free. When it had finished, Vortro panted heavily. It dragged itself to Ian's knees, rested its head against them, and closed its wide eyes.

Ian felt the weight of the head on his lap and realized that Vortro had fallen asleep.

"What... what is he?" Ian asked.

Zan swallowed audibly. "I'm not sure what that creature is, but I'm pretty sure Vortro is a girl."

"Huh?" Ian touched Vortro's head, eying the pair of antennae.

"Um, well…" Tyzak cleared his throat. "Her anatomy is female. Can we find… her… some clothes?"

A new voice broke into the conversation. "Hmm. Looks like a Mocjoa."

They all looked up to find First Mate Jani standing over them.

Jani smiled. "It matches the captain's sketches. Cute."

The rest of the group turned back to stare at the Mocjoa.

"A diaper," Tyzak said at last. "She needs a diaper."

The little Mocjoa's head remained rested on Ian's lap. Her breathing was gentle.

"She really is a baby!" Ian said, shaking his head in shock.

"More like a toddler," Tyzak said. "She was a baby as a worm, I guess."

Zan shivered. "This is so wrong."

"The captain!" Savato shouted, startling everyone. "The captain will want to see her! Ian, do you think you could carry her up to the captain's quarters?"

Eying her a moment, Ian placed his hand on Vortro's back. He felt her soft, slow breathing. "I don't want to wake her. She looks so tired."

"Of course." Savato turned to Jani. "Perhaps you could get the captain down here?"

"I will." But Jani's gaze remained fixated on Vortro. "Allow her some rest. It looks like she needs it."

Ctzo felt Jani's presence behind him and turned to his first mate. "Is all well?"

"There's someone for you to meet down in Savato's workshop."

"To meet?" Ctzo raised an eyebrow.

Jani's eyes remained downcast. "Vortro has revealed her true form. She's a Mocjoa."

"She's… what?"

At that moment, Réto appeared, landing on the railing and pointing out towards the sea. "Captain, a ship approaches."

When Ctzo turned back to Jani, the being was gone. Unclipping the spyglass at his side, Ctzo walked to Réto's side and followed his finger, bringing the lens to his eye. He squinted through the telescope and stared at the form of a tiny ship on the horizon. His heart skipped a beat. It looked black in this lighting.

Could it be? Yes. Its black sails billowed in the wind.

"Réto, prepare for battle," Ctzo said, his tone conveying authority. "An old enemy is coming."

Grey Noon eagerly leaned forward, grinning as the dot on the horizon grew and transformed into a ship with colourful sails, flanked by two five-masted ships, one orange and yellow and the other blue and purple.

"We've found him. May Tarair be at our side." Grey Noon turned to Nva. "Have the crew prepare the cannons."

Ctzo's fleet had only moments to prepare for the attack. From his place aboard the *Diversity*, the captain sent Réto off to survey the approaching enemy.

When the Kamai returned, he landed upon Ctzo's shoulder. "They have six ships: the xebec flagship *Ko'Ekua* and five large warships."

"Five warships?" Ctzo watched as the enemy grew closer. "We can't take them. Not out here in the open ocean. Send a message to all our ships: we're fleeing. Kyaté, please, help us…"

As Ian, Savato, Zan, and Tyzak gathered around little Vortro, a Scavgan crewmember suddenly entered the workshop. Each looked up to see his serious expression.

"We're under attack," the crewmember said.

Tyzak frowned. "Under attack?"

Just then, the *Diversity* rattled. Everyone in the room had to steady themselves, and each heard the loud *crunch* of a cannonball hitting the ship.

The crewmember grabbed the doorframe. "Find a weapon!" With that, he rushed off.

Ian's hand went to his side and found his strapped-on pistol, just as he'd been doing target practice. But it was still filled with practice ammo, not real bullets. He searched around the room. "Savato, where—"

Savato handed him a fistful of bullets. "Here."

"I'll grab a sword," Tyzak said just before he rushed out of the room.

Zan looked around. "Any pistols in here?"

Savato hesitated. "No, but I might have a sword..." He reached into a barrel, pulled out a short sword, and handed it to Zan. "Here." He also pulled out a musket. "And now we're all armed."

Ian's gaze went to Vortro. The little girl's sleepy eyes were open, and she appeared confused.

Another cannonball rocked the ship.

"I'll stay here with her," Ian said.

Savato nodded as he sat down on a chair facing the door. "Me as well. Zan?"

"I'll go see what's up." Zan exited the room, sword in hand.

Ctzo's fleet was outnumbered, and clearly outgunned as well. He'd ordered a retreat, but it proved futile: he could see the enemy vessels closing in. Already one was near enough to land cannonballs against the *Diversity*'s hull.

The captain gripped the rail, eyes on the black vessel as it approached. He then saw Grey Noon leap off the *Ko'Ekua*'s deck and fly up into the sky.

Ctzo gritted his teeth. "Prepare to be boarded," he called to the crew.

CHAPTER TWENTY-TWO

*A*s Grey Noon thudded upon the deck of the *Diversity*, Black Night landed before Captain Ctzo, ready to greet their Rezumi adversary.

Grey Noon eyed Black Night up and down through his skull-like mask. "Move aside," he grunted.

Black Night smiled, flexing his wings and rolling his shoulders. "Don't want to fight me, old man?"

With brutal force, Grey Noon's wing slammed against Black Night's chest. Black Night fell back, unable to breathe for an agonizing moment.

A black shape then raced by Black Night's head, flying towards Ctzo. Before he could react, Black Night heard a screeching sound as the black shape collided with Réto—or perhaps Réto collided with it.

The rest of the crew came to their captain's aid. They raised muskets and pistols and fired at Grey Noon, but if any of the bullets made their mark the pirate didn't show it.

As Grey Noon's fleet neared, Ctzo realized Grey Noon's presence had been meant as a distraction.

"To your positions!" Ctzo cried over the gunfire.

Réto had seen the black Kamai make a dash at Ctzo. If he hadn't intervened, his captain would have already been killed. Now, the two had collapsed onto the deck, and Réto found his enemy's knifelike claws cutting through the air around him. The dark Kamai tried to land a deadly blow, and her claws found his flesh just as his found hers—but the wound she inflicted proved more serious, and Réto's blood flowed unhindered.

"No!" Kyra shouted as she rushed mercilessly at their attacker, racking the other Kamai with calculated fury.

Their Kamai enemy received a few cuts, then stepped back and launched itself at Kyra. Réto, though bleeding, wasn't about to leave his mate alone in the fight, and in a mere dozen seconds of battle he had come to the conclusion that this Kami was a better fighter than either of them. It would take both Réto and Kyra to keep the creature away from their beloved captain.

Tyzak came up on deck and witnessed the chaos. Black Night was struggling to raise himself from the floor while a massive Rezumi stood facing Ctzo.

"Grey Noon," Tyzak said in realization, holding in his hand a rapier he'd grabbed belowdecks.

A black ship, its dark sails blotting out the light of a sun, had pulled up next to the *Diversity* and some of the crew were firing at the enemy's deck. Others attempted to aid Ctzo, but to no avail. Grey Noon threw them each aside with a brush of his powerful wings.

Zan came to his side. "What do we do?"

It seemed the pirates had the upper hand. Soon gangplanks were laid down and the pirates began streaming onto the deck of the *Diversity*.

A pirate rushed at them both, and Tyzak shifted his weight in time to feel a fiery pain in his leg. He cried out but didn't fall back from the attack. Zan came to his aid but found himself defending against the pirate's slashes. With practiced precision, Tyzak ran his enemy through.

Down in Savato's workshop, the surgeon and Ian remained tense. Then Vortro began to stir. She looked up at Ian through brilliant silver eyes.

"Ian?" said the bug.

Ian's eyes widened at the sound of his own name. "Yes?"

"No go!" she whimpered. She tried to stand, but then stumbled over and grabbed his leg. The tension in the room was palpable. The child, though young, clearly sensed it.

"I'm not going." Ian touched her gently. "*We're* not going. Don't be scared."

An unfamiliar sailor then entered the room, a pistol in his hand. He aimed it at Savato, but the surgeon's musket felled him before he could fire off a shot.

"That was close," Savato muttered. "Almost forgot how to shoot this thing."

"I can guard the door," Ian said quickly. He tried to move to the entrance but was held back by Vortro.

She burst into tears. "Ian! Ian!"

"It's okay." He patted her head again, then snapped to attention as another pirate entered. Ian fired before anyone else could, and the pirate fell. "Stay behind me, Vortro."

Sébérus stared down from the *Diversity*'s mast, his ears ringing with the clashing of swords and firing of guns. He caught sight of Ctzo in the commotion, dodging Grey Noon's attacks.

This isn't the way I hoped to meet the great general, Sébérus thought. Even now, he couldn't help but admire Captain Ctzo's tenacity as he boldly stood up to the massive Rezumi pirate.

Then he spotted someone else: a blue-furred Darian hiding behind the sails and hanging onto the mast.

"Hello," he called. She caught his gaze and shivered. "No need to fear me. I can tell you aren't a fighter. It's not like I need to kill you."

She frowned, tensing.

"Stay away," she ordered, but in a language he couldn't recall having heard before.

His eyes narrowed. If he hadn't heard it before, why did he understand it?

"What's your name?" he asked. "And what language are you speaking?"

The question clearly puzzled her. "My name is Katia... and I'm speaking the same language you just spoke in."

"Strange," Sébérus said, half to himself. "I know I can speak Questavan, and I know some basic Gashaian and Eastern Aziashan. But I didn't learn any other languages in Atzinus's care."

"I'm speaking what we Aziashans call a 'trade tongue.' The Athai and Reea also speak it." Katia paused, then switched to another language. "What about this tongue? Do you understand it?"

"Yes."

This latest language sparked in him a sense of familiarity and comfort. He wasn't sure what to think of this new development.

"I suppose I spoke this language before I became a Blackblood," he said. "I suppose it remained stored in my mind."

Her ears suddenly went back. "Anveil?"

He frowned. "What?"

She drew back, climbing a few steps down from the mast. "This is evil," she said, motioning to the battles upon the deck. "Stop it."

"Evil?" Sébérus couldn't hold back a grin. "That's strong wording!"

"It must end!"

"I'm sorry, friend." His grin faded as he looked again towards Grey Noon. "This isn't my fight anyway."

The pirates seemed to be coming faster now, and Ian could only imagine what was going on up on deck. But it couldn't be good...

Suddenly, a shot echoed through the room and Savato fell to the floor.

Ian fought back the panic and agony that hit him. He aimed his weapon, took out the pirate who had shot his friend, and then rushed over to where the doctor lay. He knelt on the floor next to Savato, searching for any signs of life.

He found none.

Captain Ctzo's hopes rose, his heart filling with pride as Athai and Reea from *Radiant Dawn* and *Night Light* came over to aid their comrades. The Athai stood with the wounded and defended them. Some of Ctzo's crew had already been killed, but the tide of battle appeared to be turning.

Surveying the scene, Grey Noon accepted all this with a shrug. "If the captain falls," he said, returning his attention to Ctzo, "the rest will surrender."

Ctzo remained on guard, a pistol in one hand and his sword in the other. He looked over Grey Noon's massive bulk, well-protected by his skeleton-like armour.

All I can do is dodge his attacks, Ctzo thought, staring into the eyeholes in Grey Noon's mask. *Unless I can hit his eyes!*

The captain fired and Grey Noon turned his head to shield his eyes. The bullet bounced harmlessly off the mask.

Grey Noon then charged at Ctzo, who eased backwards, trying to keep some distance between himself and his foe. Ctzo fired again, then shifted and fired once more. None of the bullets hit their target.

Come on. Ctzo grit his teeth. *This is my last chance.*

As Grey Noon charged again, Ctzo raised his weapon to fire a fourth time. This time, Grey Noon's wing thudded against the captain's arm, knocking the pistol from his grasp. The next thing Ctzo knew, Grey Noon stretched out his wing and Ctzo felt a weight like a boulder slam into the back of his head.

Then he felt nothing at all.

He awoke a few moments later lying flat on his back, blinking in confusion. Grey Noon's haunting, armoured form overshadowed him. The Rezumi wore a dangerous grin.

Ctzo reached for his sword but found only air. His other hand felt around for his pistol, and it, too, came up empty.

Leaning in, Grey Noon rested a heavy, clawed finger against Ctzo's chest.

Sébérus rushed toward the scene of Grey Noon's battle with the ship's captain.

"Wait!" Sébérus called as he attempted to push Grey Noon's claw off the captain's chest. It barely budged.

"Wait?" Grey Noon growled.

"We can't kill them," Sébérus said, aware that Grey Noon would initially disagree. "Rather, we shouldn't. I have an idea that would benefit us more. If I may speak to you privately…"

Grey Noon accepted the distraction. Soon his crew was clearing the way for them as they walked towards the captain's quarters.

Sébérus went straight to the desk and searched until he found a quill, ink, and scroll.

Grey Noon's eyes narrowed. "Are you trying to save these people from destruction out of misplaced pity?"

"No, sir," Sébérus replied. "My plans for our attack on Questava depend on fear, and fear begins as a sense of danger. You don't fear what you don't know is coming. But if you're told of something frightening long before it occurs, your fear has a chance to build. We'll tell the dear Emperor of our plans for his city—just enough to inspire panic, but not enough to give them clues as to how to wisely counter us."

"The Emperor is unlikely to take our threats seriously."

"But the seed will be planted, and it won't just be the Emperor hearing the message. His attendants will also hear."

Grey Noon shook his head. "I don't see the benefit of allowing Ctzo to live. He is a respected hero. We should kill him and slaughter most of the crew. We can allow a few to survive and take our message back."

"A message from Ctzo's own mouth will be taken more seriously," Sébérus said, dipping the quill into the ink stone.

As he wrote out a letter, Grey Noon watched from over his shoulder. Both remained silent as Sébérus filled the scroll.

Finally, Grey Noon understood. "I'll go along with your plan, Blackblood. You seem to know what you're doing. But there has to be some consequence for Ctzo, something that will hurt him."

"We've already killed some of his crew," Sébérus said.

"I want more."

"Fine. We can sink a ship or two."

Grey Noon's eyes explored the captain's quarters. "A ship is a captain's treasure, his home. I should know that well enough. If someone sank *Ko'Ekua*, I'd be furious."

Sébérus nodded. *I'll remember that.*

"We'll sink this one," Grey Noon said at last. "It'll be enough."

Without explanation, Ctzo's crew aboard the *Diversity* were forced overboard, their enemies shoving them into the sloshing waves.

Meanwhile, Grey Noon walked to Ctzo and shoved a scroll into his hands. "A message for your grand Emperor. To ensure it stays dry, I'll be carrying you to another ship."

Ctzo appeared to be in a daze. His hands folded around the scroll, and he frowned. "You're… letting me live?"

"For now," Grey Noon said simply. "The letter is for the Emperor's eyes alone. Or the Council's. Not yours. Will you be my messenger boy and deliver it for me?"

Grey Noon mounted the mast, then dropped from it, snatching Captain Ctzo's shirt in his mouth and lifting him into the air. He carried the captain to *Radiant Dawn* and dropped him upon the deck.

Ctzo landed awkwardly, still clutching the scroll. He turned to see Grey Noon's fleet bombarding the *Diversity*. The sounds of destruction resonated through the air as the cannons fell like hail upon the deck of his dear ship.

Ian felt water sloshing around his feet and his heart raced at the realization that the *Diversity* was sinking. His eyes turned to Savato one last time. He had only a moment to say goodbye.

Vortro seemed fixated on the water, slapping her hand against it and watching it curiously.

"We have to go." Ian grabbed her and lifted her up, startled by how light she felt.

Ian rushed up the stairs and onto the deck, his eyes darting around for signs of life, but none of the other crewmembers were to be found.

His gaze lifted to *Radiant Dawn* and *Night Light* in the distance. To save himself, he realized he'd have to swim.

He adjusted his grip on Vortro, trying to determine how best to carry the child when in the water. Running to the edge of the railing, he looked down into the frothy seas and hesitated.

He turned to Vortro. She watched him through silver eyes.

Taking a deep breath, he climbed the railing and leapt off into the sea. As he landed, he held Vortro above the waves, attempting to swim. But a wave sloshed them both in the face, and Ian and Vortro coughed on the seawater.

Suddenly, a scaly figure appeared beneath them. Yakara! She pushed against Ian, encouraging him to grab onto her. He wrapped one arm around her body, the other holding tightly to Vortro. Once they were secure, Yakara carried them across the waters, speeding them over to *Night Light*'s hull. Crewmembers lowered ropes to the trio and Ian let go of Yakara. He grabbed a rope and he felt himself being pulled up.

His crewmates helped him onto the deck, but once there he had eyes only for Vortro, checking her over and making sure she was breathing all right.

She coughed a little, then looked up at him and started to cry. "Ian!"

The look of shock on his crewmates' faces took him aback. They had never seen anything like her before.

Ctzo couldn't pull his eyes from the sight of the *Diversity*. Though his dear ship held on, he knew he was seeing her for the last time.

The *Diversity* shuddered, her colourful sails ripping, scraps of cloth and shards of wood landing upon the rolling waves. With one final shiver, the ship surrendered to the waters, slowly sinking into the depths from which she could never be retrieved.

CHAPTER TWENTY-THREE

"*T*hank you all for sticking by me to the end of the *Diversity's* voyage," Captain Ctzo called out to his crew aboard the deck of *Radiant Dawn*. He seemed worn, not at all the confident man he'd been when their voyage began. "As of today, we are turning back and making our way to Scavgan's Island."

Silence followed. Tyzak, Zan, and Ian exchanged glances.

"We need time to repair our ships," Ctzo continued, "and time to hopefully recruit more aid. Two months to the day after we arrive on Scavgan's Island, those of you who wish can meet me aboard *Night Light*. I would be happy to hire each of you again for the next phase of our voyage. To those who decide to call this the end of their adventure, I wish you the best in whatever comes next. It has been an honour to be your captain, and to watch each of you grow in strength and skill. May Kyaté bless you richly, and may he fill you with his peace and abiding presence."

Ian, Zan, and Tyzak sat around a galley table aboard *Radiant Dawn*. A deck of cards lay in the table's centre, yet none of the trio could bring themselves to start a game.

"So…" Tyzak cleared his throat, as though he planned to say more.

Zan's eye turned to the deck of cards. His lips didn't move. Ian fiddled with a small nick in the table.

At last, Tyzak sighed. "Our brave captain is just—giving up? Because he lost his favourite ship?"

"He's not giving up," Ian said softly but firmly. "He wants to recuperate. That battle was taxing on all of us. We lost a lot of friends, and the whole fleet is damaged."

"I'm just saying, the carpenters could always effect repairs at Aziasha," Tyzak countered. "Ships sink every day. The ocean is a dangerous place. I'm sure the captain has lost a few vessels—and crew—in his time. We're warriors. We should counterattack! Why is he set on returning home?"

"It's more than that." Zan's normally confident tone was replaced with a slight tremble. "That Blackblood and Grey Noon, they targeted Ctzo. This wasn't just some lucky attack. They were looking for us, knew where to find us. It's one thing to encounter pirates on the seas and challenge them, or be challenged by a random adversary. It's another thing when that adversary seeks you out."

At this, the table fell silent.

The tension broke only as a babbling little Mocjoa entered the galley holding someone's worn grey sock in her hand. Vortro eagerly waved this so-called treasure before her adopted father.

Ian couldn't help but smile at the child. "Hey girl. Um… where'd you get that?"

"Dis is mine!" she said excitedly, holding the sock high above her head.

"I doubt that. Seriously, where'd you get it?"

She placed the sock close to her chest. A few of the crewmembers had sacrificed clothing to sew her little diapers and shirts.

"Are you hungry?" Ian patted his lap. "Wanna come eat?"

Vortro toddled closer and Ian lifted her onto his lap.

"Right." Tyzak stood and turned towards the galley's kitchen. "I'll go fetch her something."

Deciding on what the Mocjoa child should eat had been difficult. Milk wasn't available at sea, although Mocjoa were such an alien race that it seemed possible they never drank it anyway. After all, as a larvae Vortro had been eating parasites and bugs.

It could be that, as toddlers, Mocjoa continued with that diet. However, an ironic side effect of Ctzo's strict cleaning and careful food storage regime was that the ships had few pests to deal with. Hunting down bugs for Vortro had proved time-consuming and virtually pointless.

Tyzak returned with a small bowl of diced fruit. "You should thank Black Night for offering to share his rations with you, Vortro. And feel lucky! The rest of us survive off stale biscuits."

"Don't pity us, girl," Zan said, leaning close to Vortro. "We eat well enough. Especially after visiting the Marsh Isles. We picked up some good food from them. We had fresh fruits and veggies then."

Now that Vortro was no longer a worm, Zan evidently liked her much better. Once he'd grown comfortable with the idea of a bug transforming into a child, he'd begun speaking to her freely and often.

"Yes," Tyzak said with a sigh. "Those days ended quickly."

Suddenly, Tyzak nudged Zan in the ribs. Zan glared at him, then noticed Ctzo entering the galley.

"Captain," Tyzak said with a salute. "You look weary. Perhaps you should sit and join us for a moment?"

Ctzo had bags under his eyes. He walked sluggishly, his gaze moving slowly to meet Tyzak's.

"It's… been a long day," said the captain. "Planning out the funeral for our lost crew."

The room grew quiet for a long moment. An image of Savato filled Ian's mind, followed by those of the other crewmembers who'd been lost.

Zan's hand went to the thick leather eyepatch, a corner of which had been decorated with a pattern of vines. Savato had made it himself, aware that Zan wanted something nicer-looking than a simple piece of fabric. The patch now served as a reminder of the old doctor.

"Thank you, Savato," Zan whispered.

Ctzo spent a long moment staring at Vortro. "Amazing. She really is a Mocjoa… she looks just like the ones I saw in my vision. Well, smaller, of course. I wonder why there are Mocjoa larvae on the Marsh Isles…"

Tyzak rested his fist against his chin. "A mystery indeed."

One that Savato would have loved to solve, Ian though, sighing. *I didn't even know him that well, or spend all that much time with him. Why does it hurt so much now that he's gone?*

Kyra stood over a stack of papers on Captain Ctzo's desk aboard *Radiant Dawn*. Bandages had been wrapped over her many wounds and she favoured one leg over the other. Her mate Réto, similarly bandaged, stood alongside the captain, watching as she explained her notes.

"I've gone over the finances several times," she said. "And I've spoken with the carpenters. The losses we've incurred from Grey Noon's attack are... substantial."

Ctzo nodded slowly. For all his knowledge and skills, handling money had never been his forte. He'd left the running of the business side of his quest to the Kamai.

"The numbers aren't good," Kyra said, confirming Ctzo's fears. "Between how much it cost to start this expedition, the loans you took out to make that possible—"

"They were all small enough," Ctzo said. "They seemed reasonable at the time."

"Fair enough, but we have more ships, more crew—more costs. We've managed to grab some resources at no extra cost, but it takes time and work. As soon as we arrive back in Questava, we'll have to pay those loans. Perhaps we should sell a ship or two?"

Though he didn't like the idea, Ctzo submitted to the wisdom of it. "I'll put in a request with the Emperor. Considering our finds, perhaps he'd be willing to fund our next journey. If not, we'll put at least one of the ships up for sale after it's repaired."

Our next journey. The words felt so strange on his lips. He could barely think past this journey, and how quickly it was coming to an end. *But Vortro proves once and for all that the Mocjoa exist. I can't leave unfinished the task of finding her people.*

Once Kyra had gone, Ctzo stood quietly in his quarters, the room's bright décor doing nothing to lift his mood. Nothing would ever replace the worn blankets and overall familiarity of the *Diversity*.

He had yet to shed a tear over the loss of his ship. Instead he'd wandered listlessly, trying to focus his attention on ensuring they had enough supplies for the long trip back to Scavgan's Island. He'd also checked on his injured crewmembers. He was grateful for the lives that hadn't been lost in the battle, but he felt overwhelmed by what he had lost.

Finally, he laid upon his bed. His new bed. It didn't really feel like *his*. The bed on the *Diversity* was *his* bed. This was merely *a* bed.

He closed his eyes, his mind emptying as he fell into a restless sleep.

CHAPTER TWENTY-FOUR

*H*ardly able to sleep, Ian lay upon a hammock with his eyes wide open, staring at the hammock above. He knew that any moment now one of the Kamai would come belowdecks with the news he awaited.

I wonder where Vortro is, he thought. *I'm sure someone is looking after her... right?*

Perhaps she was his responsibility; she had been for so long. However, now that she was a little girl and not a little worm, he no longer felt qualified to care for her, and so he instinctively left the task up to others.

Feeling worry for the Mocjoa, he decided to stop waiting for the Kamai and go look for her.

Just as he vaulted up the stairs, Kyra met him, landing at his feet so she didn't crash into him.

"We're almost back, Ian," Kyra announced.

Ian's heart skipped a beat. "Okay. Just let me go check on Vortro. I want to make sure someone's watching her."

"Oh, she's with my husband. Don't worry. He loves playing with her."

A sense of relief washed over him.

They made their way up to the deck, where Ian stood at the railing and absorbed the sight of approaching land. Cottages peppered the rocky shoreline and multiple docks stretched out into the water, but unlike in Questava very few of the docks harboured boats large enough to be called ships. Unpretentious tones of brown and grey likewise contrasted the capital's whites and golds.

Just looking at the village filled Ian with a sense of tranquillity and simplicity. Almost everything remained as he'd left it at the beginning of the *Diversity*'s voyage.

"Home," he whispered to himself.

After everything I've been through—fighting aboard the Diversity, exploring the Marsh Isles, wandering Aziasha—I've made it back.

As grand as his adventures had been, it felt no less grand to return to where his life had begun.

"I say," Tyzak said, jabbing an elbow into Ian's ribs, "what are the chances you'd accept a little company on your visit ashore?"

"Actually, I wanted to ask if you and Zan would like to come," Ian said. "I wanted to ask Katia, too, but I couldn't find her. Guess she's busy with something."

"I'd love to," Zan said. "After all the time we spent together in Aziasha, it would be nice to meet your family."

A jealous frown passed over Tyzak's face. "Well, I'm glad your wilderness adventure allowed you two to bond so deeply."

Zan put his arm around Tyzak's shoulders. "Believe it or not, the time away actually made me appreciate you more. There were so many situations that would have been less stressful if you had been there with your bold confidence and cocky humour. You were missed."

Tyzak's eyes trailed to the arm draped over his shoulder. "You... are touching me." He returned the gesture by wrapping Zan in a tight hug. "Friends at last!"

Before Zan could pull away, the captain approached.

"Ian, if you want to use the longboat, you'd better take off soon," said Ctzo. "The ships will be passing by this area and continuing to the main harbour. And don't worry about Vortro. Réto and Kyra are thrilled to look after her until you meet up with us again."

Ian nodded. "Thanks, Captain." He then turned to his friends. "Come on, guys."

Ian paddled the longboat confidently through the rippling sea. In his mind, he flashed back to an image of him and Tyzak paddling amongst the muddy waters of the Marsh Isles. The picture faded quickly as a simple but familiar wooden house came into view, nestled against the shoreline and linked to the ocean via a long and narrow dock.

Ian's face broke into a wide smile. *Home. Home at last.*

His older sister Katana, her green dress flapping in the wind, was the first to approach. She stood atop the dock and waved as Ian, Zan, and Tyzak floated towards her.

Tyzak elbowed Zan in the ribs. "Ian, who's the cute girl?" he whispered.

Ian frowned. "You mean my big sister?"

"Your—oh." Tyzak cleared his throat. "Is she... betrothed?"

"Not the last time I was here, no..."

"Oh, good! Do I have your permission to flirt with her?"

Zan shook his head. "You could show a little more class, Tyzak."

"What?" Tyzak said. "You're not going to take her, are you?"

Zan blushed. "We'll discuss this later."

"Ha! So you agree she's cute!"

Ian couldn't understand their reactions. "My sister is cute?"

The conversation ceased as they drew within earshot of Katana. Ian tossed her a rope, and she secured their longboat. When she'd finished, Ian climbed off onto the dock.

"Katana!" He threw his arms around her. "I missed you."

Katana smiled. "We missed you, too. Dad is off on a fishing trip, but Calyx and Mom are inside making dinner."

Zan cleared his throat as he and Tyzak joined them on the dock. "Ian, aren't you going to introduce us?"

Tyzak pushed past Zan. "Katana, it's a pleasure to meet you at last!"

Ian motioned to his friends. "Katana, this is Tyzak and Zan."

Katana bowed. "Nice to meet you both. Is the captain coming?"

"They're putting the ships in the main harbour," Ian said. "Maybe you'll get to meet the captain later."

Katana's face fell. "Oh, all right. Well, why don't you three follow me inside?"

"We'd love to!" Tyzak said.

Ian and Katana led Tyzak and Zan off the dock, along a step-stone path that inclined towards the home's back entrance. Framing the door was a set of semi-scraggly grey-blue bushes which Zan took an interest in.

"I think I've seen these before," Zan said, rubbing a thin leaf between his fingers. "But I couldn't put a name to them. They don't grow in Questava, but I've seen them in some houses."

"Kiok," Tyzak said. "They grow like weeds in Medioca."

Katana nodded. "They're not as common around here. I find them pretty, especially when they're blooming."

Though the dishevelled appearance of the kiok could hardly be deemed pretty, its unusual colour did attract the eye, and Ian agreed that the plants' massive, velvety black and blue flowers stood out.

"They do look good when they're blooming," Ian said. "And apparently their fruit is edible."

Tyzak's hand flew to his mouth to stifle a laugh. "Edible, you say? Have you yet to try said fruit?"

"Yeah, I've tried it…" Ian shivered. "Very, very bitter."

"We use it as a spice on special occasions," Tyzak said. "Whenever we commemorate a bitter experience. Such as at funerals."

Zan mumbled, "I'm getting the impression I should never try this fruit."

Katana laughed, a soft, musical sound. She opened the door and the other three followed her in.

A yellow and brown grass-woven mat, decorated with fish and other sea creatures, welcomed their feet. They each removed their boots as they entered.

"Katana made this," Ian said proudly, pointing at the mat. "She's very crafty, and very artistic."

"Lovely indeed!" Tyzak said.

Zan nodded. "Yes, well done."

Katana's face shied away. "Mom, how is dinner coming along?"

"Almost ready." Ian's mother rounded the corner, smiling warmly. She hardly looked her age, with a youthful spring to her step and a simple tan gown more in the style of Katana's generation than her own. "How was your journey?"

She hugged Ian first. He smiled, glad to feel her arms around him. He hadn't realized how badly he'd missed her until that moment.

"It's been an adventure, for sure!" Tyzak said. He put one hand on Zan's shoulder and motioned to Ian with the other. "Especially for these two. They have many stories to tell of evil bugs, losing eyes, dragons, creepy temples, blackwaters miners—"

Zan's good eye narrowed. "The bugs were venomous, not evil. Only one eye was lost. There was only one dragon. And only one temple."

"But it was creepy?" Tyzak prompted.

Zan sighed. "Yes, Tyzak, it was creepy."

"I'm jealous," Ian's mom said with a smile. "Why does my son get to go on adventures and not me?"

Another fellow appeared, taller and clearly a few years older than Ian. He cast his dark blue-and-violet eyes around the group before settling on Ian.

"What sort of trouble did you get into?" the man asked in a deep voice.

Their mom was the first to reply. "A lot less than you would've gotten into!"

"This is Calyx," Ian said to Zan and Tyzak. "My big brother."

Calyx nodded in greeting. Zan returned the nod while Tyzak extended his hand for a shake. Calyx hesitated, then reached out and took it. Tyzak nearly jumped back when he realized Calyx's right hand had been severed, and he was missing half his fingers.

"An accident," Calyx mumbled. He allowed a half-smile to grace his face. "Maybe I'll tell you the story sometime?"

Tyzak nodded vigorously. "Oh, please do!"

"He likes stories," Ian said. "Even morbid ones. He'll love yours, Calyx."

"Good to know." Calyx tipped his head towards a table in the centre of the room. "Wanna sit?"

Tyzak quickly brushed past the others, grabbed a chair, and sat. He watched Calyx with keen eyes. "So… ahem… the story?"

The others took their time finding a seat while Ian's mom returned to the brick oven to remove a pan of bread from its place over the hot coals, and Katana finished what had been Calyx's task of preparing the salad.

The house was small, with the main area housing the entryway, kitchen, and dining table. Doorways led to three separate sleeping quarters and a toilet.

As Ian's mother and Katana brought the bread and salad to the table, Ian rushed to find dishes for everyone.

"Ian!" Katana said, shaking her head. "Since when were you so helpful?"

"I've always been helpful!"

Katana put her hands on her hips. "You always said it was the girls' job to set the table."

"No I didn't," Ian muttered. "And I'm hungry."

Tyzak and Zan were already gathered around the table, listening to the story of how Calyx had lost his hand. Tyzak's mouth gaped open.

"No!" Tyzak said, gasping. "A fish did that?!"

"Death fish have terrible teeth," Calyx insisted. "My fingers were gone in an instant, cut clean through."

"Maybe you should save the gory details for after dinner," Ian's mother said as she took a seat at the table.

She, Calyx, Katana, Tyzak, and Zan all began scooping up salad and slicing bread. The conversation temporarily centred on the food, and the women received many compliments for their delicious bread.

"It's been so long since I had real fresh bread," Zan said. "Thank you so much for this meal!"

"I'm sorry we didn't have more prepared," Katana said.

"Nonsense, this is perfect," Tyzak assured her. "Before we get into describing our grand adventures, is there anything new in your life? Ian has mentioned you now and again. He's said that you like crafting."

"Um, yes." Katana sent Ian a raised eyebrow. "You actually mentioned me?"

Ian shrugged. "Maybe. I guess."

"In Medioca, you'd be old enough to be married," Tyzak continued. "Do you village folks prefer to take your time?"

Coughing, Ian gave Tyzak a disbelieving look.

Zan frowned. "Way to be subtle."

Katana's face changed colour rapidly. "Uh, I have been busy learning to fish. Now that Ian's been gone, Dad has had time to teach me."

"Right, your father." Zan looked around the room as if he might appear at any moment. "When will he return from his trip?"

"Probably not until the evening." Ian's mother sighed. "I'm sorry he's not here, Ian, but we had no idea you'd be arriving today."

"I'll see him tonight." Ian was disappointed, but he remained positive. "At least I get to see the rest of you."

His mother smiled at Tyzak and Zan. "Yes. And I'm glad we've had the chance to meet your new friends."

"Speaking of meeting people," Tyzak spoke between mouthfuls of bread. "When are you going to introduce them to your daughter, Ian?"

Katana and Calyx's eyes widened as their gazes shot over to Ian. "Your what?!"

Ian, Tyzak, and Zan trod the narrow dirt street in the direction of the village's main harbour.

"Are there any restaurants you'd recommend?" Tyzak rubbed his stomach. "I didn't wish to offend your family, but that was a rather small meal."

"There's a couple of inns that serve food," Ian assured him. "The best ones are right next to the main harbour."

"Oh, good." Tyzak whistled as he walked.

"So what's your plan from here?" Ian asked.

"The captain said he wishes to leave the ships docked here for a while so the carpenters can do further repairs. Buying supplies here is cheaper than in Questava, apparently. But while the carpenters are at work, the captain and I will be taking a carriage to Medioca."

"A carriage?" Ian's brow lowered. "You're not going by boat?"

Tyzak shook his head. "I wished for a break from the sea, and the captain wishes to visit the temple as soon as he can. So rather than sticking around during the repairs, he'll entrust the running of the fleet to the Kamai. We'll go to Medioca, I'll see my family again, he'll spend some time at the temple, and when the repairs are complete the fleet will meet up with us in Medioca."

"Oh." Ian stared down at his feet. "When are you leaving?"

"Well, I believe the captain was hoping to get underway tonight."

"So soon?"

"As I said, the captain would like to visit the temple as soon as time allows."

"And what are your plans from there?"

"Obviously I'd like to spend a little time with my family. But as for whether I'll continue on to Questava with the captain or remain in Medioca until the two months are up… I haven't settled on that one yet."

"What about you, Zan?" Ian asked. "What are your plans?"

Zan shrugged. "What are yours?"

Ian looked ahead at the fast-approaching harbour. "I really want to see my dad tonight. And I need to introduce my family to Vortro. I don't think I'll be sticking around the harbour for long."

Tyzak nodded. "Fair enough."

The trio allowed a long moment of silence. In that time, they arrived at the harbour. Though both Ian and Ctzo had called it the *main* harbour, it was certainly nothing grand or awe-inspiring, just a line of docks bordered on one side by small shops and on the other by the sea.

The fleet wasn't hard to find. Soon the three were walking up the gangplank onto *Radiant Dawn*'s deck. Several crewmembers were there to greet them: Réto and Kyra, with Vortro between them; Yakara and Chiha; and Katia, who watched Ian and Zan through wide, tear-filled eyes.

She knows it's time, Ian thought, his heart aching for her. *I'm going home, and she's sailing on.*

He knelt to the ground, and Katia rushed over to embrace him.

"Bless you," she whispered in her ever-improving Questavan.

"Bless you, too," Ian said. "Thank you for everything."

Meanwhile, Chiha and Yakara focused their attentions on Tyzak. Chiha walked up to him, nodding and tilting her head. "You and the captain are leaving tonight?"

"Afraid so." Tyzak gave a small bow. "I hope you and Yakara can get along fine without me." He reached out and gently patted Yakara's head. "Not to worry. I'll be back soon enough to join in with Ctzo's next adventure!"

Chiha's tail flicked back and forth. "Are you going to hug me?"

Paling slightly, Tyzak stammered, "Er, well, I'm not leaving yet…"

Vortro seemed reluctant to leave her babysitters. Réto was teaching her a clapping game, and she giggled as she attempted to copy his movements. Ian patted her on the head, then stroked her antennae.

Turning, her brilliant silver eyes met his and she lifted her arms. He picked her up, held her close, and then passed her back to the Kamai.

"Just a moment, girl," Ian said. "I have a few goodbyes to say. But then we're going to head home, okay?"

By this time Tyzak and Zan had found their way to him, and Tyzak's face suddenly turned downcast. "Well, I suppose this is..."

Ian wrapped his arms around his friend. "See you later."

Tyzak managed a small smile, though a tear slipped down his cheek. He returned the hug. "Right. Until later."

As the two parted, Tyzak turned to Zan and offered him a hand. "Am I correct in assuming you'd accept a shake over a hug?"

"I'll take neither, for now." Zan shuffled his feet. "I was actually hoping, if it's not too much trouble—"

"Are you coming with Ctzo and me?!" Tyzak released a rather unmanly squeal of delight. "Brilliant!"

"Well, I've only visited Medioca a few times, and never with a local. Perhaps you could give me a tour."

"Oh, of course my family will have room for you! And don't worry, we'll find some way to return you to your stately mansion in Questava after your visit. But first you must have dinner with us. And breakfast. And perhaps stay for—"

"Right. Might as well." Zan's gaze fell on Ian. "See you later, my friend. It's been a pleasure getting to know you and sail with you. You've matured so much since we met."

Ian couldn't hold back the tears streaming down his face. "Goodbye, Zan. Maybe next time I'm in Questava, we can meet at Zono's?"

Zan laughed. "Of course. I'll pay."

With some hesitation, Zan placed an arm on Ian's shoulder, but Ian converted the gesture into a hug. Memories flooded back of all the adventures they'd had together.

A small smile lit Ian's lips. "I never did get you back for that time you scared me after the Darian told that Blackblood horror story."

"No, you didn't." Zan pulled away from the hug, still smiling. "Someday, perhaps, you will."

"In two months," Ian reminded him. "After the captain gets things in order, we'll be sailing together again."

He examined Zan's face. Inwardly he already knew the truth.

Zan shook his head. "I'm sure plenty more adventures await you and Captain Ctzo. And Tyzak has made it clear he'll be joining you on those adventures. But the sea isn't for me. Still…" He tried to sound confident. "Still, I'll see you again, Ian. Soon enough."

"Right." Ian didn't know whether it was silly to hope, but he hoped anyway and allowed a bit of confidence to slip into his voice. "I'll see you again!"

CHAPTER TWENTY-FIVE

*O*tzo stood outside a small storefront, negotiating prices with a carriage owner while Zan and Tyzak waited a short distance back.

Tyzak shook his head. "Are you hearing the prices that man is demanding for driving us to Medioca? Shameful!"

"The captain doesn't seem bothered." Zan shrugged. "From what Ian's told me about this village, traveling any way but by sea is unusual. The driver probably doesn't get many requests like ours."

"I suppose." Tyzak eyed up the carriage hitches. "And I'm guessing caperos are rare in this region, too."

Leading the covered carriage were four feldas. About half the size of caperos, their comparatively light build was well-known to be deceptive; for their size, they could pull an impressive load. However, their stubbornness made them less appealing as carriage hitches.

Smirking, Zan asked, "How many times do you think we'll get stopped on our trip because the feldas decide they want a nap?"

"Too many. Anyway, I understand the value of a change of scenery, and with how the captain has been..." Tyzak lowered his voice. "It doesn't surprise me that he would wish to get his mind off the sea. But sailing would be so much more convenient. And far less expensive."

"Does it matter? Like you said, he's… well, how do you think he's doing?"

Their conversation was cut short when Ctzo turned from the carriage owner and headed towards them.

"He'll be ready to take us in an hour," Ctzo said. "He's just getting some supplies packed."

"Marvellous!" Tyzak smiled. "The sooner we leave, the sooner I'll be home! Ah, world adventures are a treat, but there's nothing quite like the thought of seeing your family again."

"Speaking of," Ctzo said, "are you sure your family will be comfortable with hosting Zan and myself?"

"Absolutely!" Tyzak wrapped an arm around Zan's shoulders. "In Medioca, we don't turn away friends. You'll receive a warm welcome!"

The trip to Medioca from the village was expected to take several days. Since travelling in a carriage for days appealed to no one, they planned several rest stops along the way.

"Almost to the first town," the driver said gruffly. Though he sat outside the carriage covering, a small window allowed him to communicate with the passengers. "We'll find us an inn and settle down for the night."

When the carriage stopped, Zan stepped out and shaded his eye with his hand. The blinding suns radiated off the sandy terrain, waves of heat enveloping the travellers. Before them stood rows of small adobe buildings, each just as pale as the sand.

A wandering merchant spotted them and seized the opportunity to make a sale. "Sun umbrellas for the weary journeyers?"

Zan nodded as he grabbed an umbrella decorated in geometric patterns. "How much?"

Zan paid the desired price, and Tyzak soon purchased his own umbrella. Meanwhile, Ctzo and the driver hung back.

"Sensitive to the sun, they are?" the driver asked. "Don't believe we'll be staying outside for long."

"It's a souvenir," Zan said, having heard the comment. He spun the umbrella in his hand. "I like the design."

"Why suffer the suns if you don't have to?" Tyzak asked.

The driver began unloading their baggage. "A hand, please, Captain?"

Ctzo helped him with the load. Zan and Tyzak came to lend aid, but the driver waved them off. "You two, go get us all some water from the well. I need a drink. The well is just a few streets down. Can't miss it."

Nodding, Zan and Tyzak did as instructed and went on their way. They found the well within a few minutes and met a woman standing over it with a pail and rope.

The woman eyed the travellers warily. "I can draw you water… if you pay me."

"People in these desert towns tend not to have much," Tyzak whispered in Zan's ear. "They probably see a dark-skinned Questavan like you and think, 'He's got plenty of money to throw around!'"

Zan managed a smirk, and agreed to pay the woman for her help. But when she handed him a pail full of water, he wasn't sure what to do with it. So he touched his lips to it and took a sip of the refreshing liquid. Realizing how thirsty he felt, he followed this with several gulps. Then he handed the bucket to Tyzak, who took his share before asking her to fill it again for their companions.

"We'll bring you back the pail when we're done," Zan promised.

As they walked back to Ctzo and the driver, Tyzak leaned close to Zan. "They have rather pale blue skin. Do you think they might be from the same race as Jani?"

"Perhaps." Zan shrugged. "Speaking of Jani, I don't think I ever saw him after the battle."

Tyzak just laughed. "Oh, that fellow knows how to blend into the shadows! I suppose he's still with the fleet."

"I suppose so." Zan sighted Ctzo and the driver and quickened his pace, careful to hold the pail of water steady.

Days later, in the early hours of the morning, Zan peered out the carriage window. Rolling hills met his eyes, lit by the suns peeking over the horizon and decorated by patches of rust-coloured grass. Small, twisted trees with lovely blue leaves dotted the otherwise rocky landscape. They grew far enough apart not to constitute a forest, but they sprouted in large enough numbers as to dominate the land.

"What are those?" Zan asked, gesturing to the trees.

"Oh, the avolia trees?" Tyzak's chest swelled with pride. "Those grow everywhere in Medioca! Though the wild ones hardly produce any fruit. Aren't they beautiful? We flavour nearly every dish with avolia oil, and we use the fruits in our salads... ah, I've missed the taste." He sighed longingly. "I am looking forward to a Mediocan home-cooked meal."

Noting that the captain hadn't joined their conversation, Zan looked over Tyzak's shoulder. Ctzo's head rested against the back of the seat, his eyes closed and his breathing deep.

"How long has he been asleep?" Zan whispered.

"A few hours." Tyzak, too, eyed their sleeping companion. "Should I wake him?"

"Wait until we get to your family's place. We're almost there, right?"

Tyzak shook his head. "Medioca isn't exactly small. There's still an hour or so to go." Leaning back, he closed his eyes. "Perhaps I'll get in a bit of a nap as well."ew

Ctzo awoke to the chatter of Tyzak and the driver. As his mind tuned into their words, he realized Tyzak was giving the man directions on how to get to his family's house.

Ctzo would have been fine stopping in the city and finding an inn. He hadn't been sure how to politely refuse Tyzak's offer of hospitality.

Truthfully, I'd rather be alone than stuck in a crowded house right now, he thought.

He sighed. It was too late for that, and perhaps the company would do him some good. The pain of his losses was still felt fresh in his mind and his mood remained low. Some friendly faces might take his mind off his sorrows.

Stepping out of the carriage, Zan approached their driver before Ctzo could. He'd pulled a bag of coins from his luggage earlier and now handed them to the driver.

"I believe this was the agreed-upon price?" Zan said.

The driver poured the money onto his hand and counted through the coins. "Yes, wonderful! Thank you!"

Zan turned to find Ctzo watching the exchange with surprise.

"The payment is taken care of," Zan said. "Don't worry about paying me back. It's the least I can do, considering how well you've taken care of all of us."

Before Ctzo could say anything, Zan began to unload the luggage. He didn't want to give his captain a chance to argue.

Tyzak's family home was grander than Zan had expected. It wasn't quite a mansion, but it was decently sized and had expensive purple paints colouring the edges of the otherwise white building.

He did say that he comes from a family of successful merchants, Zan thought.

The moment the doors to Tyzak's house burst open, Zan was engulfed in the arms of a large, laughing man.

"Ah, my son and his friend!"

The big man gave Zan a messy kiss on the cheek. Then, releasing him, he did the same to Tyzak.

"Father," Tyzak greeted exuberantly, returning the kiss. "What a joy to see you again!" He looked around the room and smiled at the men, women, and children who watched. "Brothers and sisters!"

Eyes widening, Zan counted each of them. "There's twenty people! They can't all be your blood brothers and sisters!"

"Of course they can." Tyzak chuckled, then leaned in close to Zan. "My father has two wives—my mother, and his other wife."

"Only two?" Zan exclaimed. "Two wives doesn't explain twenty-one children!"

Tyzak frowned. "Sure it does."

His siblings gathered around, chattering away in Mediocan, leaving Zan to translate their messages by their cheery voices, pushing, and hugs.

"Welcome, guests! I am Abrim!" Zan's father took the hands of the two oldest women in the room. "These are my beloved wives, Akel and Becca."

Tyzak rushed to Becca and gave her a peck on the cheek, followed by a greeting in Mediocan. He then turned to Zan and Ctzo. "This is my dear mother. Father, Mother, Akel; this is Captain Ctzo and my friend Zan."

"A pleasure to meet you all," Zan said. He folded his hands in front of him, unsure of what a proper Mediocan greeting looked like. He looked to Ctzo for a cue, but the captain was just struggling to keep his eyes open. He yawned into his shoulder.

Abrim paused, noting the string hanging from Ctzo's belt. "You wear the braided crimson chord!"

"Yes," Ctzo said. "I purchased it while I was a soldier here, during the war."

Abrim turned to his son, narrowing his eyes. "Why do you not wear your chord, my eldest son?"

Tyzak grinned sheepishly. "Oh, um, I misplaced it. I can always buy a new one."

After a shake of his head, Abrim turned back to Ctzo. "Do you know the importance of the crimson chord, the meaning behind it? It is not a mere souvenir."

"No, it isn't. I wear it to remind me of my commitment to Kyaté, and to his commands. Just as it is instructed in the law."

"You are a worshipper of Kyaté, then? Peace to you, brother!" Abrim gave Ctzo yet another look-over. "You must be aware, friend, that your accent and the colour of your skin will cause some to resent you. Questavans aren't well-liked here, even though they protected us during the war." His gaze turned to Zan. "That goes for you as well."

"Fair enough," Zan said. "You speak Questavan very well."

"Everyone in Medioca knows at least a little Questavan. Ah, you must all be hungry for a good meal after your long journey! Come, be seated in the dining room, and we will prepare you something to eat!"

The scent of strong tea met Ctzo's nose as he entered the family's dining room. The room, coloured in rich browns and reds, held a short but wide table with a colourful table-runner stretched along its wooden surface. Studying the walls, Ctzo realized where the strong odours originated; against one wall was a shelf lined with various sizes and styles of tea tins.

"Take a seat," Abrim encouraged. "I will get some water for your tea."

One of Abrim's daughters opened a cabinet and gingerly pulled out teacups and saucers, laying them on the table for his guests.

Ctzo and Zan did as instructed and sat down, with Tyzak taking his place across from them.

"Ah!" Tyzak said happily. "I'm looking forward to having a real meal again! Not that biscuits and grog aren't fine fare, but…"

Ctzo laughed. "I don't feel insulted by your desire to eat something else."

Zan's brows rose. "Captain, I think that's the first time I've heard you laugh in a while."

"Perhaps," Ctzo admitted.

"You seem tired," Zan added.

"You are both free to stay the night." Abrim said as he entered with a steaming kettle. "I can prepare you a guest room."

Tyzak nodded. "That would be wonderful, Father! Although I believe the captain would like to visit the temple before the day is through."

Tyzak's brothers began entering the room one by one, each taking a seat around the table while the women worked busily in the kitchen. Mouth-watering smells emanated from the kitchen until finally the meal arrived. Upon the table, the women and girls placed platters containing various vegetables and grains—and in the very centre, a seasoned fowl.

"The women will eat after," Tyzak said to his guests. "It's tradition."

Zan wasn't sure whether to feel guilty. His family always ate together as one, with the servants waiting their turn to eat. But the women appeared to be entertaining themselves, their chattering voices carrying through from another room.

Shrugging, Zan dug in. He piled his plate with each and every offering and savoured the flavourful feast.

CHAPTER TWENTY-SIX

The temple remained far off when the trio caught sight of it seated atop a large, smoothly sloping hill.

Zan gasped in awe. "Wow. I wasn't expecting to see anything that looks so… Questavan."

When Tyzak spoke, he had a sharp edge in his voice. "I believe you mean that you didn't expect to see a building as impressive as what your people have created in Questava."

"Well, yes." Zan face flushed with colour. "It doesn't look Questavan, very Mediocan, and very… beautiful."

Tyzak smiled. "Isn't it, though?"

Shining white in the light of the suns, the temple stood three stories high, its outer walls featuring motifs of vines and fruit painted in a rich purple hue. The temple's design seemed at once simple and magnificent, standing firmly atop a hill overlooking the rest of Medioca. A single paved path led up to the gated walls surrounding it.

Zan narrowed his eye, attempting to get a clearer view. "That path looks crowded."

"Well, yes," Tyzak said. "Why wouldn't it be? Kyaté's law encourages regular sacrifices!"

"What do you sacrifice?" Zan asked.

"Mostly birds. Recall what you were served for dinner? Our fowls are our choicest meats."

After staring up the hill a moment, Zan turned to Ctzo. "Looks like a bit of a walk. Are you sure you're up for this? You seem very tired."

"Not tired," Ctzo said quietly. He lifted his eyes to the temple. "Sombre, perhaps. This trip holds great significance to me."

As the three neared the temple, Ctzo's gaze took in the strangers sharing their path. Every detail of the temple's design had been given to the Mediocans by Kyaté hundreds of years ago. Sacred meaning could be found in every measurement, every colour, and every shape. Yet surrounded by the bustling crowds hurrying to and from the iconic building, Ctzo felt in the air only a sense of routine. The discrepancy bothered him.

Do these people still consider this holy soil? He thought about it a little longer. *The familiarity may cause them to lose their awe of it.*

They reached the stone walls and Ctzo frowned as he noted shopkeepers in their tents, crying out their wares—from sacrificial birds to red chords. Their presence had always seemed an unnecessary distraction.

I suppose I can't blame them for setting up shop here, much as I would prefer they sold their goods elsewhere.

The three passed through the gates into the massive temple courtyard. Within it was yet another courtyard, a low latticework fence surrounding the temple itself. Ctzo saw Mediocan men and women pass through a simple gateway into this inner courtyard, heading for the temple building.

But he knew he couldn't follow. This was Medioca's temple, and only Mediocans could continue through.

"If you need some time alone, Zan and I can head outside and visit the shops," Tyzak said.

"No need for that," Ctzo said. "This place is big enough for each of us to find our own spot to contemplate and pray. But I would appreciate splitting up for the time being."

Tyzak and Zan nodded, and they went their own way while Ctzo went his. He walked up to the lattice fence and knelt on the ground, facing the temple. It felt awkward, submitting private prayers in a crowded outdoor space, kneeling on the dirty ground. Thankfully, he wasn't alone. Other foreigners knelt or stood, whispering or crying out their own prayers in the direction of Kyaté's Temple. He bowed his head and closed his eyes closed, yet his ears continued to absorb the din of others' prayers.

He saw an image of Jani in his mind. He sensed somehow that Kyaté's messenger stood nearby, invisible to those around.

Ctzo gritted his teeth.

"You promised!" He tried to keep his volume low, though his voice trembled with the effort. "You said great things awaited. You said we would change the world."

His eyes roamed—there beside him, Jani stood.

The being hung his head. "First, I spoke only what Kyaté told me. I can make nothing happen by my own powers. Only Kyaté has the strength and knowledge to bring about what He has planned. Second, how do you believe Kyaté has failed to keep His promise?"

"The *Diversity* has sunk."

"But what happened before that?"

"Nothing! We stopped a few nobodies, took out only a few pirates. What did that accomplish?"

Jani allowed a silence to pass before he responded. "Whose glory were you seeking?"

"I wasn't in it for glory. I was in it for..." Ctzo stopped, reality sinking in. "No. I did it for revenge. I did it because I wanted to defeat Grey Noon. Fine, I'll admit it: I did want the glory, too. To be honest, I still do. But is that wrong?" He buried his face into the ground. "I want the Council's respect and trust so that they'll give me more resources to do more good. I want people to see that doing the right thing, no matter how hard it may be, will bring about the best results. I want Grey Noon dead, so he will never return to Questava to hurt anybody. I want—"

"Now you realize what you wanted," Jani said. "Do you know what Kyaté wanted?"

Ctzo released a long, deep sigh. "No. I don't."

"Ah, but you do. Read the scriptures. They spell out what Kyaté wants. Read them again and again. And return to your family."

Ctzo's eyes widened. "My... family?"

"Make peace with them."

"But I've tried, over and over—" Again, Ctzo sighed. "I'll try once more."

"In person, this time. No letters or money sent via courier. Face to face."

The captain allowed a long pause. When he looked up, Jani was gone.

"All right," he spoke to the air. "In person."

Zan and Tyzak's wanderings went from excited and intentional to meandering and aimless. A single sun hung low in the darkening sky and another barely blinked over the horizon.

"My, the captain is taking his time," Tyzak muttered, glancing up at the temple.

Zan noted several shopkeepers packing up their wares and tents. "I suppose he only gets to come on occasion. He takes the time to make the most of it. How often do you go?"

"Hmm?"

"To the temple."

Tyzak considered. "Well... on special holidays, everyone goes. Like for the coming Festival of Life. Everyone will be at the temple then!"

"What about when it's not a holiday?" Zan asked.

Shrugging, Tyzak eyed a departing shopkeeper. "I don't know. Sometimes."

A moment of silence fell between them. Their eyes returned to the temple.

"The captain's faith is very important to him," Zan said. "What do you think he prays for?"

"World peace?" Tyzak said it with only the slightest hint of sarcasm.

"I suppose," Zan agreed with all seriousness. "He seems like someone who would strive for that. Not just in his prayers… in his actions."

Tyzak smiled. "We have a grand captain, don't we? Been through so much, and yet faith still comes so easily to him."

The moons stood high and bright in the sky, yet Tyzak remained awake, busily catching up with his family in their native tongue.

"I slashed through enemy after enemy!" Tyzak said, regaling them with his story in an excited voice. "But then out of nowhere, boom! A bullet hit my leg and sank into my flesh!"

He presented the leg and its scar to his younger brothers.

"And that is why we're never becoming pirate-hunters," one of them said. "Standing in the marketplace selling our wares, we don't get fired at."

"Ah," Tyzak countered, "but then you haven't heard Uncle Ethaniel's story. That's for another time."

One of his siblings leaned closer, gaping. "What happened to Uncle Ethaniel?"

Tyzak frowned. "Don't you wish me to finish the first story before I begin another?"

"I wish you to finish it!" a child declared.

"Thank you! Now, where was I… ah, a bullet came out of nowhere and pierced my leg. My eyes roved the scene. And there he was: a sniper, up on the mast! Tricky fellow, I thought. I planned to take that sniper down from his lofty perch. But lo and behold, a giant winged figure swooped down from the heavens and knocked that pirate from his stand. It was Black Night, our Rezumi ally!"

"Cool!" the youngest brothers said.

An older one nodded. "I saw a Rezumi the other day. They're huge!"

"I'm glad you didn't die," one of the little brothers said, giving Tyzak a strong hug.

"My, that is sweet of you," Tyzak said with a chuckle. "But wouldn't it have made an interesting story if I had died?"

His brother stared at him, eyes wide with horror.

"Come now." Tyzak patted his brother's back. "Everyone must die, dear brother. I've seen enough death to know I must face it, too. And since I've lived to tell stories, I wish the story of my death to be equally enjoyable to tell." He rubbed his hands together. "Now, someone wanted to hear the tale of Uncle Ethaniel's adventure in the marketplace?"

His siblings remained engrossed.

"Go ahead," one said. "But after you're done, we should tell you some stories. You haven't heard what's been going on around here!"

"And tell it in Questavan," an older one put in. "The kids need the practice."

The younger brothers groaned, but conceded.

"I would love to hear your stories!" Tyzak cleared his throat, switching to Questavan. "I'll try to speak a little slower, for those of you who are still learning. And I will make this tale brief, as it isn't technically my tale, but dear Uncle Ethaniel's. Well, there he was, minding his business at his carpentry stall in the market. A Questavan guard came over and eyed up Ethaniel's exquisite wares.

Then he declared, 'I need this chair,' pointing to one of particularly fine quality. 'Of course,' our uncle said, and he named his price. But the guard became angry. 'How dare you charge me for something I need from you!' he said. 'I do a great service to your city, defending it from harm!' Ethaniel muttered, 'I feel more enslaved than defended.'"

The older brothers covered their mouths, gaping.

"He did not say that!" one gasped. "How did he get out alive?"

"Fortunately, Uncle Ethaniel is incredibly fast. The guard fired off his musket at our poor uncle, but he got away. He was too afraid to go to the market for another few weeks." Tyzak laughed. "Thankfully, the guard in question left Medioca, and Uncle Ethaniel received no punishment."

An older brother looked down at the littler ones. "Don't get any ideas in your head, kids. Uncle Ethaniel did an unwise thing in talking like that. Remember when the nationalist Cactu was speaking, and he told everyone it was better to obey the traditions of their ancestors than to obey the Emperor?"

The children were silent for a moment.

"He didn't do anything wrong," one whimpered. "And why'd they have to torture him before killing him? Questavans are evil."

Tyzak hesitated. "Not quite so. Many are arrogant, true. And we didn't really ask them to come in and 'protect' us, as they put it. But there are good men and women among them. Why, take my two friends! Ctzo has adopted our faith, and Zan is a reasonable chap." Stretching, he rose. "Pardon me for a moment, I need a drink. While I'm gone, you should use the time to decide which story you wish to tell me first!"

He departed the room, where he found Zan standing just outside the door.

Tyzak chuckled. "My, I thought you'd gone to bed hours ago!"

"I went outside for a bit. Wanted to get some fresh air." Zan looked down at the floor. "Do all Mediocans feel the way your younger siblings do about Questavans?"

"We are a proud people. Being conquered didn't suit us."

"But you were conquered a long time ago," Zan said. "And Questavan rule isn't as strict over you as it used to be, is it? I know in our government circles we talk about the freedoms we've restored to you. And, though you may not like this, if Questavan guards and soldiers hadn't been here during the War of Nine Leagues, or during Ti'te'Vikan attacks, you probably wouldn't have won those battles."

Tyzak bit his lip. "Hmm."

"Everybody in the Questavan Empire needs to obey the law. And to be held accountable when they don't, like that Cactu fellow, or there would be chaos and crime everywhere."

"Fine," Tyzak grumbled. "But it would be nice if we had our own ruler, one who understood us and the importance of our customs."

"Don't you have the Regent?" Zan said.

Tyzak coughed. "Oh, him. You mean the man who just uses his power to get rich and kiss up to the Emperor? I'll forgive you for not being aware of this, but no true Mediocan acknowledges his authority."

"Why not?"

"The same reason that you wouldn't be recognized as Emperor if someone from Medioca up and put you on the throne in Questava," Tyzak said. "You're not from the royal family, and everybody knows it. Sure, there's a place for Council members who earn their position. But people like that understand law, not heritage or legacy. And in Medioca, heritage and legacy are everything." He continued more softly. "We had a king once, even under the Emperor's rule. King Avad. And many of us miss him. The Regent just doesn't represent us well."

"I suppose that's fair." Zan sighed. "I'm sorry we Questavans haven't been the best of neighbours."

"Well, I don't hold you personally responsible. Like I said, we are a proud people." Tyzak took a deep breath. "I can see we aren't going to agree much when it comes to politics. I consider myself a nationalist. I don't believe we should be under Questavan rule."

"Maybe we should try not bringing up this topic too much," Zan suggested, sensing his friend's anger. "I should head to bed."

"Sweet dreams," Tyzak said. "I suppose we'll have to leave tomorrow, so get your rest. As for me, I'll sleep in the carriage. I still have more catching up to do with my brothers!"

"Good night." Zan began to walk down the hallway. But then he stopped.

"Did you want something else?" Tyzak asked.

"May I ask you a personal question?"

"Be my guest!"

"Is... is that what your faith is to you?" Zan asked. "Heritage?"

Tyzak frowned. "I don't understand..."

"Well, for Ctzo, his faith in Kyaté isn't heritage. His ancestors, his parents, never worshiped Kyaté. But his faith influences how he sees the world, how he lives, and how he makes decisions. For you, though... I get the impression that belief in Kyaté is just a tradition. Am I wrong?"

Tyzak hesitated. "It's... well, my family believes in Kyaté. It's... it's important to us, going to the temple on holidays. Things like that. It's part of our family."

"Oh." Zan nodded. "Have a good night, Tyzak."

CHAPTER TWENTY-SEVEN

"So, we're back in Questava," Zan whispered to himself as he stared out the carriage window at the pale desert city stretching before him. Several days after leaving Medioca, they'd finally arrived at their destination.

Tyzak smiled from the seat beside him. "You're home! Excited? Disappointed? Uncertain?"

"More so the latter." Zan caught himself fiddling with his eyepatch. "I suppose I had to return sooner or later."

"Don't worry, friend." Tyzak wrapped a comforting arm around Zan's shoulder. "This time you'll have me with you!"

"Right." Zan gently removed Tyzak's arm. "Just so you're aware, my parents might not consider that a plus." He looked over at Ctzo. "Are you glad to be home?"

"Yes," Ctzo said slowly. "There's a lot of work to be done before we head off in search of the Mocjoa."

"Of course," Zan said. "I... wish you well in your efforts."

Ctzo studied him. "Will you be joining us?"

"Afraid not," Tyzak interjected. "Zan has had enough of the sea. But I'm looking forward to our next quest!"

"Good." Ctzo turned to look back out the window.

Zan jabbed Tyzak in the ribs. As Tyzak turned to his friend with a frown, Zan narrowed his eye at him.

Shrugging, Tyzak leaned back and closed his eyes.

"So, where to now?" the driver called.

Zan swallowed. "My house, sir."

Zan let out a big sigh as the carriage came to a stop in front of a shining cobblestone path. It led up a hill, past immense and stately gates, along manicured gardens, toward an impressive white house.

He reached out his hand towards Ctzo. "Have a good trip home, Captain. Thank you for everything."

Ctzo took the offered hand and shook it. "I hope we meet again."

Zan and Tyzak climbed out of the carriage, each grabbing their luggage. Zan gave a fistful of coins to the driver.

"That's not your house, my dear friend," Tyzak marvelled. "That's Parliament. Driver must have dropped us off at the wrong place!"

"It's my house," Zan said in a grating tone. "Do you happen to have a mirror on you?"

Pulling a shiny, flat object from an indiscernible pocket in his green cape, Tyzak handed it to Zan.

As Zan examined himself, Tyzak looked on curiously. "Aiming to look our best, are we?"

Zan released another deep sigh. "Checking that my eyepatch isn't... unstately." He adjusted it a tad.

"Dear Zan," Tyzak placed a hand on his friend's shoulder, "anyone would be jealous of an eyepatch like that."

"You don't know my father." Zan narrowed his good eye at the sight of a capero and rider approaching quickly from down the path. "That's probably my father now."

Tyzak coughed. "Not unless your father wears a skirt."

Frowning, Zan realized his friend was right; the rider, dressed in dark grey, was clearly a woman.

One of the family servants, Hana, pulled on the capero's reins, bringing it to a stop alongside the carriage. She rapidly dismounted and bowed low before Zan.

"My master, I am glad to see you well." Though Hana tried to hide it, her voice choked with emotion.

Zan watched her through a wide eye. "Um… hello. Where is my father?"

"Oh… yes, I suppose I should have given him the news that you're here," Hana stammered. "It's just that when I saw you alive and well, I wished to greet you. I'll fetch your father right away."

"No need." Tyzak pointed beyond Hana and her steed to another capero and rider. "I'm guessing that's him now. Dressed in off-white, a very nice outfit, to be sure…"

"That's him." Gulping, Zan listened to the sound of the carriage driving off. It was too late to turn back now. "Stay behind me, Tyzak. Father may not take well to your attire."

Tyzak gave himself a look-over. "I dressed in my very best shirt and pants and fine jewellery. How is it I'm not impressive enough for the likes of you?"

"Not me. Just my father. Hana, please prepare a guest room for my friend here."

Hana bowed again. "As you wish, master." She mounted her capero and led it back to the house.

Meanwhile, Vasitan rode up to them, halting his muscular steed and jumping down.

Zan's stare journeyed further up the path and saw his mother also coming down towards the street. He then returned his gaze to his father, clearing his throat.

"Now, I know you're angry—" His eye widened as he felt Vasitan embrace him, weeping softly.

"I thought..." Vasitan coughed on his own words. "I thought I would never see you again."

Tears slipped from Zan's own eye as he wrapped his arms over Vasitan's shoulders. "Father."

His mother soon joined them. Sobbing, she hugged her son.

Tyzak watched the tearful reunion with a smile. "So much for a cold reception."

CHAPTER TWENTY-EIGHT

Aziasha is a long way from here now, Katia thought as her feet landed against cold stone. She crossed the sidewalk in the heart of Questava City.

She nervously ducked as a carriage noisily raced by, pulled by two muscular monsters with proud heads atop strong necks—caperos, she'd been told. Their fiery blue eyes sent a shiver down her spine. The claws on their well-padded paws clicked against the pavement as they strode forward with confidence. She relaxed only after they'd turned off the street and out of sight.

Katia raised her gaze to those traveling with her: Black Night, with Oti atop his shoulder, and Chiha, her long tail flinching. The four travellers had decided to go exploring, leaving behind the guest rooms at Ctzo's house to search for the city's core landmarks.

Of the group, she knew only Black Night had ever been to Questava. Because of this, and his massive size, she felt safest when he was near. She adjusted her pace to match his.

She took a deep breath. Why was the air so dry? The ground so sandy? Was this whole area a massive inland-reaching beach? Why all the wind? Why so few trees? Being aboard the ship had been shocking enough. Questava was something else entirely.

Chiha was most bothered by the shortage of trees. Though occasional palms grew here and there, they couldn't compare to the massive trunks and tangled branches of the Marsh Isles.

"This place is ugly," she stated.

Black Night smiled at a passing Scavgan child. The child stopped in his tracks, jaw hanging open at the sight of the visitors, until his mother pulled him away.

"I like it, even though it's nothing like my home in Gashaia," Black Night eyed the horizon. "The sunsets here are beautiful. They fill the whole sky with colour."

Chiha snorted. "The suns do that everywhere."

"Not like here," Black Night insisted. "I guess there's less scenery to distract from the sky. Anyway, we should be able to get to Parliament from this street. At least, I think it's this way…"

"So many huts." Chiha sighed in amazement at the many storefronts and houses. "But where are all the people?"

"What do you mean?" Black Night asked, looking around at the various passersby. All were Scavgans, and each generally gave the foreigners an odd look before moving on. "There's plenty of people here."

"Plenty?" Chiha lifted her arms. "So many big huts, yet this place isn't filled with uncountable numbers!"

Black Night shrugged. "Guess people here like their space. More so than in your village."

"Space? Space is to be filled. Not wasted like this!" Chiha looked about, then shook her head. "Didn't you say Ctzo's house isn't too far from this Parliament? Are we not repeating our path, Black Night?"

He sighed loudly. "Fine, you try leading the way."

Halting, Chiha gazed out across the street. With sudden speed and practiced grace, she dashed over the ground and raced up the wall of a building.

"Hey!" Black Night yelled after her. "I'm all for new paths, but choose one we can follow!"

Katia ran after her Chiha, afraid she might miss something.

"Wait for me!" Oti leaped off Black Night's shoulder and rushed past Katia and over the wall.

Black Night watched, dumbstruck, as all three of his companions disappeared from sight.

"All right," he muttered. "I guess she just chose a path *most* of us could follow."

Hours later, Ctzo sat on a cushioned chair in his house, quietly sipping a warm cup of tea. His butler, Alez, a young but distinguished fellow, stood motionless a few feet away. Alez was his only servant, and truthfully he was more of a companion to Ctzo. However, the lad never stopped taking his job seriously; he remained stern-faced most of the time.

Ctzo's two-story house, though less grand than the houses of many Questavan aristocrats, was still spacious. A simple paint scheme of brown, orange, and pale aqua gave it a warm, cozy feel despite its size.

Both Ctzo and Alez took notice at the sound of the double doors creaking open. Ctzo stood while his butler strode ahead to greet the visitors.

Chiha was the first to step into the house, followed by Oti and Katia. Black Night had to duck and fold in his wings to fit through the doorway.

Ctzo nodded their way. "How did your exploration go?"

"This village is big," Chiha said simply. "Please, Captain, may I return to my room for rest?"

"Of course."

He watched Katia meander around the house. She still appeared to find the captain's home interesting to wander.

Even before they'd landed upon Scavgan's Island, Ctzo had been diligent in assuring that each Athai and Reea of his crew had a place here to call home until the return trip to the Marsh Isles. He didn't want them to be alone as they experienced the culture shock.

Ctzo felt especially responsible for Chiha, being Chief Orthel's own granddaughter, and he also had a soft spot for Katia and Oti. Adding Black Night to the mix, he now had six guests taking up his three guest rooms, with Oti sharing a room with Black Night. Réto and Kyra were also staying together; they and Alez had been responsible for the guests while the captain had taken his detour in Medioca.

Ctzo looked over to Alez. "Would you let Réto know that I'm headed out for the evening?"

Alez nodded but raised an eyebrow. "Of course, sir. I will find him straightaways."

"Good." The captain sighed. "I have a task I've been putting off for too long."

Not long after, Ctzo slid off Wind-Drummer's back. The dark capero pawed at the ground, and Ctzo calmly stroked her, then went about tying her to a nearby post.

He looked around the dirt streets running alongside grey brick houses. Not the worst neighbourhood he'd ever seen, but certainly not the best.

He stared at the home before him. A company of flowerpots, each with a unique plant, sat outside the wooden door.

Taking a deep breath, he forced his feet forward. His mind returned to the day he'd first entered Parliament to receive his acceptance into Questava's privateer forces.

This was far more terrifying than that.

Lifting his hand, he knocked twice against the wooden door, then paused. Part of him hoped no one was home.

No, I've waited too long to do this.

The door creaked open and Ctzo stared into the aqua-green eyes of a woman nearly his age.

"Hi, Qeysta," he managed at last.

The woman stared back silently.

"Mother," someone called from further into the house. A younger woman, barely an adult, suddenly slipped next to Qeysta. She frowned up at Ctzo. "Father?"

Ctzo smiled down at his daughter Warrah, chuckling lightly. "My, you've grown."

"Get out." With that, Warrah turned and walked briskly back into the house.

"So my husband returns," Qeysta said sharply. "Is the great Captain Ctzo so short on women vying for his attention that he dares to darken my door?"

"Qeysta…"

"How long has it been since you last came begging for forgiveness? Years?" She shook her head, body quivering. "Look at what being conscripted into the war did for you. No more vandalizing shops for the fun of it, no more starting fights just because you felt like punching someone." She smiled insincerely. "Now you get congratulated for stabbing people and destroying what others have built!" Her eyes searched him up and down. "Looks like you get paid well too. Nice uniform."

"It was a gift." He cleared his throat. "I… I brought presents. Thought that might… smooth things over."

Qeysta sighed, widening the doorway. "Bring them in. The least you could do is offer me payment for the years you've been gone."

"My love," Ctzo said, "last time I came, you said you never wanted to see me again. You wouldn't even let me come inside. So I thought—"

"Yet somehow here you are." She turned and headed into the house. "And never call me 'my love' again."

Ctzo sighed, closing his eyes. *Not a great start. Kyaté, please, let this get better.*

He returned to Wind-Drummer and rummaged through the saddlebag, taking out two bottles of perfume, a bracelet, and a necklace. He brought the gifts into the house.

The dwelling was humble; he'd forgotten just how humble in the years he'd been gone. Ctzo studied the mostly bare walls and simple yet snug décor.

"You took down the old paintings?"

"Sold." Qeysta sat at the dining room's small wooden table. "You were the one who liked them. And right after you were taken to jail, well, I didn't have a job, so money was a little tight."

"Of course." Ctzo joined her at the table, pulling up a worn seat. "Where do you work now?"

"All those connections of yours," Qeysta said briskly, "and you never bothered to use them to find out what your wife and daughter have been up to?"

Ctzo paled. "I—"

"Not that it's any of your business, but I'm working as a seamstress." Her eyes narrowed. "I've always wondered: how did a drunk inmate become the great General Ctzo Mainaia, hero of the War of Nine Leagues?"

"The last battle of the war... I heard it hit this part of town. Were you and Warrah all right?"

"Don't change the subject." Qeysta studied a small candle on the table. "It was scary at the time, but I suppose we weren't hit that bad. There was a small contingent of Augai soldiers, yelling and dragging any men they could find out of their homes. They were never there to kill anyone, just to wave muskets and swords around and look threatening. Warrah and I were fine."

"I'm glad." Ctzo sighed. "As for your question about how I came to be a general, it was an act of the God Kyaté." Qeysta stared unblinkingly at him, so he went on. "After I was taken to jail, as the war against the Augai dragged on, not enough Questavans volunteered for the army. The Emperor had the jails emptied and each of us conscripted. The troop I was part of moved to Medioca. There, while at the temple..."

"...you found the Mediocans' God." Qeysta sounded unimpressed.

"He... found me. We worked alongside some Mediocans, and they shared with me their faith and the commands and scriptures given by Kyaté to his people. My change in attitude caught the attention of my superiors. Over the course of the war, I was promoted again and again. Early on I captained ships, but I soon moved to commanding land troops. I guess Kyaté had his plans for me. When General Unio fell deathly ill before a vital battle—"

"He recommended you as his replacement." Qeysta shook her head. "How memorable you must have been to your superiors. Are you sure it was your God and not your skill at killing that got you to the top?"

"Without him, I'd have never come up with the strategy that won us the war," Ctzo insisted. "It was a risky and unorthodox one, but it worked. I certainly wouldn't be called a hero if we had failed. Our victory was Kyaté's doing."

"Well, at least you're not arrogant about it."

Ctzo cleared his throat. "I want to do more than just send money. I want... to make amends." His gaze went to Warrah. "To smooth things over, if I can."

Warrah looked away.

Qeysta ran her hands over her skirt. "Fine. There is something you could do for me that might help smooth things over, as you put it. Maybe you could take me to one of those grand parties the Emperor throws?" Her eyes sparkled. "I've always dreamed of seeing the inside of Parliament."

To Ctzo, her sparkling, aqua-green eyes were like the gentle waves of a calm sea. No, they were more beautiful than any sea.

"I would be honoured to have you accompany me," he whispered affectionately. "In fact, the Emperor is throwing a party tomorrow night, and my presence has been specifically requested."

"I want to come, too," Warrah spoke up. "What should I wear?"

Ctzo's gaze remained on Qeysta. "Wear your nicest dress. That silver and pink one will work. And I can have a carriage come and pick you both up."

"We can find our own rides," Qeysta said curtly. "We'll meet you there."

"Yes, very well. I'll meet you outside Parliament's doors."

CHAPTER TWENTY-NINE

"*Y*ou're going to a party at Parliament tomorrow?" Black Night asked, frowning at Ctzo's news. "Sounds stuffy."

Ctzo and his houseguests sat around the dinner table. Chiha had quickly finished her meal and now paced back and forth within the room. Alez stood at attention, ready to receive the slightest cue from his guests or master.

Though the Kamai technically could feed themselves, for much of the meal they accepted bits of food tossed at them by Ctzo. He didn't treat this as childish or odd: for Kamai, bonding with their master in this way was an important aspect of the meal.

"I've been planning on attending since I arrived," Ctzo said. "I received an invitation from the Emperor himself after my quick talk with the Council about Grey Noon's letter and my discoveries."

"I'm guessing none of us are invited," Black Night said. "Not that we'd want to. Who wants to hang out with a bunch of politicians?"

Chiha stuck her long, lizard-like nose into the air and twisted her hips. "I am going to the party. I am the daughter of a chief."

"She's right," Ctzo said. "The Emperor himself asked that she come. He wants to meet her."

"Of course," Black Night mumbled, folding in his wings. "It will boost her already mega-sized ego."

"And what do we do?" Oti pouted.

Ctzo's eyes widened upon hearing his voice. "Well, your Questavan has improved quickly!"

Blinking, Oti simply stared at him, saying nothing.

"Right." Ctzo addressed the group as a whole. "You may continue to explore. Do as you please. There's plenty to see in Questava. Make the most of your time here before we leave. Buy anything you want for the trip…"

Katia, perched upon a chair, nibbled quietly and tried to follow the conversation as best she could. She ran her hand along the chair's cushioned seat, noting the smooth texture. Everything in this city seemed so alien.

She yawned, suddenly realizing just how worn out she felt from their day of exploring. She looked over at Oti, smiling as she noticed for the first time that he spent more time fingering and playing with his food than eating it.

I'm glad he's here, she thought. Back in the tribe, Oti had been self-absorbed and a bit of a nuisance. But she'd come to enjoy his company. It was nice to have someone familiar, someone from a culture she knew well, to share her thoughts and experiences.

Speaking of the tribe, she wondered when she'd have the chance to reunite with them. Sina had believed that Katia needed to go into the world of the Scavgans, and Katia felt like she'd done that in coming to Questava.

Even if I don't need to go back to my old tribe, doesn't Oti need to be returned with his family?

Chiha had told Katia that Captain Ctzo planned on going back to the Marsh Isles. Perhaps from there the Athai could help her and Oti get to Aziasha.

After finishing his meal, Black Night left his spot at the table. Stretching his wings to their full length, he sighed. "Bit cramped in here. Oh well. At least it's not as bad as belowdecks on the ship."

"Keeping up your exercise routine will probably be a good idea," Ctzo said with a nod.

Black Night grinned. "I'll have more energy and time to put into exercise now that you'll be going easier on me."

Ctzo frowned. "Going easier on you?"

"Yeah. You know, since I'm a returning crewmember, you won't be expecting me to work as hard, and you won't be giving me as many rules to follow as you did before, right? I mean, I've already been through the hard part. No more practice and training sessions..."

"The rules aboard my ships do not change the longer you're aboard," Ctzo said. "As for practice sessions, it's important you stay fresh and ready for action."

"Aw, come on." Black Night shook his head. "Are you serious?"

"Yes."

Black Night allowed a small pause. "Think about it. Do you know how much time I spent practicing fighting and running the cannons? If I didn't have to do those things, it would free up a lot of time for other things."

"Like what?"

"Well, maybe I could help out around the ship more."

"Everyone has a four-hour watch," the captain said. "That's your time to help out around the ship. If you want more, you're free to give more. But remember, it's a warship, and knowing how to fight is part of your job."

Silence hung in the air.

Finally, Black Night spoke. "You know what? I've been thinking… maybe I'd be better off in someone else's employ."

"I'm sorry you feel that way."

"You don't have to be sorry. It's just, I know the basics of being a sailor now. Maybe it's time for a change of scenery."

Ctzo nodded. "Fair enough. I wish you well."

Black Night walked towards the stairs. "I'll get my stuff."

"Your stuff?" Ctzo raised an eyebrow. "You can stay as long as you need. Or at least, until I depart."

"That's fine. I'm already packed." Black Night went up to his room and returned a short time later with a large bag slung over his shoulder. "Thanks for letting me stay for a while."

"You're welcome." Ctzo appeared unsure how to react. "Perhaps we'll meet again someday."

"I look forward to it." Black Night waved to the others. "Goodbye all! It's been nice knowing you!" He patted Oti's head affectionately. "Stay safe, friend."

"What's going on?" Katia asked, sensing the tension in the room. She still didn't understand enough of the language to get what was happening.

"Black Night is leaving," Chiha explained. "He will not be sailing with us."

"Leaving?" Oti watched as Black Night opened the door to the house and stepped out. "Wait!"

The Darian rushed towards the door.

"Oti!" Katia called, following him.

Oti turned, frowning at her. "What?"

"Are you asking him why he's leaving?"

"No. I'm going with him."

Katia's ears folded back. "What?"

"I'm going wherever he goes," Oti stated firmly.

"But what about going back to Aziasha? What about trying to find and rejoin your tribe?"

He shrugged. "I never fit in with them anyway. Besides, do you really think we'll ever find the tribe again? They're nomads. They could be anywhere in Aziasha."

"I thought you... never mind." Katia wished to say that she'd thought he'd finally come to think of her as family. That he'd want to stay with her. She must have misunderstood. "I can't stop you."

"Nope, you can't."

"I wish you well."

Oti nodded, then rushed off to follow Black Night through the door.

Katia watched him go, then turned and slunk off towards her room, attempting to hold back the flow of tears that threatened to fill her eyes.

Her mind returned to a moment that seemed to have happened so long ago. Black Night had held her and comforted her when she was a stranger aboard the *Diversity*. It had meant so much to her to be welcomed by the then-unfamiliar creature. And Oti had helped her relax at the presence of the two Kamai, beings she'd once feared but now felt safe around.

Why does every good friendship have to end? she asked herself. *Sina is gone, far off in Aziasha. Anveil...*

No, she wouldn't think about him. Ever since the encounter with that Blackblood who served Grey Noon, she refused to think about her husband. Because she knew. She wasn't sure how she knew, but her instinct persuaded her: that Blackblood, that creature, had once been Anveil. And if that's what Anveil had become, she was better off not accepting that it was him. She was better off forgetting and leaving the memory of her beloved Anveil behind.

She stopped in her path, no longer able to hold back the sobs. She pressed her face into her arm and wept.

CHAPTER THIRTY

*L*ym watched as the small island with simple shacks built upon it drew closer. Above him flew black sails, rippling in the wind.

Ever since that Sébérus creature had returned to Atzinus's abandoned fortress, Lym's life had changed at a rapid rate. Sébérus had told all the Blackbloods that they were now free, no longer anyone's slaves. But Sébérus had announced big plans for his race, and if they wanted to be a part of it they could stick around.

Lym hadn't even thought to say no. Not until recently.

But as the ship pulled up next to the island and the anchor was dropped, he decided this was where he wanted to be.

Grey Noon's pirates had tracked down this island, one full of captured Blackbloods. At this very moment, an island guard, dressed in protective gear and carrying a musket, approached the ship. He was shot down quickly, and other guards rushed to take his place. But even as one of the Blackblood ships came into view, cannons firing, Lym knew the battle would end quickly.

Grey Noon had one goal, and he'd brought aboard Blackbloods like him to help with that goal: to free the Blackblood slaves and convince them to return peaceably to Atzinus's old fortress.

From there, they'd be asked—not forced, but asked—to join their building army.

And I doubt many will say no, Lym thought, the sounds of battle echoing in his ears.

Sébérus briefly looked over the map of Questava once more. By his side was August, a Scavgan who was familiar with the capital city.

"So this paved stairway is really the only way of carrying wares up into the city?" Sébérus asked, pointing to the map.

August nodded. "Yes. The harbour is bordered by a cliff which has a wooden walkway along it. The cliff overlooks the beach, and the walkway leads down to the docks. But it's too narrow and crowded to carry crates up it. The stairway is carved into the cliff, sloping down to the beach."

As Sébérus and August discussed the layout of the city, Kaio sat nearby, watching them quietly.

"That'll be all," Sébérus said at last. "August, would you please have Jair sent in? I need to speak with him."

"I'm not your servant," August muttered. At Sébérus's annoyed look, he added calmly, "Why not? He'll be here in a moment."

August left to carry out his task.

Kaio's eyes remained on his leader. "Jair… he's the Scavgan Blackblood who talks funny, right?"

Sébérus gave a slow nod. "My old master Atzinus thought Jair was a lunatic."

"Do you think he's a lunatic?"

"Yes." Sébérus's gaze rested on the map even as he spoke to Kaio. "But he's a useful lunatic. He's not as good as my old master at working with blackwaters, but he's better than anyone else in the world. Between his experience and my aid, we can bring something never previously imagined to our fellow Blackbloods: hope."

"And the war that Grey Noon promises…"

Sébérus tensed. "Wasn't my idea, remember?"

Looking at his leader through soft, surprised eyes, Kaio faltered, "B—but don't you think it'll make the world a better place for us?"

Sighing deeply, Sébérus turned from the map. "At the end of the day, friend, Blackbloodism is an illness. I can ease our suffering, with help from Jair. But I cannot cure us. No one can. At least… not yet." He closed his eyes. "Maybe not ever."

They were suddenly interrupted by Jair's entry into the room.

"Good morning, dear captor!" Jair said in a cheery voice.

Sébérus's ear went back. "What?" he snapped.

"Don't be so grouchy." Jair harrumphed. "I actually don't mind being your captive, in case my tone did not convey—"

"What have you gotten done? How is the rehab going?"

After a moment of hesitation, Jair said slowly, "Well, um, I've been assessing the different Blackbloods…"

"Have you made any headway on understanding Atzinus's notes?"

"Hmmm? Headway? Why, a decent amount, yes." Jair left it at that.

"And?"

"And…" Jair bowed his head. "Forgive me. I've been out of sorts lately. If I may be completely frank, I've been self-reflecting."

"Self-reflecting?" Sébérus inwardly groaned. Was he always this absent-minded? "And where have your self-reflections led you?"

Jair's voice trembled. "I know I'm not sane. I was in denial, but I know it now. And… it scares me."

Sébérus wasn't sure how to take this. He wasn't prepared to deal with this creature's emotions. "Sane or not, you are intelligent. And your intellect is what I need."

"What if… I'm not intelligent?" Jair asked mournfully. "Not anymore?"

"That's ridiculous. If you could make yourself into a coherent, capable Blackblood—"

"Coherent and capable, but insane."

"Whatever." Sébérus hissed. "You're an improvement on most of the Blackbloods out there. I'm not looking for perfection. I'm looking for…" He sighed. "I'm looking for more than moving and breathing and being able to complete basic tasks. I'm looking for Blackbloods to engage, to question, to create, to understand, to learn, to dream… to love." A picture of Katia flashed through his mind unbidden. "I'm looking to live again."

"For yourself?" Jair asked softly. "Or for them?"

"For all of us."

"Us?"

"You're a Blackblood."

"True." Jair chuckled. "I suppose I don't imagine myself to have flown to your heights, dear Sébérus. You are an exceptional being."

"No," Sébérus replied grouchily, imagining Grey Noon's shadow hanging over him. "I'm just another ill slave attempting to make the most of his life."

"Then I suppose we share the same boat."

August re-entered the room. "Blackblood, Grey Noon would like an update on your plans."

Sébérus frowned. "He's back already from retrieving Blackbloods? He's coming here then?"

"Why should the priest have to come to you?" August asked. "He's in the top room of the main tower. Go meet him there."

With that, August exited the captain's quarters.

"Of course. Kaio, follow me. And you," he said, turning to Jair, "return to your work in the laboratory."

Jair bowed respectfully. "Right away." He left the room without another word.

Sébérus sighed. *A useful lunatic. That's all I need Jair to be. I don't need him to be an encouragement. I don't need him to be confident.*

He felt both annoyed at Jair's unexpected respect for him, and a bit ashamed of how he'd spoken about Jair to Kaio earlier. But why should he be ashamed? Jair was just a tool. An admittedly broken one at that.

And what are you? a voice inside him countered. *Are you something greater than Atzinus's final pet project? Greater than the disease that defines you?*

He pushed the questions away. There was nothing to be done about them now. Grey Noon expected a progress report, so Sébérus headed off to deliver one.

CHAPTER THIRTY-ONE

Zan was seated in his family's spacious tea room when Tyzak finally came down from his guest room to visit.

"Did you sleep in or were you just enjoying the room?" Zan asked. He blew on the cup of tea held in his hand.

"Yes and yes," Tyzak said with a grin. "My, what a wonderful home you have. Hmmm… where do I find breakfast?"

"I'll fetch it, sir," said one of the waiting servants.

Tyzak looked around, his gaze pausing on each of the other servants and then resting on Zan's mother. "Good morning, Zelda!"

"You may call me ma'am," she said hastily. "Zan, would you like anything else? I can get you some more food, or perhaps get a warm bubble bath started for you. Poor thing, you look like you've weathered a storm!"

"A few." Zan chuckled, then straightened his face at Zelda's worried look. "Don't worry, I am well, Mother."

Vasitan soon joined them.

"Good morning, sir!" Tyzak said cheerily. He then turned his attention to Zan. "What are the chances I could have a bubble bath? I mean, I've weathered a few storms myself."

Zan just shook his head and turned towards one of the servants.

"It shall be done," the servant said quickly, just as another servant entered with a platter of food for Tyzak.

Tyzak settled down into a well-cushioned chair. "Looks delicious! My gratitude to you all!"

After he'd eaten a few bites, Tyzak turned towards Hana. He frowned, watching her closely. "You're Mediocan?"

She looked around. "You're asking me?"

"Yes." Tyzak then asked, in Mediocan, "Do you and I not share the same heritage?"

Blushing, Hana answered slowly: "My mother is Questavan, but I'm Mediocan on my father's side. Apologies. I don't speak Mediocan well."

While this was going on, Zan took another sip of his tea, watching the two converse.

"You're half-Mediocan then," Tyzak said, switching back to Questavan. "What's your father's story? How'd you two come to Questava?"

"It's... not a very good story, sir." She looked from Zelda to Vasitan. Neither seemed prepared to interrupt.

Tyzak smiled. "That's for me to decide! Do tell!"

"Well... things didn't work out with my parents." Her voice trembled. "My mother was—is—very powerful. She and my father had a bad fight, and she had him thrown in prison. He... he died there."

"Oh," Tyzak said meekly. "That is very sad. I'm sorry. But surely there's a happy ending to this story?"

Her gaze briefly went to Zan before returning to Tyzak. "My mother's father is very, very powerful. Too powerful to argue with.

So when they had me disowned... I suppose there is a happy part." She bowed. "I serve my masters here, and that is good enough."

"Why not return to Medioca?" Tyzak asked.

"People would make a big deal about it," Hana said. "I... I don't want to start an uproar. My family there wouldn't understand..." She sighed. "Never mind. That doesn't make any sense, does it?"

Tyzak narrowed his eyes. "Hana? Would your father's name happen to be Avad?"

Hana swallowed, nodding.

"I don't think you've ever told me about your parents before," Zan remarked.

"Excuse me," Hana said as she backed out of the room. "I forgot to... I have work to do in the stables. Beg your pardon."

She departed hastily.

"I need some air," Tyzak muttered. He stood and left through a different doorway.

Turning to Zelda, Vasitan shook his head. "I suppose in some cultures people are very friendly with their servants."

"Oh, there's no harm in it," Zelda said. "Is there?"

Zan frowned, eying the door from which his friend had departed. What had just happened?

Some time later, Zan found Tyzak on a balcony off the second floor of the house. "I was wondering where you'd gone off to."

Tyzak acknowledged him with a small nod. "Well, you found me."

"What was that about? I don't think I've ever seen you leave a conversation like that. And I definitely haven't seen you this angry before."

"Oh, it's nothing." But Tyzak's tone was unconvincing.

"Does our use of servants make you uncomfortable?"

"Nothing of the sort. I'm just thinking of a sad tale, one you clearly haven't been told."

"What tale?" Zan asked.

"It's not worth your time, I'm sure."

"Come on," Zan pressed. "I thought you loved telling tales."

Tyzak stared out over the balcony at the bright sky. "It's not a story our people are very fond of."

"Tell me."

Sighing, Tyzak closed his eyes. His fists gripped the railing. "Do you remember King Avad?"

"The Mediocan king?" Zan said. "He married the Emperor's daughter, Princess Nela." He paused, waiting for Tyzak to speak. When his friend said nothing, Zan continued. "But King Avad had an affair."

"There was no affair," Tyzak snapped. "Your princess married our king and had a daughter with him. Then she betrayed Avad and had him tossed into a Questavan prison, never to be seen or heard from again. Which, we Mediocans suspect, was the Emperor's plan all along. And their daughter, who would have been our princess? Declared illegitimate and thrown out on the streets like garbage."

Zan bristled. "Well, whether or not you're right, what does that have to do with Hana?"

"You really don't see it, do you? Hana *is* the princess."

Frowning, Zan mused this over. Then his face broke into a grin. "You're either bluffing or crazy! There's no way our servant girl is a Mediocan princess."

"Ask her. Better yet, ask your sweet mother how you came to hire Hana."

Setting his shoulders, Zan turned and walked away. "Be like that. I'll ask my mother if your story is true. But if it isn't, you owe me. I'll invent an appropriate punishment."

"Stop right there!" Tyzak barked.

Zan halted in his tracks. "Yes?"

"If I'm right," Tyzak said, clenching his fists, "then *you* owe *me* something."

"Fair enough. What would you have me do?"

"You take both me and Hana to the celebration at Parliament tonight."

Zan sighed. "I told you—"

"You can make it happen." Tyzak crossed his arms. "I know you're allowed two guests. There's nothing stopping you."

"There's *someone* stopping me," Zan corrected. "My father."

"You're an adult, and you can't take whomever you wish to the party?"

Chuckling, Zan considered his friend's point. "You don't know my father! Either way, *if* you're right about Hana being a princess, which I still doubt, I'll do what I can to get you and Hana into the party."

Zan returned to the eastern living room to find both his parents and a scattering of servants, though Hana wasn't among them.

"Mother, it's been a while since I visited the fish pool," he said, approaching her. "Would you accompany me there?"

She stood quickly, exchanging a look with Vasitan. Vasitan said nothing.

"I would love to," she finally said.

Zan and Zelda walked together to the room holding a pool of colourful fish. Zan could still recall the day during his childhood when his father had bought him the pets. He smiled as he watched them swimming around.

"I'm sure those fish will live to be a hundred," his mother said as the two settled down on a bench beside the pond.

"Mother, I have... an unusual question."

"Yes?"

"Is our servant girl Hana... is she a princess?" When Zelda didn't immediately answer, he explained. "Tyzak has gotten it in his head that Hana is the daughter of Princess Nela, from her marriage to King Avad. It's silly, but..."

"I didn't think the Mediocans recognized her as a princess anymore. I know Questava doesn't." Zelda shook her head. "Politics was always your father's business. I could never make sense of it."

Zan frowned. "Wait, are you saying... he's right?"

"Hmmm? All I said is I don't think she's recognized as royalty anymore, not since Princess Nela disowned her."

His mouth dropped. "Hana *is* the princess's daughter?! Then how did she come to be our servant?"

Zelda stared out into space, thinking back. "Well, when she was disowned, Hana was still a child, but old enough for work. She went to begging on the streets. It seemed such a waste, someone who understood fine culture begging for handouts from passersby. I asked her why she didn't work for her living, and she said no one would hire her. So I said, 'That's enough of that. You're working for me now.' I took her home, and she proved very loyal and caught on to her responsibilities well." She paused. "I suppose, in a sense, we raised her. Don't you recall having her around while you were a child?"

Zan remembered that he'd been rather snobbish as a boy and hadn't paid much attention to his servants, except when he wanted something.

"I suppose I forgot that. Nobody questioned you taking her in as a servant?"

"Over the years, I suppose people just forgot about the whole thing." Zelda smirked. "Princess Nela has had more than one dramatic relationship. Have you heard that she's engaged again?"

Zan shook his head. "Why didn't you ever tell me about Hana's history before?"

Zelda appeared confused by the question. "Since when do I explain how we came to hire any of our servants?"

He stared down at the fish for a moment. "Well," he muttered, more to himself than to his mother, "I guess that means I owe Tyzak after all."

Zan heard Hana humming to herself as he approached. She stood over a washbasin in the stable, her back turned to him, scrubbing something with a rag. For a few moments he simply watched her, hands held behind his back, trying to decide what to say.

She turned unexpectedly, caught his gaze, and gasped. "Oh, master! I'm sorry, I didn't hear you come in." She dropped the item back in the basin and bowed. "What can I do for you?"

Finding himself wordless, Zan looked her over for an awkward moment.

She doesn't look like a princess, he thought. His mind turned to Chiha and her confident presence. *Hana just doesn't have that same air of royalty.*

He looked into her eyes and noticed her worried expression. He cleared his throat. "No, I don't need anything."

He allowed another silent moment to go by.

"Master?" she asked. Zan opened his mouth to speak, but Hana missed it and burst out, "I'm very, very glad you've returned. It's such a relief to see you alive and healthy." She bit her tongue, blushing. "Ahem... may I ask how your journeys went?"

Funny, Zan realized. *She's the first person to ask me that.*

Neither his mother nor father had even hinted at wanting to know more about his adventures. Perhaps they were just too focused on his return to care.

"Actually, it would be nice to talk about my time aboard Ctzo's fleet," Zan said, his tense posture relaxing.

Hana nodded enthusiastically, taking a seat on the floor. When Zan made a move to do the same, she quickly got up.

"Oh no, master, I will get you a chair."

Zan laughed. "Hana, I've been eating stale biscuits and sleeping on an old, smelly hammock for months. Not to mention all the time I spent trekking through the jungle, sleeping on bare earth, and drinking next to nothing. I can handle a few minutes on the floor."

She looked him over, squinting, seeming to analyze him. "I would feel bad making my master sit on the floor."

"All right," Zan relented. "Pull up two chairs then. It'd be awkward having you sit beneath me while I'm trying to carry on a conversation."

Hana nodded and departed. It was several minutes before she returned with two chairs. She waited until Zan was comfortably seated before easing into her own chair.

"Well," Zan said, grinning as he cocked his head. "Where to begin…"

Zan didn't sense the hours passing as he conversed with Hana, telling her about his time at sea and in Aziasha. His clue that he'd been talking with her a long while came when his mother suddenly entered the stable and gasped.

"Hana!" She sounded angry. "Why didn't you help with preparing lunch?"

Hana bolted to her feet, stammering, while Zan waved his hand dismissively. "Mother, she was entertaining me."

His mother placed her hands on her hips. "You could have warned us. The other servants thought you must be feeling unwell, Hana."

"I'm—"

Zan cut off Hana's apology. "Do I need to warn you before I busy any of our servants, Mother?"

The two locked gazes. Zan knew from the look in his mother's eyes that she was thinking about their earlier conversation.

Finally, she nodded. "Lunch is ready, Zan. Please come and eat. It's been so long since we've had you here. I was afraid your father and I would be eating alone forever."

Zan got up and wrapped his arms around his mother. "I know. But I'm back."

Her eyes widened, then filled with tears. She patted his head affectionately and wiped away an escaped tear with the back of her hand. "Yes. You're here."

"And looking forward to lunch." Zan turned back to Hana. "Coming?"

She nodded.

"Of course, she will eat when the other servants eat," Zelda said as though he'd forgotten how things worked around here. "After our family has finished."

"I'm aware, Mother. I haven't been gone *that* long."

Though he'd had lunch with his family thousands of times, Zan's many months away from home left him unprepared for the feast presented in his honour. The table was so large that the four seated around it—Zan, his parents, and Tyzak—each had a gracious amount of space between them. Each also had a servant standing behind them, ready to bring new napkins, refill drinks, replace plates, and pass dishes brimming with rich delights.

"I've never seen so many kinds of meat on one table," Tyzak noted, keeping his servant busy passing each and every item of food and drink available. "It's an honour that you would share this bounty with me, my kind hosts."

"Think nothing of it," Zelda replied politely. "Please, eat as much as you like." She eyed her son with some concern. "Not hungry, Zan?"

"I suppose that's it." Zan passed her a warm smile. "It's been so long since I've eaten this well that I feel as though my stomach has shrunk!"

"Well, I'm not having any difficulties," Tyzak said as he savoured another mouthful. "Good servant, do fetch me another one of those cakes."

Zan continued, keeping his tone calm. "I realize I just returned, but I was considering going to the party this evening at Parliament."

Vasitan exchanged a look with his wife. "The party had slipped my mind. I'm sure all your old companions will be cheered greatly by seeing you there, alive and well. Feel free to go for as long as you like."

"I'm glad you're comfortable with it, Father," Zan said. "It also crossed my mind to bring… Hana… with me."

"Hana?"

"Our servant girl."

"Oh, yes." Vasitan nodded. "Of course, take her with you."

Zan frowned, raising an eyebrow. "You... you don't have a problem with me taking her?"

"Why would I have a problem with you taking your servant to the party?" Vasitan appeared puzzled. "I'm guessing that eye gives you trouble now and again. It'd make sense to have a servant tending to your needs."

Zan looked over to Tyzak, who merely shrugged.

"Dear, will you be attending the party?" Zelda said to her husband.

"I wasn't planning on it, my love."

Zelda turned her smile on him. "Well, it would be good for Zan to have a chance to reconnect with his friends on his own."

"I'll be bringing Tyzak as well," Zan pointed out.

"Your friend will be welcome, of course," Vasitan said warmly. "And I'm sure he wouldn't mind borrowing some of your old clothes to wear. It'll make you feel like a king, won't it, Tyzak?"

Tyzak grinned widely. "Oh, yes. He could share his clothes. And jewellery." He turned his eager gaze towards Zan. "I'm sure you have some old jewellery you wouldn't mind me borrowing, just for tonight?"

Zan rolled his eye. "Yes, of course."

Zelda got up from the table, then leaned over to whisper in her son's ear, "I will ensure Hana is properly attired. You just deal with your friend."

Zan was surprised by the comment, but his mother departed the room before he could ask her about it.

Tyzak posed in front of a large mirror, arching his hips slightly. "What do you think? Too much?"

"The posture is too much," Zan muttered. "Stand straight. Like you're important."

Tyzak harrumphed. "If I'm going to look impressive, I'm going to flaunt it."

"Then you can get back into your own clothes."

"Fine, fine." Tyzak examined himself again. "No, this is too much. I need something a tad simpler." He went to Zan's closet and browsed through it. "Why aren't there servants to help you?"

"To help me get dressed? I'm old enough to dress myself, thank you. Besides, they're right outside the door if I need them for anything."

"Well, I would like to have servants helping me pick out an outfit."

"I pick out my own outfits," Zan said. "Decide what robes to wear after you pick your jewellery. You'll want something that matches."

"Of course!" Tyzak leaned over Zan's desk, nearly drooling as he examined the assortment of necklaces, earrings, bracelets, and rings laid upon it. "You have good taste, my friend. Now, where to start…"

"We don't have all night." Zan picked out a few pieces and put them on. "How's this?"

"Marvellous! You look splendid! Now, help me pick something…"

But Zan's mind wandered to Hana and his mother. He knew they were getting ready together, but he didn't know what exactly they were doing. How did Mother plan to dress Hana?

Zan returned to the present, catching sight of Tyzak's hand waving before his eye.

"You zoned out. Thoughts?" Tyzak asked.

"I was just wondering about Hana, and what she'll be wearing."

"Ah." A broad smirk coated Tyzak's face and his eyes sparkled. "Well, you can think about that more in a moment. First, how do I look?"

Zan and Tyzak met Hana and Zelda in the large entryway of the mansion. Zan's mouth fell open when he saw how she looked.

"Oh, Hana!"

Hana blushed intensely. "Is it bad?"

"Nonsense," Zelda said. "You look wonderful."

"Y—yes."

Zan looked Hana over, realizing that his mother hadn't held back. Hana was dressed beautifully in white lace and shining gems. She still seemed a little nervous and hesitant, as always, but seeing her in something other than her dark grey servants robes did make her look more royal.

"You look lovely, Hana. Thank you, Mother."

Zelda allowed a half-smile, though she seemed unsure about the situation.

"Enjoy yourselves, you three." She turned to Hana. "Be on your best behaviour." She then addressed her son playfully. "You too, young man."

Zan pointed to Tyzak. "He's the only one you need to worry about, Mother."

"Oh, I will behave." Tyzak bowed at the waist and took Zelda's hand, kissing it. "You have a wonderful evening, ma'am."

Zelda frowned. "I see what you mean, Zan." She then gave her son a hug. "I know you were never really a fan of me touching you all the time, but—"

"The newness hasn't worn off yet," Zan said, patting her on the back. "I'm still too glad to be back to find it annoying."

"Good. Now, the servants are readying the carriage. You'd best get outside before your Father sees Hana dressed like a family member!"

Hana nodded quickly. "Thank you, my mistress. I'm most flattered that you'd allow me to wear this tonight."

Zelda's gaze remained on Zan. "Yes. Just... be on your best behaviour, all right?"

Zan wasn't sure what his mother meant. "I'm not planning on staying out long. We'll be back in a few hours."

Tyzak's face fell. "Aw. Well, I'll enjoy the night while it lasts. Come now, Zan! I'm looking forward to a ride in a fancy carriage!"

Zan's attention had turned to Hana, who was fiddling with the folds of her dress.

"You look lovely," he assured her. He offered his hand. "Come."

CHAPTER THIRTY-TWO

Stepping into Parliament's first corridor, Ctzo heard Qeysta take in a sharp gasp.

"It's… huge!" she breathed.

Ctzo took a moment to appreciate the vaulted ceiling and gemstone-inlaid floor. "This is where the Emperor holds his parties. We can spend some time here together, until I'm summoned into the Emperor's presence. He's usually at the far end of the hall, surrounded by his attendants."

"So we can wander?" Warrah said hopefully.

"If you wish," Ctzo said. "Though it would be nice to have some time…"

Warrah briskly walked off, acting as though she hadn't heard him.

He sighed and turned to Qeysta, standing by his side. "You look lovely."

"I'm underdressed," she said, her tone sharp. "You still find new ways to embarrass me."

Ctzo was taken aback. "To me, you look perfect. Isn't that all that matters?"

She frowned. "Not perfect enough to stick around for."

"Please, Qeysta, I'm trying. I know I've made a mess of things." He sighed. "I just want a second chance to earn your affection."

Tyzak and Zan stepped into the brightly lit halls of Parliament and gasped. Captain Ctzo stood not twenty paces away, a woman in a simple dress by his side. Ignoring all other partiers, the duo made a beeline for their old captain. Hana followed behind.

"Captain!" Zan called.

Ctzo looked up, his wide eyes betraying shock. A small smile slipped onto his lips. "Zan? It's good to see you again."

Zan returned the smile. "It's good to see you, too!" He looked at the woman by his captain's side. "Who is this?"

Ctzo turned to the woman, opening and closing his mouth. "Uh… this is Qeysta. My wife."

Zan's jaw dropped. "I didn't know you were married! Welcome, Qeysta."

"Excuse me," Qeysta muttered, pushing away Ctzo's arm. "I need a drink."

With that, she walked off. Ctzo sighed deeply, watching her go.

"What was that?" Zan asked.

The captain shrugged. "How should I know? Women can be impossible sometimes." He shook his head. "I'm sorry, Zan. How have you been?" He looked over Zan's shoulder. "Tyzak! And who's your friend?"

Tyzak smiled warmly at Ctzo, then turned to Hana.

She blushed, bowing meekly. "Hana. I'm Zan's servant girl."

Tyzak rolled his eyes. "Zan, correct her."

"Huh?" Zan asked.

"Tonight," Tyzak said, bowing towards Hana, "you are Medioca's princess."

Hana shook her head violently. "I, uh... I need a drink, too." She rushed off.

"You're right, Captain." Tyzak put his hands on his hips. "Women are impossible sometimes."

Zan chuckled. "And to think, Tyzak, your father handles two of them!"

"*Handles* might be stretching it. Well, Captain, what's new with you?"

"I'm here for an audience with the Emperor. I gave my report to the Council, along with the letter from Grey Noon and his Blackblood ally. They requested I speak directly with him."

Tyzak whistled. "Impressive! Will this be your first face-to-face encounter with the Emperor?"

"No," Ctzo said. "Remember, I did win a war for him."

"Lucky you." Tyzak looked around, suddenly realizing that Zan had disappeared. "Where'd he go?"

"I believe he went after the young lady you two brought. Hana, was it?"

"Did he?" Tyzak smirked. "Good on him! I suppose I'll allow them to have their own time together."

"Hana?" Zan called.

Hana stood by a table overflowing with enticing appetizers. Not feeling quite peckish enough to eat, she admired the fancy arrangements without touching anything.

When Zan came up to her side, she took a deep breath, straightened, and gave him a fake, well-practiced smile. "Yes, master?"

"What's wrong? Why'd you leave us?"

"No reason, sir. I simply assumed you'd wish for time alone with your friends."

"Stop," Zan said sternly.

Hana's pulse quickened. "Stop what?"

"You're not fooling me. You're upset. Why?"

Staring at Zan, Hana couldn't help but admire his costly robe. He looked very handsome in that.

Finally, she whispered, "Do you really think I'm a princess?"

Zan frowned. "I thought it was an established fact."

"Why did you never say anything about it before?"

"I didn't know about it. Tyzak just enlightened me."

"And?"

"And what?" Zan seemed confused. "What do you want to know?"

Whether you think of me as a princess, she thought. *Isn't that what I asked?*

Hana couldn't recall what exactly her query had been, so she decided to change the topic. "I have a question that's been bothering me."

"Name it," Zan said.

"Joining Ctzo's crew: why did you do it?"

Zan's eye turned down to the floor, and the movement drew her attention to his eyepatch. Sadness washed over her as she realized he had lost something to that journey. What other scars did he carry from his choice? She half-expected him to admit that he regretted sailing with Ctzo, to rage against the world for his loss.

Instead, as his eye met hers once more, he smiled. "You know, someone asked me that question not long after I joined the crew. I don't remember what answer I gave, nor what answer I gave Ctzo when he asked. But after trekking through Aziasha, and after our failure against Grey Noon, I believe I've come to know myself better than I ever have before. I think my real reason for going was... to know that I was more. More than the pampered son of a Council representative. More than a man who'd been made arrogant by his Questavan heritage. More than the sum of my parts, I guess."

Hana considered this answer. "What does 'more' mean? What does it look like?"

"First, it means knowing that I really am a man. That I'm strong. That I don't need to be pampered, to be babied. That I can handle the pains and labour of ordinary folk, and pull through when life gets tough. After that..." His eye briefly wandered. "After that, I wanted to know that I could help. Once I knew I wasn't helpless, I wanted to help others. Oddly, though, that's when I learned that not being helpless doesn't mean never needing or accepting help. On the journey across Aziasha, I needed to rely on Katia and Ian."

He touched his eyepatch.

"To me, the loss of this eye is a physical reminder of the humility I've learned," he continued. "I discovered that I don't always know the way forward. Sometimes I need others to guide me." The smile on his lips grew. "It's funny. I left Questava thinking I was going out to find a way to solve people's problems for them. Instead I learned that I need them, that others have something to offer me. Who would have thought the rich kid could benefit from the strengths of others? I've discovered what real friendship, real trust, true interdependence is." His smile relaxed. "Sorry, I guess that's a rather long answer to a simple question."

Her eyes glowing with amazement, Hana stared at him as though seeing him for the first time. "You've... grown."

Zan stared back at her, saying nothing.

Shifting her feet, she continued. "What will you do now?"

"That's the hard part," Zan said with a short sigh. "I only thought as far as getting back home and waiting out my father's anger. And he doesn't appear to be as angry as I expected. How about you?"

Hana frowned. "Pardon?"

"Do you really plan on being a servant your whole life?"

"I... I don't really have another option." Hana studied the lavish décor of the room, the elegant, pale grey clothing of the guests. She'd often thought about the strange twist of her fate. Born a princess but lowered to a servant's position, she was still surrounded by the powerful and well-to-do.

She almost jumped as the sound of music floated in from a nearby room.

"Ah," Zan said, turning towards the melody. "They've opened the dance hall."

A warm feeling engulfed Hana's hand she looked down to find Zan holding it. He gently pulled her, guiding her towards a wide open doorway. As he did, the music grew clearer, and at last they entered a circular room filled with the light of golden candles standing upon candelabras. Musicians played off to one side while dancers glided over a smooth silver floor.

Zan gently placed his hand on her waist and began leading her in a dance. Awkwardly, Hana attempted to keep in pace with him. It had been a while since she'd danced. Zan soon noticed this and slowed the dance to a crawl. Meanwhile, Hana's gaze wandered the room, never resting on him for more than a few seconds.

Finally, Zan sighed. "So neither of us really has an answer."

"To what?" Her gaze met his.

"What our plans are for the future."

"I know my plan. Continue to be your servant." She paused. "You don't have anything in mind?"

"I want to help people. Make a difference in how the high-class act towards those they see as beneath them. You've been on the receiving end of our mistreatment. What do you think needs to be done?"

"Zan, I don't think about the past," Hana said firmly. "I don't want my feelings about the past to hold me back from reaching to the future."

"The future that's exactly the same as today?"

"Well… yes." Hana frowned. "Fine. The future that will be exactly the same as today. Except not *today* today, because today has been unusual. I'm dancing with one of my masters while wearing the dress of another."

"Maybe it's just Ctzo's influence," Zan said thoughtfully, "but it seems to me that we should try to make tomorrow better than today."

"Sounds like work," Hana said flatly.

"It probably will be."

"Where will you start?"

"I think the Mediocans would be happy to have their princess back."

Hana shook her head. "Do you really think that would make the world a better place?"

"It would certainly improve our relationships with them."

"Maybe." She sighed. "Some people just can't let past wounds go."

"Why don't you return to Medioca?" Zan asked. "It seems like you would be better off there."

"First, it's not a 'return' if you've never lived there," Hana said. "I grew up here in Questava. This is what I know. And I've heard some unwelcoming stories about the nationalist rebels in Medioca. I don't trust them not to trick, manipulate, or even force me to further their goals, their way."

"Do you trust me?"

Hana stared into his eye. "Yes."

"Hana, I'm more than old enough to marry and start a family. If I married a woman from below my class, it would raise her up, and it would say to the world that I'm not half-hearted in my commitment to considering the welfare of the lower class. Besides, to be honest, the women of my class bother me. They all come across as money-grabbers and—"

"Where are you going with this?" Hana interrupted.

Zan stared at her.

I already know where you're going with this, she thought. But she wanted to hear him say it. "Well?"

"Well, what if... *we* got married?"

Her heart skipped a beat. "I don't know. There'd be a lot of complications to work out. Your father wouldn't be impressed. I'm not sure about your mother, either."

"As far as I'm concerned, you're already part of the family. Why not make it official?"

"That's very kind of you." Hana forced her voice to remain flat. "I suppose... I could consider it."

"Consider it then."

Hana tried to keep her feelings bottled up, but she couldn't take it. Before any words could leave her mouth, though, a sigh escaped his lips.

"You're... beautiful," he exclaimed.

The two stared awkwardly at each other, blushing. Then their smiles returned, larger and brighter than before.

He pulled her closer.

She held him tighter.

Ctzo found Qeysta wandering aimlessly amongst the other partiers.

"Did I say something wrong?" Ctzo asked his wife. She didn't turn to him. He touched her wrist. "Qeysta..."

She pulled away, glaring at him sharply. "Don't touch me."

"Forgive me, I forgot myself. I just... what did I do?"

"Nothing." Qeysta's hands rushed to cover her face as tears poured down. "I... I've missed you."

Ctzo stared at her.

Her words were barely audible as she continued. "When we got married, I was so proud of you, so proud to be yours. And I want to be proud of you again. But that's stupid. I don't trust you. I won't trust you." Brushing away the tears, she straightened. "I'm sorry I asked anything of you. That was a mistake. You owe me nothing, and I owe you nothing. Let's just have a clean split. All right?"

Tears filled his own eyes. "I love you!"

Perhaps his voice was a little loud, because other partiers stopped for a moment to watch them.

Ctzo and Qeysta stared awkwardly at each other.

A man in a very pale robe, a man of the Council, stepped in next to Ctzo. "Ah, you are here, Captain Ctzo! Did you bring that foreign princess you mentioned?"

"Yes. She's here." Ctzo looked around. "When I last left her, she had asked to wander around outside Parliament. I don't believe she's come inside yet."

If Chiha had returned, he expected she would be standing out from the rest of the partiers.

"Fetch her then," the Council member said. "The Emperor would like to see you both now."

CHAPTER THIRTY-THREE

*A*fter finding Chiha and bringing her inside, Ctzo walked to the far end of the hall, into the Emperor's presence. He stood before the Emperor only a moment before falling to his knees.

"Rise." The Emperor's voice was calm, perhaps bored. He sat in a decorated chair surrounded by advisors and servants and a few members of the Council. Less important partiers crowded nearby, soaking in the Emperor's every action. "Welcome back into my presence, Ctzo Mainaia. What have you been up to lately?"

The question was asked merely out of courtesy, Ctzo knew. As was proper, he brushed it off. "Oh, nothing worth taking up too much of your time."

Ctzo looked over to see that Chiha had followed his lead and knelt.

"Arise," the Emperor said.

Ctzo did as instructed, then motioned to Chiha as she rose. "My great Emperor, this is Chiha, granddaughter of Chief Orthel of the Marsh Isles, of the race called the Athai."

Chiha stiffly faced the Emperor. Ctzo guessed she felt tempted to look around at the various gawking Scavgans as they studied her, but she understood that to turn her attention from the Emperor would be disrespectful.

The Emperor leaned forward in his chair, his eyes narrowing as he studied her. "Fascinating. You are the princess of your people?"

Chiha hesitated. "I am the granddaughter of the chief. And I may become chief after him, though I have relatives who could become chief instead of me."

"So, Chiha," the Emperor asked, "was Captain Ctzo here the first Scavgan you ever saw?"

"No, Emperor. I met many Scavgans before him. All, I have been told, were pirates who do not represent your greatness." She paused. "My brother was murdered by these pirates."

"That is a tragedy," the Emperor said. "I'm sorry you had to meet such scum before meeting the greater members of our race." Chiha remained silent. "I do hope that we can now establish a more legitimate trade between your people and ours. We'd heard rumours of your race, but to see you before us for the very first time—you are quite an athletic-looking creature!"

Again she remained silent, even though his voice dripped with admiration.

Finally, the Emperor's attention returned to Ctzo. "As for you, Captain, I have reviewed with the Council the letter you delivered from Grey Noon. Rest assured that he poses no threat to us. Our city will not fall to the likes of him. Is there anything else you wish from me, my servant?"

"You have given me much by allowing me to be part of your pirate-hunting unit, to sail distant seas in pursuit of your enemies," Ctzo said. "Because of this gift, I have made new discoveries. I have confirmed the existence of the Athai and their allies the Reea, who had been known to pirates but never humbly brought before you. And I discovered another previously unknown race: the Mocjoa. With your blessing, I wish to search for the islands of the Mocjoa." He kept his voice calm and strong. "However, this journey will require funds. With your blessing, I could also receive the kingdom's best cartographers and scientists to aid in our quest. I do not wish to waste your time, but I know that the discovery of the Mocjoa's islands would be a glorious thing indeed for you and for Questava."

Ctzo allowed silence to envelope the room.

The Emperor put a hand to his chin. "A new race? Now, we have suspected the existence of the Athai and Reea for years now, decades even. To confirm it is wonderful, though hardly earth-shattering. But now you present to me the idea of a wholly new race, on wholly new islands. Is that correct?"

"Yes, your greatness."

"On what evidence?"

"We've encountered a child of these creatures," Ctzo said. "A toddler whom our crew named Vortro. She—"

"And the islands?" the Emperor interrupted. "Why do you believe these creatures don't exist on any known islands?"

Ctzo paused for a moment, knowing the next part was going to be complicated. "I had a vision of sorts."

The Emperor said nothing. Ctzo knew the Emperor to be a spiritual fellow who wouldn't mock the mention of visions and supernatural encounters outright. But the captain would still need to choose his words carefully in order for his interpretation of the experience to be believed.

"I was infected by a Blackblood," Ctzo continued. "Before the infection could take hold, however, an angel grabbed me and lifted me into the sky. He asked Kyaté where I should be placed, and—"

"Kyaté?" The Emperor turned to an advisor, who whispered in his ear. "Oh. The God of the Mediocans."

"Yes."

"Interesting." The Emperor sounded guarded. "Continue."

"I looked below me and saw four islands in a sea of grey. I was then lowered onto one of the islands where I met two of the Mocjoa. They treated my wound and my Blackblood infection was healed. After this, I was returned to where I had been."

"Fascinating." Again, the Emperor looked at the advisors on his right. "Do you have anything to say about this?"

The advisors exchanged looks, then whispered amongst each other.

Finally, one spoke. "Sir, given the captain's great stature among our people, we do not wish to say anything against him. However, he is a man of war, not a prophet that he should be able to properly interpret a vision. So his understanding of these events should be called into question."

"The grey of the waters could have a spiritual meaning," another said. "It may not be a physical reality. The captain's entire experience was more than likely a step into Morpha, the afterlife of those affected by blackwaters. We know from various experiments and visions of prophets and seers that when a person becomes a Blackblood, their soul leaves them and ends up in Morpha. If he were a learned man, he would be familiar with this world and understand that his soul went there. But when it was deemed by the gods that he should be returned, the spirits there pushed him out."

There were nods and whispers throughout the room. This explanation clearly made sense to those standing around.

Ctzo didn't know how to argue against it.

"These Mocjoa then," the advisor continued, "were the souls of Blackbloods."

The Emperor turned back to Ctzo. "What do you say to these remarks?"

"They sound very intelligent," Ctzo admitted. "I have no doubt that your advisors are more learned than myself. However, I must disagree with the conclusion that the Mocjoa were spirits. When I asked the one I saw what race she belonged to, 'Mocjoa' is what she called herself. Second, she looked identical to the Mocjoa child I found on the Marsh Isles."

The Emperor's eyes searched the crowd. "And where is this Mocjoa child, that we may see her for ourselves?"

Ctzo's mouth went dry. "I. . . did not bring the Mocjoa child to Questava, your greatness. I left her in the care of her closest companion, in a seaside village far south of here."

His face flushed as he heard scattered whispers and chuckles around the room.

"Convenient." The Emperor tapped his foot. "Pray tell, what do these Mocjoa look like?"

"Their skin is black as night," Ctzo began. "And their eyes glow."

"They are Blackbloods then?"

"No. Their blood is like liquid silver."

Now it was the Emperor's turn to laugh. "Liquid silver, you say? How poetic." Ctzo remained silent. "Look, Captain, you needn't fear my anger. You're not the first to bring me news of impossible wonders on distant islands in hopes that I'll fund an expedition. I am, at least, amused. Though I did expect better from you."

The Emperor signalled a nearby servant holding a plate of drinks. The servant quickly offered the platter to his master.

That's the end, Ctzo realized.

"I won't waste any more of your time," he said quickly. He bowed once more. "Thank you, your greatness, for allowing me to speak with you."

Tyzak walked into the dance hall to find Zan and Hana together. He stepped up next to them, smirking. "Having fun?"

Hana blushed.

Zan rolled his eye. "Yes, in fact." He gently pulled away from Hana. "I would like a drink, though. Would you like one, Hana?"

"That would be welcome, thank you."

"If I may." Tyzak offered his hand. "I know I'm not your handsome master, but maybe you could do me the honour of dancing with me?"

"Yes," Hana said slowly. "But if you don't mind, I think I'll sit for a moment and catch my breath."

"Very well."

While Hana went to find a seat, Tyzak and Zan walked over to a servant carrying drinks. Zan took two glasses and Tyzak one.

"I forgot how thirsty dancing makes me," Zan mumbled. He took a sip, then nearly choked on his drink as he caught sight of a familiar face amongst the partiers. "Uh, Tyzak..."

Tyzak turned to follow Zan's gaze. "Uh-oh. Um, didn't your father say he wasn't planning to attend?"

"Yes." Zan sighed. "Yes, he did."

"Well." Tyzak took a calm swig. "Perhaps you should ask him about his change in plans."

Zan looked around the room. "Perhaps. If Hana returns, please keep an eye on her. It's probably best if my father doesn't see her wearing one of mother's dresses."

That could have gone better, Ctzo thought. He felt ready to leave this party, ready to escape the mocking gazes that were cast his way. *But I can't, I won't, leave without speaking to Qeysta.*

He turned his eyes to Chiha walking alongside him. Her pace seemed stiffer and her movements more restrained than normal. Her fists were clenched.

"We'll figure something out," Ctzo said encouragingly. "If nothing else, we'll sail back to the Marsh Isles so you can see your tribe and grandfather again."

She nodded. "Who is that man standing with Zan?"

Ctzo searched the crowds and found the man she meant. Zan was speaking to Vasitan.

"That," Ctzo said, "is Zan's father."

The captain walked their way, and soon the two were close enough to hear.

"I thought you weren't planning to attend this party," Zan was saying.

Vasitan frowned. "I wasn't. Is it wrong for me to change my mind?"

Spotting Ctzo, the Council representative turned and scowled. Stepping away from Zan and closer to Ctzo, Vasitan spoke harshly.

"You!" Vasitan said. "I hope you understand the life-altering damage you've caused my son. He's lucky to have survived. And the loss of his eye needs to be recompensed!"

"Father, please don't," Zan said with embarrassment.

"Your son is a hard-working and responsible man," Ctzo said, "and I was proud to have him on my crew."

"Oh, so you think flattery will turn away my anger?" Vasitan took another step closer. "It won't. Are you so blind to the damage you've caused? Does the loss of his eye not even bother you? You should be ashamed!"

Ctzo caught sight of Qeysta vanishing into the crowd. "Perhaps, dear Council Representative, we could discuss this on another occasion. If you and Zan would meet me at my home—"

"You will discuss this with me here and now! Perhaps you're forgetting my position, and how easily I could ruin you!"

Chiha pushed herself between Ctzo and Vasitan, shoving Vasitan out of the way. She planted her feet firmly as she stood and faced the Council representative.

"You disrespect my captain, you disrespect me!" Chiha hissed. "Shame on you!"

"And what would you be?" Vasitan looked down on the reptilian creature. "Is Ctzo bringing talking lizards aboard his crew now? How many animals does he need?"

He staggered back as Chiha's fist landed forcefully against his jaw. The room dropped into dead silence as all the partiers turned to the scene.

Warrah covered her mouth, snickering.

Vasitan glared at Chiha, his eyes as sharp as daggers. "How dare you!"

"How dare *you!*" Chiha snapped. "I should have known better than to trust the race that murdered my brother. Apologize to my captain, or I swear there will be no peace between my people and you barbaric Scavgans!"

"Enough!" Zan stepped between the two of them. "Give yourselves a moment to calm down before you say something you'll regret."

"Indeed," spoke an authoritative voice. It was the Emperor, bringing renewed silence to the room and chasing away any plans of retaliation held by either side. The group turned as one to see that the Emperor had left his chair to mingle with his visitors. "Calm yourselves. I, for one, am here to party. And you're both throwing off my good mood."

Vasitan stammered a half-coherent apology. Chiha hung her head.

"Captain." The Emperor's gaze landed on Ctzo. "Perhaps you should take your guest and return home?"

Ctzo swallowed. That was definitely an order. "At once, your greatness." The captain then walked over to Chiha and whispered in her ear: "It's all right. We'll return here another time."

"I can walk by myself," Chiha said quickly. She then ran off in the direction of the entrance, not giving Ctzo a chance to hold her back.

Ctzo instinctively wanted to search for Qeysta and Warrah, but he knew the Emperor wouldn't take well to him dawdling. He would have to visit his family later. Instead he followed after Chiha.

CHAPTER THIRTY-FOUR

*W*arrah lifted the skirt of her dress so it wouldn't touch the ground, her eyes roaming Parliament's vast courtyard. It consisted of a wide stairway, leading down to a cobblestone plaza framed by tall, decorated walls.

Further down the stairs, still within the courtyard, Captain Ctzo was untying his steed. She rushed down the stairway towards him. She had to catch him before he left Parliament.

"Wait!"

Ctzo had already mounted Wind-Drummer and begun to ride away when his daughter's voice reached his ears. He turned to her, watching as she half-tumbled down the stairs and ran to him, stopping mere feet away.

"I want to go with you," she demanded. "On your quest for the Mocjoa."

Ctzo pulled back on the reins, bringing Wind-Drummer to a halt. He regarded his daughter with surprise. "You are interested in restoring our relationship?"

"Hardly," Warrah said coldly. She softened her tone as she continued. "I want to go on an adventure. I want to explore new lands. I'm sick of Questavan scenery and Questavan food and

Questavan jobs and Questavan men. I want to see what other places have to offer."

He raised an eyebrow. "How much experience do you have with scenery, foods, jobs, and *men* that aren't Questavan?"

"I've done some traveling! Mom tried moving us to Medioca after you went to jail. It didn't work out, but I got a taste of travel, and I liked it."

"Let me get this straight." Ctzo swung his leg around and slid off his capero. He stood before his daughter. "You don't want to make peace with your father, but you do want to journey with him across vast seas to uncharted lands?"

Warrah glared up at him. "I'm not asking to travel with my father. I'm asking to travel with the war hero Captain Ctzo. I understand he's a much more likable fellow than my father."

Ctzo flinched. He stroked Wind-Drummer's neck, attempting to calm his heightened emotions.

"I can't take you without your mother's permission." He sighed, thinking back to how he'd taken Zan abroad without Vasitan's consent. "Rather, I *won't* take you without your mother's permission."

"I can get her permission. What I'm asking for right now is your promise to take me."

Ctzo folded his hands, contemplating.

"You don't need the Emperor's blessing," Warrah continued. "Your old crew will follow you. And it's not like the Emperor is going to hold you back from a fruitless search for imaginary islands."

"Don't you make our odds sound hopeful..." Ctzo sighed as he eyed a black bird soaring overhead.

And what's worse, she's not being unrealistic, he realized.

He looked down and saw that she, too, was watching the bird.

"Captain," she said wistfully, "I want to go on your quest. I don't care if it's hopeless. It's worth it." Her gaze met his. "Don't you think it's worth it?"

"Even if I do, getting together a fleet capable of such a journey may take years. It's too costly to maintain the ships I had. I've already sold most of them."

His shoulders sagged at the sad realization. The *Diversity* was at the bottom of the sea, and now he'd have to sell *Radiant Dawn* and *Night Light* as well.

"You'll figure things out," Warrah said confidently. "You're the great Captain Ctzo, aren't you?" She didn't give him a chance to reply. "When you are prepared to leave, please take me with you."

"Ask your mother," he said firmly. "And then I'll be speaking to her to confirm the truth."

Warrah sighed. "Fine. But you'll take me?"

"If she'll allow it." He remounted Wind-Drummer. "Is that all you wanted from the great Captain Ctzo?"

She stared up at him and bowed slightly. "Yes. That is all. Thank you for your time, Captain. Until we meet again."

After returning home from the party, Zan caught Vasitan writing at his desk.

"Father, I need to speak with you."

"Of course." Vasitan finished signing a document. He pushed his quill a little forcefully into the parchment, Zan noted. He then looked up at his son. "You need something?"

"You sound… tense, Father."

Vasitan swallowed. "I—I suppose I should be more lenient when you make mistakes like that: stealing your mother's clothing and allowing a servant girl to wear it to a party. That's… unacceptable."

Zan decided it best not to get his mother in trouble over the incident. "So how did you find out?"

"I saw her dancing with your friend. But you did just spend months aboard a ship with Captain Ctzo. What should I expect, except that you'd learn a few bad habits along the way?"

Zan frowned. "You sound angrier with Ctzo than with me."

"Please." Vasitan got up from his chair and rounded the desk. "Let's not talk about him anymore. You've returned to your life here in Questava. Right?"

"What do you have against Ctzo?"

"Nothing," Vasitan said briskly. "He's a venerated hero. Who could hold anything against him?" He lowered his voice. "He only took my son into dangerous territory and nearly got him killed."

"That was my choice, Father." Zan pointed at his eyepatch. "Ctzo wasn't even present when this happened. This was me making a foolish decision because I was too stubborn to let an escaped prisoner go."

"And where did you learn that stubbornness from?" Vasitan insisted.

Zan smiled. "You." Silence filled the air and his smile faded. "Ctzo doesn't control me, Father, and I won't blame him for my own mistakes. I respect him. I don't always agree with him, but still, you shouldn't speak so angrily about him. I think people are starting to forget all that he's done for this empire." He muttered, "The Emperor included."

"Fair," Vasitan said, though he didn't sound sincere.

"And this next decision I've made is one I came up with all by myself. No one suggested it to me." Zan paused. "You're going to hate it, but please, at least hear me out. I don't want to do this behind your back, though it would be much easier. It's only fair you know."

Vasitan took a deep breath. "All right."

"I'm marrying Hana."

An intense silence followed. Vasitan's expression didn't change. Zan waited for a response.

"The servant girl?" Vasitan said at last.

"Yes, Father."

"That's idiotic."

Zan sighed. "Could you explain how so?"

"Maybe the girl is charming, or pretty, and you've 'fallen in love.' But marriage isn't just about love. Romantic feelings wax and wane, my son. Marrying for political reasons, finding someone who will strengthen your sphere of influence, that is wisdom. It can benefit your family for generations to come."

"I am marrying for political reasons, Father." Zan managed to keep his voice calm. "I've thought through this carefully, and I believe—"

"Your heart deceives you!" Vasitan snapped bitterly. "You're making a big mistake, letting that servant girl charm you. I tell you, all she wants is to marry into money and prestige. You'll be miserable, and you'll have no one to blame but yourself. Let the record show that I did my best to talk you out of it."

Still, Zan remained patient. "Father, she's a princess in her own right. And as far as Mediocans are concerned, *I'll* be the one marrying into prestige. But please, throw off the façade. You're not worried about me following my heart and then becoming miserable with the results... you just don't like that I'm growing my 'sphere of influence,' as you put it, in Medioca instead of Questava. To you, they're just a slave nation."

"A slave nation? Hardly. But think about all the benefits they've received from being a part of the Questavan Empire: wealth, culture, improved infrastructure. Don't tell me you want to risk sending them back to the dark ages by causing a political upheaval."

"I've been to Medioca, Father." Zan put up his hand as Vasitan started to argue. "Not just with you. I went with my friend, Tyzak. And he—"

"Is clearly a rebel who wants nothing but trouble," Vasitan spouted. "A nationalist who aims to stir you to his cause."

"First of all, aren't we proud of our nationality? Why is it that our nationalism is virtuous and his troublesome? Second, I'm not here to argue about who has a better nation. I've seen that we've caused them pain. I want to set things right—for Hana and for Tyzak, if no one else."

Vasitan peered over Zan's shoulders, his eyes narrowing. "Ah. Our lovely princess awaits."

Turning, Zan found Hana standing there, dressed in her usual servants robes, blushing mightily as she looked at her feet. "M–my masters. A guest is at the door."

"Hana," Zan said his tone soft and sad.

She ignored him and focused her gaze on his father. "Warrah, the daughter of Captain Ctzo, requests the honour of your presence, master."

Brushing past Zan, Vasitan sent his son one final glare. "We'll finish this conversation later." He then took a seat at his work desk. "Hana, bring Warrah here."

Zan took the hint and walked out of the room while Hana obediently went to fetch Warrah.

At the sight of Warrah standing in front of his desk, Vasitan frowned. Ctzo was a noble, intelligent-looking figure, but Warrah was dressed plainly. A mischievous smirk lit her face. She didn't fit his vision of how the great captain's daughter should comport herself.

"Miss Mainaia," Vasitan said curtly. "Something you wish to discuss?"

"I know you want Captain Ctzo gone." At Vasitan's shocked look, Warrah leaned forward, smiling. "Now, how badly do you want him gone? As in, how much money would make it worthwhile to you?"

Vasitan frowned. "Are you asking me to pay you to kill your own father?"

"I'm asking whether or not you want Ctzo to leave on his impossible quest."

Catching on, Vasitan laughed. "You want me to finance Ctzo's ridiculous expedition!"

"If it's that ridiculous, you should be eager to send him off on it. But if it's not worth your money, he can stay here, meddling in your affairs, chatting with your son…"

Vasitan made a rather undignified growl. He folded his hands, and his expression softened.

I do have all that money saved up from blackmailing pirates, he thought. *I was going to give it to Zan, but do I really want to give him coins that he'll turn around and spend on his wedding to a servant girl? Hardly!*

The Council representative smiled. "Young woman, I'll not only give you money to use as you see fit, I'll even buy Captain Ctzo another ship! A big, fast ship that'll take him as far as his heart desires, for as long as it takes to find those islands in a grey sea."

CHAPTER THIRTY-FIVE

"*Introspection is probably a healthy alternative to gloom,*" Jair wrote. He sat within Atzinus's old lab, a healthy scattering of notes, charts, and books lying over the large desk before him. Paper had always been his friend. Give him a quill and a notebook, and even as a child he'd contentedly pass the hours writing, sketching, and doodling to his heart's content. His random dreams and voluminous thoughts could become something concrete, something focused and sharable.

Now more than ever he needed the chance to explore his own mind. Yet now more than ever he felt his mind had little of value to offer. Jair sighed as he continued scribbling his thoughts:

> Perhaps my fear of my own mind is freezing me, but I have struggled as of late with tasks that commonly come without difficulty. For example, that dear little Kamai-Darian, Sébérus, has granted me the freedom to determine the unique needs of each and every Blackblood under his paternal care. Usually, I would be drooling, eager to jump at the chance to invent a custom potion for each one. Alas, I find my creativity lacking, and only a

few separate potions have been completed. Poor Sébérus; I know he requires and expects more from me.

I suppose I'm scared. Scared of failure. What was I thinking when I opted to turn myself into a Blackblood? I suppose I know what I was thinking—Blackbloodism presented an opportunity to become something greater than I was. What I mean is, how did I ever have so much confidence that I could brave such a drastic alteration to my life?

And worse, I doubt my previous conclusion: that it would be a change for the better in all respects. In transforming myself into a so-called god, did I drive myself to insanity?

Tears slipped down his cheek.

Was I always insane? Everything I've ever thought and believed seems to be uncertain, on shaky ground. If I know that my mind can feed me lies and turn myth into reality, can I ever trust my mind again? Is there any good to be had from imagining or thinking or pursuing faith or philosophy?

Is there any good to be had from...

Jair stopped himself. He closed his notebook, abandoned it on the desk, then stood and walked away. He didn't even want to finish the sentence. To finish it was to admit the truth, to make it concrete and real and inescapable.

He fell to the floor, a sense of numbness filling his mind.

I don't want to be alive anymore.

Sébérus walked in to see Jair crying on the floor, unimpressed by the sight.

"Forgive me." Jair hastily got to his feet and brushed his tears aside. "I was just working through the formula for another potion."

"I see." Sébérus rubbed his forehead. He then checked outside and closed the lab's door. "I have a new request."

Jair kept his voice low. "Your wish is my command."

"This pain..." Sébérus sighed deeply. "This pain needs to go away. I can't think with it, and I need to be able to think."

"Truly? I've found that I think clearer without the shots I'd been giving myself. I may not be as happy, mind you, but perhaps clarity and suffering—"

Sébérus let out a growl. "But you can make something, can't you?"

"Are you sure you wish me to? I'm simply concerned about our dear host's response to such a request." Jair motioned to a shelf full of chemicals. "The fact that Grey Noon allows us to keep these elixirs at all is precarious at best. He has permitted them to remain only for the purpose of improving the condition of the Blackbloods."

"I am a Blackblood," Sébérus snapped, "and my condition needs to be improved."

"If I may clarify, I meant the physical condition, not the mental—"

"The two overlap. The condition of the mind affects the condition of the body, and the condition of the body affects the condition of the mind."

"True," Jair said. "I suppose what our good captain finds distasteful is the use of chemicals as a coping mechanism, when a problem needs to be faced and not run from. However, you argue convincingly. If you're so sure of the need for physical relief to ease your mental symptoms, why do you fear Grey Noon's response? Why not ask him to allow an exception, as he has for the other Blackbloods?"

Sébérus groaned. "Shut up and make me something, Jair. I don't care what Grey Noon thinks anymore."

As they heard Grey Noon's mighty bulk approaching, both fell silent.

Sébérus moved to the door, his piercing gaze remaining on Jair. "We'll continue this conversation later."

With that, he turned his back and exited the room.

Sébérus was beginning to get a sore neck from constantly having to raise his head skyward just to see Grey Noon's face. "Sir, are you here to speak with me or Jair?"

"You," Grey Noon said. "Come with me."

He led Sébérus towards the docks, Kaio following behind. The massive Rezumi said not a word until their arrival.

Grey Noon spread one wing, motioning around Atzinus's harbour. "Consider this a reward for your labour. Any one of the ships I haven't already outfitted, you may claim as your own. You captain it. You pick the crew. You rename it to your liking."

Sébérus looked around at the ships, puzzled. "As a reward for my labour?"

"You've done as I asked. You came up with a plan. You've outlined a way to put it into action. The Blackbloods are eager to join us, not out of numb obedience but with joy for the battle ahead—joy you've inspired."

By now, Sébérus had mostly tuned out Grey Noon's words; instead he eyed each of the vessels. Three remained from Atzinus's previous force, all of them large, well-equipped warships. The others, Grey Noon had already claimed as his own.

Sébérus hadn't expected such a generous offer.

What do I want in a ship? he asked himself. *Well, I know what I want in battle: for the enemy to fear my blackwaters and for the Blackbloods to paralyze my foes.*

"I'll give you time to decide," Grey Noon said at last. He wandered off, barking orders to a few of his pirates as he walked away.

"What will you name your ship?" Kaio asked.

Sébérus turned to him. "That's the easy part."

"You know of a name?"

"Yes. In the Ti'te'Vikan's interpretation of history, a dark sword pierces the dark waters of the early world. A sword that masters blackwaters seems a fitting symbol for us." Sébérus's gaze came to rest on one of the frigates—large, solid, sitting proudly atop the waves. "The sword was named Moakoko. An acceptable name for a ship, don't you think?"

"I don't know," Kaio admitted. "I don't know what sorts of names are normal for ships."

Sébérus smiled at his companion. "I like it."

CHAPTER THIRTY-SIX

A month later, Ctzo heard knocking on the door to his house and rushed to answer. He expected to find a member of his old crew had come for a visit. Instead, as he opened the door, his brows lowered.

"Council Representative Vasitan?" he said. "Forgive my abruptness, but I wasn't expecting you."

"No need to apologize." Vasitan's voice was cheery, almost unnervingly so. "I have wonderful news to share with you."

Ctzo braced for impact. After the events at the party, he didn't have high hopes for this so-called wonderful news. "Yes?"

"I have purchased for you, at my own expense, a new ship."

Silence followed.

"What?" Ctzo asked after a long pause, his confusion evidenced by his blank stare.

Vasitan continued undaunted. "And if I may say so, I do believe I made a fine choice. Of course, you'll need to affirm that the ship is truly seaworthy. But I believe you will be impressed." He watched Ctzo a moment, his smile finally easing. "Well? Don't you have anything to say?"

"Um… what?"

Vasitan cleared his throat. "Would you like to come and inspect the ship I purchased for you?"

"Why... would you purchase... for me... a ship?"

"I'm sorry. Your daughter gave me the impression you needed a vessel if you were going to tackle the gargantuan task of finding that new race you spoke of."

"My daughter spoke to you?" Ctzo shook his head. "We'll get to that point later. First, I was under the impression that you thought little of my goals."

"Nonsense! Why, I'm all for you leaving Questava and setting out to change the world. Provided," Vasitan said with a forced chuckle, "that you don't take my son with you this time. Fair enough?"

Ctzo wasn't sure what else to say. "Where's this ship?"

"I'm told it's fast." Vasitan kept his hands folded behind his back as he led Ctzo along the harbour. "An all-new design. One of a kind. And of course, if anyone asks, you'll mention I helped support your vision of discovery, won't you?"

"Of course," the captain muttered. "Where is my... *our* ship, Council Representative?"

"Be patient. Ah, there!"

Ctzo's jaw dropped at the sight of his new ship. Its five masts rose into the sky and armour plates stretched over its hull. Ctzo counted the windows to the cannons hidden inside—four on each side, eight total; each was large, suggesting heavier firepower than the *Diversity* had ever been capable of carrying.

"It's a warship?"

"The old captain assured me that it'll do great for exploration," Vasitan said. "After all, you never know what kind of people you'll meet on your travels, right?"

Ctzo had never seen a ship with so much armour. He frowned, unsure what to think of the design. "You said it's new, but it's already been floated and captained. It's not in the shipyard, so it's been sailed previously. And you mentioned a prior captain?"

"Oh, yes. He's the one I bought it from. At a handsome price, too, but I'm sure it'll be worth it." He noted Ctzo's frown and continued hastily, "But you can't really judge a ship from the dock, can you? Just wait until you come aboard!"

A gangplank had already been lowered and a man stood guarding it—one of Vasitan's servants, Ctzo guessed. He bowed at Vasitan and stepped aside, allowing his master and the captain to climb onto the ship's deck.

Ctzo stared at the tidy deck of his new ship. He ran his hand along the ship's smooth wooden railing. As Vasitan gibbered on about the unique design of the vessel, and its builder's assurance that it would do marvellously well at crossing the ocean, Ctzo absently took in the ship's every nook and cranny, each nail and rope.

It isn't the Diversity, he had to remind himself.

Stepping into the captain's quarters, the distinctive scent filled his nostrils. He took each breath slowly, soaking in the aura while noting sadly that it just didn't have the same feel as his last vessel.

It would have to do.

Nearly anyone would have been shocked at his blasé reaction. This ship was far larger than the *Diversity*. It was truly a beautiful piece of work, crafted from a near-white wood that seemed to repel stains.

Vasitan, too excited at the prospect of sending Ctzo away and proud to show off his purchase, didn't catch on to the captain's mood until the very end of the tour.

"What do you think?" Vasitan asked as he passed Ctzo a glowing smile. "Are you... disappointed?"

"I'm just remembering." Ctzo closed his eyes, sighing. "I appreciate the gesture, Council Representative. I'll take her for a short sail outside the harbour."

"Of course!" Vasitan chuckled nervously. "I'm sure I could get an exchange if you don't like it. Maybe. Do shipbuilders do exchanges if you don't like the ship you bought?"

"It's fine," Ctzo said dismissively, not even looking Vasitan's way. "I just really wish to take it for a sail. Could you send my crew aboard?"

Nodding, Vasitan took a few steps towards the gangplank, then sent another look Ctzo's way. "What's troubling you? Aren't you happy? You'll get to sail on your grand quest now, to discover these... Mocjoa. Collect a diverse crew. Isn't that what you always dreamed of?"

"Yes." Ctzo straightened. The sinking of the *Diversity* had seemed the end of his dream, but now... Again he touched the smooth wood.

Perhaps I can still do something special on this vessel.

At last Ctzo smiled, even allowing himself a small laugh. "You're right, Council Representative. Thank you. I never would have seen it without your help."

Vasitan lowered his brows, shrugged, then turned and walked off the ship.

Closing his eyes, Ctzo took in a deep breath. "Yes indeed. This will be called the *Diversity II.*"

Ian stared out the window of the small kitchen as Vortro sat playing on the floor, chattering to her wooden blocks as if they were little people. He'd been back home for about a month and half, but he couldn't stop thinking about the world outside.

His mother entered and noted his faraway expression.

"It's almost time," she said as she walked over to him. "It's almost time for you to meet Captain Ctzo back in Questava. Are you still set on going?"

"Yes. More than ever."

"All right."

She sighed as she looked over to the Mocjoa toddler. Vortro had been dressed in proper baby clothes for the last few weeks. Ian had played chase with her, read her stories, and helped clean up after her messy meals.

"She can't go with you, you know," Ian's mother said firmly. "It's too dangerous for a child."

"I know. I'm just not sure how I'm going to tell her. Or if she'll understand."

"She won't." His mother patted Vortro's head. "But don't worry about her. Your dad and I are happy to be parents again. Though it is weird returning to the diaper stage after all this time." She knelt down by Vortro and spoke softly to her.

A sad smile appeared on Ian's face. It would be good to get back to Ctzo, and good to know that Vortro was well looked after. However, he would miss the little girl.

"I guess I should start packing," Ian said.

His mother frowned. "You haven't packed yet? Ian, you've had plenty of time!"

"It'll only take a moment!"

Determined to prove his point, Ian rushed to his room and hurriedly stuffed clothes and other desired articles into his bag.

Evidently hearing him through the thin wall separating their rooms, Katana called out, "Don't forget my gift for Tyzak."

"I'm not forgetting the gift!" Ian yelled back at his sister. "Though I still don't understand why you got him one."

"Don't damage it," she added. Then, as an afterthought, "Please."

Ian returned to his mother a short time later with a smile on his face. "Done!"

His mother still sat on the floor with Vortro. She looked up and frowned at him. "You sure you remembered everything?"

"Yes, Mother," Ian droned. "It's not like this is my first time traveling!"

"Do you have your travel plans worked out?"

"Yes, Mother. I'm leaving early tomorrow morning."

Ian joined her on the floor beside Vortro. "I'll be leaving before she gets up, though."

Vortro remained absorbed in her toy blocks, now banging two of them against each other.

"Vortro?" Ian said, caressing her antennae. "Do you want to play with me tonight, before you go to bed?"

The little girl looked up at him. "I got blocks!"

"Yes." Ian smiled. "Yes, you do. Do you want to play with them together?"

Vortro stood. "Outside! Shoes!" She rushed off to the entryway and returned with Ian's shoes. "Shoes! Let's go!"

"All right, we'll play outside," Ian agreed. "But you're going to need your shoes, too."

Vortro retrieved her little boots and set them on Ian's lap.

His mother stood. "I suppose I should get back to chores." She smiled down at Vortro. "Have fun with Ian outside!"

Once her boots were on, Vortro rushed to the door excitedly, attempting to turn the latch.

Ian slipped on his own shoes and followed her to the door. "Coming!"

That night, Ian laid a wornout Vortro into her bed, tucking her capero stuffie under her arm.

"Have a good night sleep," he whispered. "I'll miss you."

He hesitated, feeling like that just wasn't enough of a goodbye.

"Kyaté, bless little Vortro, and may she sleep well and have sweet dreams. Keep her safe while I'm far away. Amen."

Vortro watched Ian until he slipped out of the room, closing the door behind him.

CHAPTER THIRTY-SEVEN

*C*tzo knocked once on the worn wooden door before Qeysta opened.

She nodded at him. "Warrah said you'd be coming."

"May I come in?" he asked hesitantly.

She stepped aside and led him to the dining table, where Warrah awaited.

"I'm guessing that she's asked you about coming aboard," Ctzo said, looking at Warrah.

"Yes." Qeysta looked down at her feet. "It's... a difficult decision."

"Fair enough. That's why I waited this long to come for your answer." Ctzo watched his wife's face, attempting to read her. "Do you need more time?"

"No." Qeysta turned to Warrah. "We've already decided that she's going. The question is whether or not I'll be joining as well."

"Really?" Ctzo's eyes widened. "I'd love to have you aboard."

"I don't know." Qeysta sighed. "I would need a housesitter."

"I could ask my friends to look after the place for you."

"It's a dangerous trip."

Ctzo couldn't disagree. "But you're allowing Warrah to come?"

"She talked me down," Qeysta said.

Warrah wore a big smile across her face. "So when can I pack up and move onto the ship? I've never been on a ship before. I should probably get used to it before we leave."

"I have other crew already spending their nights aboard *Diversity II*," Ctzo said. "You're free to join them whenever your mother allows."

Warrah looked hopefully at Qeysta.

"Yes," Qeysta said, relenting. "Get your things packed up."

"Done!" Warrah headed off down the small hallway and out of sight.

"Qeysta, about what happened at the party," Ctzo whispered. "I'm not trying to intrude on your life or force us back together. I just want you to know that I care. And… I miss you. And I've been awful to you and Warrah. I'm just not sure how to start making things right."

Qeysta sighed deeply. "You win."

Ctzo frowned. "Pardon? I win what?"

"We can talk." Qeysta searched his eyes. "And we'll have plenty of time to do that on a trip across the world."

Warrah barely held back an undignified squeal of glee as she pranced aboard *Diversity II*. It seemed far too girly to squeal, and as of this day she considered herself a true woman, about to challenge the world by sailing impossible distances on an impossible quest.

Yes, she recalled her mother's whispered question from not long ago: *Are we sure we're not headed to our doom?*

Warrah laughed at the thought. Ctzo wasn't stupid. Should the quest fail, she was sure they'd be back within a year. And who cared if they weren't? Everyone had to die some way, and dying at sea sounded adventurous enough.

Her heart skipped a beat. *No, I'm not fearless. But I don't have too much to fear, do I?*

As she leaned against the railing and absorbed the salty sea smell, she allowed her mother's worried expression to fade from her mind.

"Do you like the ship?" Captain Ctzo voice came from behind her.

She turned to face him. Having him here would take some getting used to. It'd been years since she was that naïve teen who'd assumed that all the bad things Daddy had done were normal, and she just had to live with them. He looked older now… not weather-beaten or wrinkly, but somehow stronger, standing to a fuller height and dignified in cleaner, pricier clothes.

It made her angry to see him this way, better off than he'd ever been. It seemed unfair that he'd been so successful after everything he'd put them through.

"The ship is lovely," Warrah said, trying to keep her tone casual.

"Have you had a chance to study the rigging?" Ctzo's eyes filled with an almost dreamy quality. "Quite a work to behold!"

"Uh… right…"

Rigging? she asked herself. *What's that again?*

His gaze held hope. "Would you like me to show you?"

"I'm sorry," she said as politely as possible. "I really don't know that much about ships. You'd have to dumb it down quite a bit for me to understand."

"Oh. Of course." He sighed, obviously disappointed. "Fair enough. How about studying the sea charts?"

Warrah felt her eyes widen in concern. "Um… am I going to be expected to work on this ship?"

Ctzo frowned, then smirked. "Lesson one about being aboard a ship: everyone works, dear."

The way he said "dear" made her blood boil. "I'm not a child," she snapped.

"No." Ctzo now spoke firmly and without fear. "You aren't a child, and that's my point. You can work as hard as anyone else. And you will be expected to. No favours."

"Of course not." Warrah crossed her arms. "I wouldn't ask for any."

"Good. Because this isn't a vacation, Warrah, and you're not just an explorer—you're my crewmember. I expect you to respect and obey me. Understood?"

"Got it."

Warrah sighed. *Do the others aboard your ships actually like being pushed around this way?*

Perhaps it was fair. Ctzo had once been a general. What had she been expecting? Her eyes returned to his face, and she noticed how calmly he regarded her.

I guess I was expecting the old Ctzo, the man who was barely around, who yelled at Mom, who got into fights, who went to jail.

She cleared her throat. "With your permission, I'd like to go in search of some food."

"All right, I'll let Réto and Kyra know." Ctzo raised his hand, looking into the sky, then lowered it. Shortly, a reptilian creature landed on his shoulder: the black-scaled male Kamai, Réto.

"Warrah is heading off to eat," Ctzo explained, "and I'm going to search the harbour for any crew that may have arrived. Look after things while we're gone."

"Will do," Réto said hesitantly. "But when you have a minute, there's some news Kyra and I would like to share with you."

Ctzo frowned. "I can spare a minute."

"Good." Réto smiled. "Kyra's pregnant!"

"Oh! Congratulations!" Realization began to sink in. "Wait, is she still planning on coming aboard?"

"That was the idea…"

"On a trip across the world? One where we don't know how long we'll be gone?"

Réto sighed. "Well, we don't want to leave you…"

"You two should stay in Questava," Ctzo said. "Don't worry about me. Kyra is going to need the freedom to relax, not to mention better food and care than we'll have aboard ship. We can talk more about it tonight, but I strongly believe you two should stay behind."

Ian jingled the coins in his pocket, hoping he'd brought enough to last him until the fleet departed. He walked along a busy street on his way to the harbour. He'd already found an inn and spent one night in this grand city. When he'd arrived in Questava by boat, it had been late, and he hadn't had a chance to look for *Radiant Dawn* or *Night Light* in the dark harbour.

Today I'll search for them, he decided.

Soon he stepped along the wooden walkway that hugged the cliff overlooking the harbour. He sidled past busy workers and people-watchers alike. The harbour was such an important place for Questavans.

"Ian!" called Ctzo's familiar voice.

Ian looked around the busy crowd, catching sight of his captain further down the walkway, closer to the docks.

Ian rushed to his side. "Captain! It's good to see you!"

"Good to see you as well, Ian," Ctzo gave him a warm smile. "I'm glad you decided to rejoin the crew! Come." Ctzo began walking towards the docks. "The ships are this way."

Though it was less crowded on the wide docks themselves, Ian still found himself squeezing past sailors and their cargo as he hurried after his captain.

"I'm glad I found you," Ctzo said as he led the way to his fleet. "We're going to have to keep an eye out for other crewmembers, so we can direct them to the ships."

"Have the ships changed that much?" Ian asked. He had assumed the repairs wouldn't leave them unrecognizable.

"Getting this mission going turned out to be more complicated than I'd envisioned. *Radiant Dawn* and *Night Light* have been sold."

Ian nearly stopped in his tracks. "Sold?"

"Yes. Funding from the Emperor didn't come through, so I sold the ships to start saving up for the next trip. But thanks to a generous donation from Zan's father, I now have a new ship: *Diversity II.* I think she's just right for the job."

"So did you sell *all* the ships?" Ian asked, hesitant.

Ctzo smiled. "Well, we still have the little cutter. I couldn't find a good price for it."

"You mean the *Cherish*?"

"Yes. Would you be interested in steering her again?"

His heart racing, memories flooded into Ian's mind of sailing that sleek vessel and competing against the Kamai. "I would love to!"

"I'm glad." Ctzo paused. "There's another... surprise of sorts this time around. My daughter Warrah and my wife Qeysta will be joining us."

"Oh?" Ian couldn't recall Ctzo ever mentioning that he had a family. "They're going to be part of the crew?"

"Yes, although I'm getting the impression my daughter doesn't really know what that means or entails. Try to help her fit in. And don't let her get away with anything you wouldn't get away with."

Ian wondered what he meant by that and hoped the girl wouldn't be too much trouble. It would be uncomfortable having to tattle on the captain's own daughter.

Ctzo took a final look around his house, ensuring that everything was ready for his departure.

He smiled at his butler Alez. "Anything I'm forgetting?"

"All is ready," Alez said simply. "Sir."

Ctzo could tell the man was loathe to say goodbye. "Until next time."

Alez bowed briefly.

The captain approached Réto and Kyra, who sat waiting for him partway up the stairs.

Kyra looked up at him sadly. "I'm sure there's a way we could come with you…"

"You're staying here," Ctzo said firmly. "Rest. I can't take you aboard in good conscience after the recent news." He smiled. "I'm looking forward to meeting your child when I get home."

Réto looked up at his captain. "I—"

"You need to stay with her," Ctzo said.

"Yes," Réto agreed, "but I worry about you."

"Kyaté will be with us." He probably sounded less confident than he desired. "I leave all that I have in your hands."

"Until next time, master."

Chiha stuffed the clothes she'd strewn over the floor into her bag. She rummaged through the blankets one last time, in case she'd forgotten something on the bed. Satisfied, she folded the blankets neatly.

The captain will appreciate this sign of respect, she thought.

She stepped out of the bedroom, closing the door behind her. It was time to leave Ctzo's home and move aboard the new ship.

Halfway down the hall, Chiha met Katia.

"Are you ready to go?" Chiha asked cheerfully.

Katia hesitated. "I've decided to stay behind."

Chiha frowned. "Stay behind? Why?"

"I... I need to rest," Katia muttered. "To refocus."

Eying Katia a moment longer, Chiha asked, "Does the captain know?"

"Would you tell him for me? It would be easier than me trying to explain. I still have difficulty speaking his language."

"As you wish," Chiha patted Katia's head fondly. "I will miss you."

Katia smiled. "I'll miss you, too. Perhaps we'll meet again someday."

CHAPTER THIRTY-EIGHT

*D*ays later, the first morning sun rose over the ocean, scattering rays of shimmering white light over the waves and brightening the sails of the *Diversity II*.

Down in the ship's sleeping quarters, Warrah's eyes fluttered open and her lips lifted into a smirk. She threw herself out of her hammock and grabbed her coat, slipping into it as she bounded up the stairs and onto the deck.

Leaning against the railing, she took in a deep whiff of sea air. Then her gaze landed on her father across the deck.

She bristled.

No, she reminded herself, forcing a smile as her eyes returned to the waves. *Not my father. Captain Ctzo.*

In mere moments, they'd be rounding the southern edge of Scavgan's Island, the only island Warrah had known her whole life. Medioca itself seemed a world away. Leaving the island felt like sailing off the face of the planet—in a very good way.

"Ah, a fellow adventurer!" Tyzak said, his voice floating towards her from behind. "You have that sparkle in your eyes that says, 'A grand story awaits, and I get to be part of it!'"

"Is that what my eyes say?" Warrah folded her hands behind her back, attempting to maintain eye contact instead of staring at the fellow's chest. He was handsome, but now wasn't the time for such thoughts. "You're Tyzak, right?"

He gave a charming bow and Warrah had to bite back her enamoured smile.

"Pleased to meet you once more," Tyzak said, his eyes meeting hers. "What an honour it is to have aboard the lovely daughter of our grand captain!"

Warrah's lips turned to a frown. *Oh. So that's what makes me interesting.*

Next, Ian came over and smiled her way.

"Hi Warrah," Ian said, his gaze resting on Tyzak. "Are you two busy? There's something I've been meaning to give you, Tyzak."

"Lead the way," Tyzak said cheerily, nodding and grinning at Warrah. "Till we meet again."

"Of course." Warrah found herself sighing in relief as the two departed. Men weren't worth her time anyway.

She caught sight of Chiha climbing amongst the mast and sails and approached her.

"Good morning!" Warrah called up to her.

Chiha stared down through shiny black eyes. With a single leap, she landed on the deck beside Warrah. "Are you the captain's daughter?"

Bristling, Warrah at last spoke her mind. "I'm more than just the captain's daughter."

"You look like him," Chiha said. "I do not know why you would need to be more than the captain's daughter. He is a great man."

"So I hear." Warrah crossed her arms. "Who's your father?"

"My father was a great chief." Chiha stood tall and proud as she spoke. "Brave and daring. I believe I am just as he was: an adventurer."

Catching the *was* in Chiha's answer, Warrah measured her words. "I'm… sorry he's not here anymore."

"I am as he was," Chiha said again. "That makes me proud."

Warrah briefly glanced over her shoulder at her father, then returned her attention to Chiha. "It's nice not to be the only woman on this ship."

"What do you mean by that?"

"Well, usually sailing is a guy thing. Some superstition about women being bad luck."

"I was not aware of that. There are other Athai women aboard. You are in good company."

"Thanks!" Warrah smiled. "By the way, it was really cool how you stood up to Vasitan at the party."

"I understand I should be ashamed of my behaviour." Chiha seemed to stare out into the distance a moment. Then she chirped, "But I am not!"

The two shared a laugh.

Ctzo couldn't help but watch his daughter as she chatted with her fellow crewmate. The girl had grown up so fast. Where had the time gone?

He already knew the answer to that question.

I spent so much time away. He sighed. *Well, she and I are here now. That's something.*

Ian led Tyzak belowdecks and into the crew's sleeping quarters.

"You know," Tyzak said as they walked, "even without Zan here, it feels like we've gotten the old crew back together: you, Chiha, Yakara... so many familiar faces."

"Zan really isn't coming?" Ian said sadly.

"Fret not. I think he has a few new adventures of his own to keep him busy. Now, what was it you wished to show me?"

Ian reached into his pack and rummaged around before pulling out a leatherbound book.

"Katana bought this for you." Ian handed it to Tyzak. "To write down all the stories you want to tell, so you can share them with her later." He shrugged. "Don't know why she decided to buy you a gift."

Tyzak pulled the journal close to his chest. "How romantic of her!"

"Yuck."

"Your sister is a sweetheart. I'll be sure to thank her for it when I get the chance."

"That could be a long time from now." Ian sighed. "This adventure hasn't even started, and already I miss Vortro and wish I could have her here."

"She's become like a daughter to you, hasn't she?"

"In some ways, yes."

"Then pray tell, why did you decide to join this quest instead of staying home?" Tyzak asked.

"Because of her," Ian said. At Tyzak's frown, he continued. "It finally occurred to me: she's someone's child. I mean, someone else's child. And we barely know anything about her people. I need to go on this journey, for her sake—to find out where she comes from, and how to care for her better."

"A noble goal!" Tyzak smiled broadly placed a hand on his friend's shoulder. "We both have our missions to complete then."

"You have a mission?"

"Obviously!" Tyzak rubbed his hands gleefully. "More stories to hear, more stories to make, and more stories to tell. And now," he added, fingering through the journal, "I have a special place to write them all. Not to mention, of course, that I made a fair profit selling those bracelets from the Marsh Isles to people in Medioca. Trade is in my blood! And I'm sure these Mocjoa, assuming we find them, will have plenty of interesting wares."

Ian sighed, a pang hitting his heart. "Right. Assuming we find them."

"Oh yes," Tyzak said, winking encouragingly, "I assume we will."

A mass of towering constructions materialized out of the blinding sunlight of midday, forcing Warrah to hold her hands over her eyes to block out the rays of the silvery sun. She took in the sight of the city off the bow of the ship. Buildings of tan stone and decorated spires filled the landscape, here and there interrupted by bushy greenery.

"Ush'qua," Ctzo said, coming to her side. "The southernmost city on Scavgan's Island."

Warrah narrowed her eyes. "It's bigger than I imagined. I never thought it could compare to someplace like Medioca, but it looks almost as big."

Soon Ian joined them, standing beside Warrah. She took the moment to gaze his way. Secretly, she'd been hoping at least one individual on this adventure would catch her attention as a possible romantic interest, but all her options had been disappointing thus far. Tyzak was handsome, sure, but could she stand being one of his multiple wives if he chose to follow the traditions of his land? And Ian… how old was he? She knew he was the youngest aboard, and she guessed he might still be a teenager. She wasn't sure she wanted to be with someone that young.

She turned back out to sea, watching as the city of Ush'qua grew nearer. Before long *Diversity II* came into harbour and the gangplank lowered. Warrah was among the first to rush to the plank, although she tiptoed along it cautiously until she reached the wooden dock. She felt small pebbles crunching under her feet as she stepped ashore. Around her, the beach was mostly barren, with no paths leading from the docks to the city.

Ian and Tyzak followed behind her, and she heard their eager conversation.

"So are we going to the lake?" Ian was asking his friend.

Warrah nearly jumped as Chiha leapt in front of her. The Athai's dark, glossy eyes turned towards Ian.

"What lake?" Chiha asked.

Tyzak spread out his arms dramatically. "This city was built around a lake with water as still as glass."

"It's beautiful," Ian agreed. "I really enjoyed watching the birds there the last time we came through on our way to Aziasha."

Warrah smiled at him. At least he enjoyed nature. He got points for that.

She decided to stick close to Ian and Tyzak so she could follow them to this lake. Chiha apparently had the same idea, so the four of them became natural traveling companions.

The people of Ush'qua, Warrah soon realized, were themselves lovers of nature. Though the streets were paved, each path was narrow and bordered by bushes, wildflowers, and trees. The tall buildings were painted generously with motifs of animals, plants, and mountainous landscapes. Several times she stopped to gape in awe at the works of art—and she wasn't alone in her amazement; Tyzak and Ian also paused when something caught their eyes.

As the four walked along, Warrah couldn't help but smile watching Chiha. The Athai woman was always five steps ahead of the group, leaping up the trees dotting their path and then rushing back down before the others had caught up.

Tyzak and Ian conversed almost nonstop, with Ian doing more of the listening and Tyzak more of the talking. Occasionally, Chiha threw in her own brief but firm opinion on their topics.

Warrah felt a little isolated. These people had had plenty of time to establish their relationships, and here she was, trying to squeeze into their group.

She sighed, and Ian must have heard, because he turned to her instantly.

"What about you?" Ian asked. "What do you think we should look for? Local cuisine, or something like a Questavan or Mediocan eatery?"

Chiha snorted. "Your home foods are not found everywhere."

"She has a point," Ian said, eyeing Tyzak.

Tyzak frowned. "I desire a good Mediocan meal."

"We might not be able to find that," Ian said. "Or we might need to search a long time."

But Warrah wasn't about to abandon her invitation into the conversation. "Shouldn't we try what the locals eat? When are we ever going to get another chance to try food from Ush'qua?"

"I agree," Ian said. "Sorry, Tyzak. You're outvoted."

Tyzak shrugged. "Well, I suppose eating can be an adventure. But first, the lake!"

"Yes." Ian eagerly looked ahead up the path. "Almost there!"

Warrah, too, could see glimmers of water beyond the nearby streets, buildings, and bushes.

Soon the four stood at the edge of a darkly coloured lake. The water lapped calmly against the shore and birds of unfamiliar and smooth shapes floated, dived, and called all around them, their voices reminiscent of bittersweet dirges or haunting melodies.

Warrah took in a deep breath of the fresh air, her eyes following the movements of the foreign birds. Moments like these were why she'd joined this quest. They were opportunities to experience something new, something beautiful… things she would never have seen if she hadn't gone looking for them.

In the romance of the instant, she didn't think about the various men on her trip and whether her affections for them would grow. None of that mattered. The world awaited her affection, and the world had it.

Ctzo stared at his ship from where he stood upon the pebble beach, reading the ship's name as painted across the hull: *Diversity II.*

But it wasn't quite the *Diversity*, was it? He'd named his previous ship the *Diversity* because he'd planned to include every race aboard it as crew. Though he still had Scavgans, Darians, Reea, and Athai, he'd lost their only Rezumi and the Kamai—not to mention the very first Mocjoa any of them had ever seen.

Ctzo felt no guilt about leaving Vortro in Ian's village. True, not bringing Vortro along to his audience with the Emperor had cost him the Emperor's trust, but at the time he had been doing what seemed best for her. He'd considered going back to get her, and even to force his way in to see the Emperor again, but the more he thought about it the more he realized such an action could have proven disastrous. The Emperor wasn't one to stand being mocked. Rather than admitting he had been wrong to cast Ctzo out without support, he might have grown angry and had Vortro executed as a monster. She did resemble a Blackblood in some ways—the glowing eyes and jet-black skin—and it wouldn't have taken much to convince the world that Ctzo had tried to pass off an unusual Blackblood as an entirely new race.

His falling out with Black Night, on the other hand... he couldn't decide what he should think of it. True, it would do no good to have a crewmember he couldn't trust to obey orders. Black Night's willful attitude had already caused much friction, and perhaps it would be better to be without the rebellious Rezumi. Chiha, for all her arrogance, was at least submissive to Ctzo.

Still, was there a better way I could have handled that? Ctzo wondered. He sighed, coming to the same conclusion once more: *What's done is done. Black Night no longer wants to be part of the crew, and Kyaté hasn't given me a Rezumi for this trip. I don't need a Rezumi just for the sake of having a Rezumi; I need people who will contribute to the crew and to our quest.*

Ctzo thought back to the early days of their adventure, when he'd told Black Night he'd be glad to have him by his side. Ctzo had felt confident he would see great things from the Rezumi. It hurt to have been proved wrong.

Surprisingly, though, when it came to disappointing crewmembers, Black Night was no longer at the top of the list. Ctzo looked around the harbour for Jani; he hadn't seen or heard from his first mate since his time at the temple.

The captain was so convinced that Jani wouldn't show that he had already settled on a new first mate to replace him.

Ian is young and inexperienced, but I can sense his potential, Ctzo thought. *And his loyalty has become more valuable to me than ever.*

Finally Ctzo stepped back aboard his ship, and as he did so a weight settled over him. This would be their final stop before reaching Aziasha. If all went well, after today the crew wouldn't be seeing land again for weeks.

With that in mind, he walked around the *Diversity II*, giving orders and examining the ship from bow to stern. Everything had to be properly prepared for their long stint at sea.

Although he was confident in his own abilities, an uneasy feeling continued to grow within him. He couldn't help wondering whether another tragedy like the sinking of the *Diversity* lay along their path.

Sighing, Ctzo prayed. *Kyaté, forgive my doubt.*

Instinct told him to turn back, to abandon his current quest. Perhaps Kyaté would send him towards doom again.

But no—he had set his course and he wouldn't turn back now. Whatever lay ahead was in the Creator's hands… whether glory, failure, or death. He would follow through to the end.

Soon the sails were open and catching the wind, and the *Diversity II* floated out from the port of Ush'qua. She then turned south, carrying her crew away from the city and the island.

Ctzo held his telescope over his eye, watching as Scavgan's Island shrunk to the size of a speck. At last, though he concentrated, he could see it no more.

He took a deep breath, lowering the spyglass and noticing Warrah standing by his side.

"Our new adventure begins, my daughter."

"First, it's just Warrah," she said, arms crossed over her chest. "Not 'my daughter.'" She stepped forward and leaned over the railing. "At last! My whole world is nowhere to be seen! Can you still see the island through the telescope?"

The captain shook his head. "No. We're out to sea now." He turned to face the opposite direction. "Straight to the south is

Aziasha, and beyond that is the Marsh Isles. There, we should find more clues in our search for the Mocjoa."

CHAPTER THIRTY-NINE

*I*n the deepening twilight, a fleet of dark ships slipped through the seas, their sails of black rippling in the wind. Captain Sébérus held his eyes closed, trusting his Blackblood senses over his sight.

The wind is in our favour, he thought. *And I can feel it now, in the distance…*

"We are approaching Questava's defences," cried out First Mate Kaio.

Sébérus's eyes snapped open, his glowing amber gaze locked on the distant warships he saw circling the capital city's harbour, ever on the lookout for suspicious vessels. Shortly the *Moakoko,* and the fleet of black vessels in her wake, would meet Questava's defenders.

But who would fire first? That remained to be seen.

Behind them sailed the rest of the fleet, including the *Ko'Ekua.* Grey Noon had wanted Sébérus's ship, and the ones carrying their Blackblood allies, to begin the attack. Well, so be it.

A ship approached waving the flag of a Questavan pirate-hunter. As it got closer, it lowered its flag and raised communication flags. Grey Noon had told him to expect this, having taught him what the various flags meant.

This ship's message was simple: *Lower your sails and prepare to be boarded.*

Sébérus took a deep breath. There was only way to respond.

"Load the cannons," he told his first mate.

Katia wasn't sure what had caused her to stay in Questava City, nor was she sure what had drawn her to the shore that evening. The docks were ever a busy place, even into the early hours of the night. She dodged the busy feet of sailors and merchants moving crates along the walkways and docks. She avoided them and instead set her own course along the beach, a course that led through sand and spray, one that reminded her of the ceaseless ups and downs of navigating the jungle back home.

It felt nice to squish her toes in the wet sand. A change of pace from the city's cobblestone walkways.

Every now and then she'd pass a small tower lit by lanterns. Upon each, a walled patio housed cannons aimed towards the sea. It made her think back to the day she'd arrived in Questava and noticed all the similar towers built upon the rocky islets further out at sea.

She paused next to one tower, frowning, her ears moving around to catch the sounds resonating from it. There were a lot of men there. Why were there so many people at the tower all of a sudden? In the light of the lanterns, she saw them gazing through telescopes, chattering animatedly about something they saw.

Then she caught other sounds carried over the waves—the blasts of cannon fire.

INDEX OF NAMES

Jani. A spirit-being and Kyaté's messenger to Captain Ctzo.

Kaio. A Blackblood, once a Darian.

Katana. Ian's older sister.

Katia. A female Darian with blue fur and orange stripes. Kind and gentle, she nevertheless can be stubborn.

Kyaté. The God of the Mediocans. His name means "Uncreated Maker."

Kyra. A female Kamai with green scales and brown wings. Faithful and curious, she's usually with her mate, Réto.

Lym. A strong Blackblood, once a Darian.

Orthel. The chief of his tribe.

Oti. A young male Shadowmacer Darian whose fur changes shades of grey depending on the shadows around him.

Pace. An ex-slave trader, now a member of Ctzo's crew.

Pazu. An elderly Ti'te'Vikan priest.

Qeysta. A woman from Ctzo's past.

Réto. A male Kamai with black scales and loyal servant to Ctzo. He's usually with his mate, Kyra.

Ryan. A captain and friend of Ctzo.

Savato. A doctor.

Sébérus. An intelligent Blackblood, once a Darian.

Terr. A young Ti'te'Vikan priest.

Tersera. A Mocjoa whom Ctzo met in a vision.

Tyzak. A twentysomething male Scavgan with purple skin. He enjoys storytelling, has a playful attitude, and wears attention-grabbing outfits.

Vasitan. A representative of Questava's Council; Zan's father.

Vortro. Ian's little bug companion.

Warrah. A woman from Ctzo's past.

Yakara. A female Reea.

Zan. A twentysomething male Scavgan with navy skin and a Questavan accent.

Zelda. Zan's mother; Vasitan's wife.

INDEX OF TERMS

Athai (race). Beings with long, lizard-like faces, a squirrelly tail and mannerisms, and black eyes that shine like polished gemstones. Their native land is the Marsh Isles, where they dwell in treetop villages alongside the Reea.

Aziasha (place). A jungle-covered land far south of Questava and home to the Darian race. The Questavan Empire claims it as part of their territory, though Questava's influence over Aziasha is weak.

Blackblood (race). Comprised of those who have been affected by blackwaters and survived. They have black skin and glowing yellow eyes, but otherwise their features vary by individual and according to what race they were previously.

Blackwaters (chemical). A toxic liquid that causes sickness, death, and physical and mental alterations to those creatures who come in contact with it.

Capero (animal). In Questava, these creatures are used as mounts and carriage hitches.

Cherish (ship). The smallest ship in Captain Ctzo's fleet. Painted in greys and blues.

Darian (race). A small race native to the island of Aziasha. They typically dwell in wilderness clans or simple villages and are covered in fur. Their colour varies by heritage. Males have horns, females have pouches, and both have tails which they use for balance when climbing.

Diversity (ship). Ctzo's flagship, featuring blue ropes for rigging and colourful sails. It contains design elements from both a sloop and a cutter.

Erra (deity). A Ti'te'Vikan goddess.

Felda (animal). A smaller, cheaper alternative mount to caperos.

Kamai (race). Small, serpentine race with large talons and fangs, known for their intelligence. They have bat-like wings and are swift and agile fliers. Though very capable, their instinct is to bind themselves in service to someone of another race. They are native to a distant region of the Gashaian Islands.

Ko'Ekua (ship). Grey Noon's flagship. A xebec with black sails.

Kyaté (deity). The almighty God of the Mediocans.

Medioca (place). One of the kingdoms ruled by the Questavan Empire. The Mediocans are called the "people of Kyaté," as they are the nation specifically chosen to receive Kyaté's laws and build his temple.

Mocjoa (race). A previously unknown people whom Ctzo is hoping to find. They are short, with spidery fangs, antennae, and glowing eyes.

Night Light (ship). Part of Captain Ctzo's fleet. It features five masts and a dragon carving at the bow. It's painted in deep blues, purples, and greens, with moons across her sails.

Questava (place). The empire of the Scavgans, and also the name of its capital city. The people of the city of Questava conquered and absorbed all the other Scavgan kingdoms.

Radiant Dawn (ship). Part of Captain Ctzo's fleet. It features five masts and a dragon carving at the bow. It's painted in silvery and golden colours, with suns across her sails.

Reea (race). A secretive race of serpent-people. Their native home is alongside the Athai on the Marsh Isles. They are long-bodied, have many legs, and can change colour at will, allowing them to effectively turn invisible. Though capable, their instinct is to bind themselves in service to someone of another race.

Regalt (animal). A large species of fish.

Rezumi (race). Giant bat-like people, often twice the height of the average Scavgan. They generally live in peace-loving villages, and only a few have chosen the path of a warrior. Native to a region of the Gashaian Islands near Scavgan's Island.

Scavgan (race). A bipedal race with blue to purple, starry-patterned skin. They have large black eyes and diamond-shaped pupils. They stand upright, six to seven feet tall, and are known for being innovative kingdom-builders, native to Scavgan's Island.

Scavgan's Island (place). The island on which the city of Questava and the Mediocan Kingdom, among other Scavgan kingdoms, are located.

Tarair (deity). A Ti'te'Vikan war god.

Ti'te'Vika (faith). The polytheistic religion of the pirate Grey Noon.

Yupetas (deity). A Darian goddess of water.

Zaia (animal). Large, blubbery marine animals.

Born and raised in a small town in northern British Columbia, Karlissa grew up feeling it'd be hard to ever call one place home.

While young, she travelled with her family across Canada, across the northern United States, to the Dominican Republic, and to a village in the mountains of Guatemala, and later to Africa and England. With a family who enjoyed exploration and a father with a passion for global history and geography, Karlissa came to love discovering diverse cultures and places, though her primary passion would always be the diversity of the animal kingdom.

As a young adult, Karlissa continued the travel lifestyle on her own, taking a school trip to Europe, then completing a YWAM DTS program in Belize and the Philippines, a communications school in Switzerland, and graphic design school in England.

She finally found a reason to call British Columbia home when she decided to marry her best friend, Jason. The two live in Fort St. John, a city not far from where they both grew up. They've recently added two kids to their family.

Karlissa's favourite pastimes include writing, designing, researching, and watching superhero shows with her husband. Her favourite creatures are bats, but she also loves little-known animals, bugs, and the diversity of aquatic life. Recently, she's been kept busy with Project Fsjmoths, designing educational materials about the moths and butterflies in British Columbia's Peace Region.

TALES OF THE DIVERSITY
BOOK ONE: THE QUEST

Captain Ctzo starts his pirate-hunting quest with a less than impressive ship and a crew that can't seem to work together. Still, he has something going for him: a spiritual helper at his side and a diverse collection of crewmates, each with something unique to offer. As new challenges arrive, both his vessel and his comrades prove to be more than appearances suggest.

Coming Soon
TALES OF THE DIVERSITY
BOOK THREE: THE PROMISE

Ctzo's quest for the Mocjoa will continue in the trilogy's final installment!

KINGDOM OF BATS

Chitolla, a swallow from a land of talking animals, suddenly finds herself in another world: a world of bats, where a cannibalistic and deified warlord spreads fear to the entire population. She meets up with Patas, a vampire bat who's trying to escape the warlord's wrath. Together, they and their new traveling companions set out on a dangerous journey.

DWELLING IN DARKNESS

Animal worlds link to one another via supernatural spiderweb portals. But one world has been closed off, the Sealed Realm, where a dying island is fought over by eerie monsters and a diminishing set of heroes. Meanwhile, a lemur dreams every night about escaping to another place, only to find her dreams riddled with challenges and darkness.

BLACK MISTS

A case of amnesia is only the beginning. A young woman believes someone intends to kill her, but who? Without her memory, the riddled clues of a person who signs each message with the words "Black Mists" are her only warnings of the danger that follows.

www.ingramcontent.com/pod-product-compliance
Lightning Source LLC
Chambersburg PA
CBHW051059030726
47504CB00006B/1700